"Nancy J. P   delight!"

—Peg Cochran, national bestselling
author of the Gourmet De-Lite Mysteries

"A delightful heroine, cherry-filled plot twists, and cream-filled pastries. Could murder be any sweeter?"
—Connie Archer, national bestselling
author of the Soup Lover's Mysteries

"A mouthwatering debut with a plucky protagonist. Clever, original, and appealing with gluten-free recipes to die for."
—Carolyn Hart, national bestselling author

"A lively, sassy heroine and a perceptive and humorous look at small-town Kansas (the Wheat State)!"
—JoAnna Carl, national bestselling
author of the Chocoholic Mysteries

"This baker's treat rises to the occasion. Whether you need to eat allergy-free or not, you'll devour every morsel."
—Avery Aames, Agatha Award–winning
author of the Cheese Shop Mysteries

"Maybe you should call for backup?" I asked.

He shot me a look of disgust. "I'm a trained officer of the law. I can handle this." Then he hitched his gun belt again and took three steps toward the drunk. "All right," he said. "Fun's over. Get out of the trough."

The wind blew and rustled the guy's coat but the drunk didn't move.

Officer Fife, as I thought of him, had red creeping up his thin, pale neck. His giant Adam's apple bobbed in his skinny neck. "I said, show's over, pal. Get out of the trough." He took out his nightstick and poked the drunk on the back. The guy didn't stir.

I pursed my lips. I could feel the customers behind me staring out the window. "Maybe if you remove his Stetson? Sun shining in his eyes might help."

Barney gave me another evil look. But he did what I said. He reached down and took the hat and we both gasped. The drunk was facedown in about an inch of water and the back of his head was covered in blood.

"That can't be good," I muttered. I dialed 911 again because Officer Fife stood frozen and stared at the guy.

"Nine-one-one dispatch, how can I help you?"

"Hello, Sarah, this is Toni again down at the bakery. I think you need to send a second squad car and possibly an ambulance. I think the drunk guy might be dead."

Gluten for Punishment

NANCY J. PARRA

BERKLEY PRIME CRIME, NEW YORK

THE BERKLEY PUBLISHING GROUP
Published by the Penguin Group
Penguin Group (USA) Inc.
375 Hudson Street, New York, New York 10014, USA

USA / Canada / UK / Ireland / Australia / New Zealand / India / South Africa / China

Penguin Books Ltd., Registered Offices: 80 Strand, London WC2R 0RL, England
For more information about the Penguin Group, visit penguin.com.

GLUTEN FOR PUNISHMENT

A Berkley Prime Crime Book / published by arrangement with the author

Berkley Prime Crime Books are published by The Berkley Publishing Group.
BERKLEY® PRIME CRIME and the PRIME CRIME logo are trademarks of
Penguin Group (USA) Inc.

For information, address: The Berkley Publishing Group,
a division of Penguin Group (USA) Inc.,
375 Hudson Street, New York, New York 10014.

ISBN: 978-0-425-25210-9

PUBLISHING HISTORY
Berkley Prime Crime mass-market edition / May 2013

PRINTED IN THE UNITED STATES OF AMERICA

10 9 8 7 6 5 4 3 2 1

Cover illustration by Patricia Castelao.
Cover design by Rita Frangie.

ALWAYS LEARNING   **PEARSON**

This one is for Ashley.
Thank you for putting up with crazy writers your entire life.
Your insight and wit constantly amaze me.
May you find happiness always.

ACKNOWLEDGMENTS

So many wonderful people have helped me in the making of this and all my books. In particular, I'd like to thank Jaci Charbonneau for the best title in the history of cozy mysteries. Jaci's brilliant puns light up my life. Next I want to thank Joelle Charbonneau for encouraging me to write cozy mysteries and to write what I know—gluten-free living. Thanks, too, for your top-notch coaching talents and generosity with your time. Thanks to Liz Powell whose encouragement and brilliant mind have lifted me up and helped me to keep going when things felt bleak. For Paige Wheeler, my awesome agent, whose excellent advice and wisdom help me in all aspects of my career. For Faith Black, for loving what I write enough to buy the series and guide me through the entire editorial process. For all the wonderful people at Berkley Prime Crime for your love of books, your vision, and your careful eye in creating the best book possible.

Finally, thank you to all the many friends and family—you know who you are—for believing in my talent every step of the way. A book is never created in a vacuum. Instead it is born from the generosity, hard work, and helping hands of an entire lifetime of people. I hope I can make you all proud to be a part of it.

CHAPTER 1

"Turn the house into a bed-and-breakfast." My best friend since grade school, Tasha Wilkes, pursed her lips and eyed the 1970s decor of the rambling, 1885 Victorian house my mom had left me.

"No." I shook my head and grabbed my car keys. "B&B's are your thing, not mine. I've got my hands full with the bakery."

She followed me down the hall, past the formal parlor, the small den, the dining room, the butler's pantry, closet-sized powder room, and into the large kitchen and out the back door. Twenty years before, my dad had replaced the gravel driveway with old brick pavers. Since weeds were hardy in Kansas, I now had to mow the driveway as well as the lawn.

"But it's perfect, Toni," Tasha muttered as she opened the passenger door of my small white delivery van. "You can remodel the carriage house apartment and live there, leaving the main house with all seven bedrooms for guests. The right decor, the right advertising, and you'll have a steady income—which by the way, might come in handy."

"One of those bedrooms currently belongs to Tim and one is my office."

"That still leaves five bedrooms."

I hopped up into the driver's seat. I'd bought the van pre-owned with over seventy-five thousand miles on it, but it was sturdy and the back could hold a lot of cakes and cookies.

"I've always loved riding in your van," Tasha said, taking a deep breath. "It smells so good from all the sweets you transport to your catering gigs."

"Too bad there aren't too many of those yet." I turned onto Third Street. The bakery was basically still in the start-up phase. I'd begun offering gluten-free baked goods online right after my divorce, but my small Chicago apartment was terribly cramped.

I'd been determined to grow my business no matter how small my kitchen. Then Mom had passed in January, leaving me the family house in Oiltop, Kansas, complete with a very mom-like addendum—any family member who was in need of shelter got to stay with me.

Yippee.

With three sisters, two brothers, and forty-five cousins, there was never a lack of family in the house. Too bad none of them remembered how to run a vacuum.

Now here I was, stuck in Oiltop, determined to keep my change of address from altering my entrepreneurial spirit.

"You would think that with a name like Oiltop, the town would be filled with oil-wealthy townsfolk ready to spend their money on specialty foods—especially with the price of gas today," I muttered.

The sad truth was that the oil heyday in our town had ended nearly a hundred years ago, leaving a small town surrounded by wheat farmers and cattle ranchers. Don't get me wrong, we still had two refineries on the edge of town. It's where most of the townspeople worked. But the biggest part of the oil field was depleted long ago, leaving farmers to grow wheat around the grasshopper-like oil pumps dredging out what was left of the black gold.

"They ought to rename it Wheatville." Tasha giggled. "Or Cattleton."

"Or Hicksville," I added as I turned onto Central Street. "Oiltop makes it sound as if we all live near the country club with the bankers, the doctors, the lawyers, and the remaining oil-elite."

"Yeah, don't we wish." Tasha let out a long sigh. "Shoot, Toni, you grew up here. You know that most everyone in town either works for the refinery or the college. That's why the chamber is pushing so hard to get tourism to our town. An influx of any kind of income would be good—like the new dam project—and the great idea of turning your mom's home into a B&B."

I shook my head at the thought. Ever since I opened my storefront, I'd barely had time to sleep. A bed-and-breakfast was the last thing I needed.

"Aren't you afraid of competition?" I asked. Tasha owned and ran the Welcome Inn, the only B&B in Oiltop.

She shrugged. "Pete Hamm says there'll be all kinds of tourism come spring. All those fishermen, boaters, and antique shoppers have to have someplace to stay. I'm already turning away guests for this spring's Prairie Port Festival." Tasha turned her wide blue gaze on me. "You could have your place remodeled and ready by then."

"No, I couldn't." I stopped at the light on the corner of Central and Main. "What would I do with my family?"

"Tell them to pay rent."

The thought made me laugh.

"No, really." She crossed her arms and tossed her long blonde hair. "It would make them think twice about walking in, tossing their stuff down, and raiding your fridge. Seriously, Toni, you can't afford to feed the masses. They should pay rent."

"I'm not allowed to ask for rent." I took off down Central. "Remember Mom's open-door codicil?"

"The door will be open," Tasha pointed out. "It simply won't be free. Did she say you couldn't set boundaries?"

"No." Tasha had me there. But setting boundaries was not my strong suit, one of the many reasons for my divorce.

"Then set boundaries. The noise and dust of remodeling will drive them out of the house, and when they come back you can tell them there'll always be a room for them . . . for half price."

I laughed. "Who'll run it?"

"Most of my staff is part-time. We could pool our funds and hire them full-time to care for both places. I'd manage it and you . . ."

"Have got a bakery to run."

"And there's your angle." Tasha was relentless. "Your bakery is gluten-free, right?"

"Yes. . . ."

"We can remodel the house in all allergy-free materials and sell it as a low-allergy, natural B&B. It's perfect. The breakfasts can come right from the bakery and you'll gain twice the publicity."

I pursed my lips. She made it sound . . . reasonable. Except launching the storefront version of Baker's Treat, my online, gluten-free bakery, had left me with my hands full and no time for a seven-bedroom, 150-year-old Victorian house.

"Think about it. It's extra income . . . and allergy-free is the next niche market; you said so yourself."

"I did say that, didn't I?"

"Yes, you did." Tasha relaxed beside me and fussed with her collar. She wore a white shirt and black vest with black slacks and a skirt apron, just like I did. Baker's Treat had been open for two weeks, but today was the Chamber of Commerce ribbon cutting and coffee. Pictures would be taken and an article written in the *Oiltop Times*. And everything, absolutely everything had to be perfect.

"Speaking of your family, are your sisters coming to the coffee?"

"Eleanor and Rob are at Disney this week. Joan called last night, her two littlest, Jennifer and Emma, have chicken pox."

"What about Rosa?"

I blew out a breath. "Rosa has a standing hair appointment."

"Really?" Tasha raised an eyebrow.

"I didn't want her here, anyway." I turned down the alley behind the Main Street stores and pulled into my parking spot. A quick glance in the mirror told me the copious amount of Freeze hairspray I'd choked on this morning was doing its job of keeping my wild hair plastered into a low bun at the back of my neck. At least I'd look professional for the picture. All bets were off after that.

"You look great," Tasha said, reading my mind.

"Until I step outside." I glanced at the tiny tornadoes the Kansas wind was making in the gravel parking lot. Taking a deep breath, I said, "Okay. Let's do this."

I crunched through the gravel in my black sneakers, unlocked the back door, and turned on the lights. I had less than an hour to get the place ready for the Chamber of Commerce Coffee.

"What's on the menu?" Tasha asked as she looked inside the giant refrigerators.

"Cookies, small tarts, and some quiches as a nod to the ten A.M. time frame." I tossed on a huge apron to keep my serving outfit clean. Everything had been made in advance and was in the freezer waiting to be put into the ovens or the display case.

Tasha pulled out loaves of bread for the proofer. I took out frosted cakes and cupcakes and a variety of ready-to-eat pastries. The bakery was small by choice. The first rule in the bakery business was to never have an empty display case.

"I think I could get fat just off the smells in here." Tasha sighed as she filled the display case while I put cookies in the oven. The smells of fresh yeast, cinnamon, vanilla, and chocolate filled the air. The display and counter took up over half the front.

There were racks of gluten-free mixes, flours, pastas, spices, and flavorings for sale. Another rack held coffee mugs, travel mugs, tee shirts, and other promotional items. There were three small wrought-iron café tables with glass tops and a variety of Victorian, velvet-covered chairs near the windows.

When the weather was nice, I would add some extra tables for outdoor seating. Beside the counter was a self-serve coffee bar complete with three kinds of fair trade organic coffees in carafes along with almond milk, soy milk, and organic cream.

Once the case was full, Tasha looked around. "I still can't get over how different this place looks since you redecorated. I love the warm yellow/green you chose and the black wrought-iron accents. Aren't you glad I suggested buying student artwork?"

"Very glad," I said as I went over to straighten the paintings of rural English scenes commissioned from students at Oiltop State College. I'd gotten the art for a song. Plus, it never hurt to start up a bakery storefront near a small college, even if the college itself was located on the other side of town. College kids loved baked goods.

The English library decor went well with the bakery name. It was sort of an inside joke. I had married Eric Holmes, which made me Marie Antoinette Holmes. I hated my name, of course, and demanded from an early age that everyone call me Toni. Only my grandma Ruth got away with calling me Marie and only when she was complimenting me. But the last name always had people asking if I was related to Sherlock, and so the name Baker's Treat.

My ex-husband on the other hand, started making guillotine jokes the day I caught him cheating with his best friend's wife. Really? I thought. Your best friend's wife? Why are men so limited in their imaginations?

Eric was a handsome man with dark hair and blue eyes and a killer smile. He used that smile well in his job as a pharmaceutical salesman. It seemed everyone fell for it. Even other married women. Sigh.

I shook off the bad memory and pulled the first two batches of cookies out of the oven, chocolate chip and cinnamon oatmeal raisin. One thing I noticed after being diagnosed with celiac disease was that people who must eat gluten-free are drawn to simpler foods that remind them of being a kid.

Next were GF sugar cookies cut out in the shapes of pumpkins and black cats. After all, it was October and it never hurt to offer seasonal cookies.

The tarts were filled with either rich caramel custard or pumpkin custard. We stacked them on the serving trays, along with two dozen little quiches.

I had spent two hours the day before talking with the local reporter, Candy Cole, about why the bakery was gluten-free. Tasha understood. Her son, Kip, had been diagnosed with Asperger's when he was four. Special-needs children did better on allergy-free diets. It's why I offered peanut butter baked goods but only as a special order, and those I cooked up at home, keeping them separate from the store. Cross contamination was a big concern, and I did my best to keep it from happening. Thankfully none of my nieces or nephews had special needs.

Tasha arranged the cookies on big black platters. "Oatmeal raisin are Kip's favorite."

"Take a half-dozen and set them aside," I said and brought her a box. "I would hate to run out before he got any."

"Thanks." She boxed the cookies, set them aside, then artfully stacked bottles of sparkling water. The sun sparkled through the big front windows, showing off the giant red ribbon blocking the door.

"People are gathering outside," Tasha warned me.

I checked the English mantel clock, which sat on the shelf on the far wall. "They're ten minutes early."

"I told you, when it comes to Chamber Coffees everyone shows up for the free food and drink. Remember not to stand too close to Lois Striker. She might be a chamber icon, but she has a tendency to spit when she talks."

I stuck my tongue out in an exaggerated gag reflex and Tasha laughed.

If I were smart, I'd buddy up to Lois and try to find an in with the country club set, as they were the people in town who set the trends. Their kids were always the most popular in school, and even the senior citizens listened when a member of the country club spoke. Except my grandma Ruth, who never cared a lick about what anyone else thought, least of all the Oiltop society people.

When I saw the photographer setting up outside, I whipped off the oversized apron and checked myself in the mirror that hung on the door to the kitchen. "And we're on . . ." I muttered as I tried to keep my hands off my hair for fear if I touched it, it would spring free.

"You look great." Tasha patted me on the shoulder. "Everything looks picture-perfect and smells fabulous. You'll blow them away."

"Here's hoping." I crossed my fingers and opened the front door. At least ten people milled about on the sidewalk. Most of them were elderly or other small-business owners looking to schmooze. To my left, Lois Striker talked to Pete Hamm, the chamber president and a personal injury lawyer. Pete smiled with relief when I waved for his attention. As he hurried away, he took a linen handkerchief out of his breast pocket and wiped his round face. He wore an imported blue suit with pale blue shirt and striped tie. He was balding but obviously had a hairdresser who knew how to deal with it as the cut looked expensive.

"Hi, Toni." He held out his hand—the hand he'd just used to wipe spit off his brow. Great. I plastered on a big smile and shook it. Rocky Rhode, the chamber's official photographer and owner of the local photo studio, Perfect Portraits, snapped a quick photo.

"Hi, Pete." I turned for a second shot. "Is everyone here?"

"Still waiting on Alisa Thompson. She was promoted to community liaison for the chamber, you know."

"Yes, I know."

"Of course you do. Alisa does great work, but she's not known for being punctual." Pete looked through the crowd. "Ah, there's Sherry, let's get her in on the ribbon cutting." He waved over the fashionable brunette, who smiled like she'd just won the Miss Kansas Pageant—which she had when we were both in our early twenties. I wasn't jealous. I simply couldn't figure out how pageant girls did it: the pageant figure, the pageant smile, the right tone in their voice when they insisted on world peace.

When I was in my early twenties, I wanted to be an astronaut or an architect or a paleontologist. My college counselor, on the other hand, thought my love of science made me a great candidate for weathergirl. After two semesters of learning things like the fact that humidity was actually measured by a machine mapping the amount of curl in a human hair, I dropped out and went to culinary school, where I learned that, even in the world of cooking, females still had to work twice as hard. Unless, of course, you looked like Sherry.

"Pete, glad to see you." She gave him a hug and a kiss on both cheeks as if she hadn't seen him for years. Odd since they worked in the same office and, if I wasn't mistaken, Pete was Sherry's boss.

"Toni!" She turned her sparkling blue eyes on me and her killer smile. "Don't you look so cute in your outfit!" Before another thought could enter my head, she'd grabbed me and squeezed me tight with her toned arms. I awkwardly patted her shoulder. In high school, Sherry, then Waters (now Williams), ran with the popular crowd while I ran with the honors kids, the debate squad and, worse, the pep band. Good times.

She ran her hands down my arms and took my hands in hers as she stepped back. "You look fabulous."

"Thank you." I think.

"You must be so proud of your little store. You know, gluten-free food is all the rage among the young and fit." She nodded. "I can't wait to pick up some more of those yummy crusty rolls I bought last week."

As if anything close to a crusty roll had ever passed through those lips. Really, the old saying is true: When you get to be fortysomething you must choose between your face and your figure. I chose my face. Sherry, it seemed on closer inspection, preferred a plastic surgeon.

"Ah, there's Alisa, the gang's all here." Pete puffed up as Alisa Thompson arrived. Alisa was in her mid-fifties and had been with the chamber her whole career. Her husband was a professor at the college, and while they didn't live in my part of town, they weren't exactly country club material either. She wore her bottle-blonde hair in a high pouf ending in an outward flip at the shoulder. Her dark glasses had rhine-stones at the cat-eye tips. Her fall green suit was well-tailored and hit her hip at the right proportion to make her thick legs look slimmer as she tottered on four-inch stilettos with red bottoms. The flash of red was supposed to show off her good taste in designer shoes, but, having lived in Chicago for fifteen years, I knew a knockoff when I saw one.

She clipped forth at snail speed, her hands full of several pairs of oversized gold scissors. "Good morning, pets." She smiled to show off her capped teeth. "Perfect weather for a grand opening, isn't it?"

I glanced up at the puffy clouds in the bright blue sky. She was right. With the crowd gathered around blocking the wind, it was rather nice out.

"Here you go, darlings." Alisa handed the scissors to Pete, Sherry, and I, leaving one pair for herself. "Now, places, everyone."

We all ducked behind the ribbon in front of the open door and waited for Rocky to give us the thumbs-up from behind his camera.

"Before we cut the ribbon," Pete straightened, "let me thank you all for coming. It's a wonderful thing to see Oiltop grow with new businesses. Niche bakeries like Baker's Treat are exactly what we need to keep the downtown vibrant. With the addition of the new dam and lake, we at the chamber continue to bring new opportunities to Oiltop."

The crowd gave a polite round of applause. Pete smiled and waved like a politician. I wondered if he'd already started his campaign for mayor.

"Ms. Holmes, why don't you tell these wonderful citizens what makes your bakery special?"

I blinked at Pete, who smiled encouragingly and waved a hand to the crowd. Darn it. I didn't know I would have to talk. I swallowed my fear of public speaking and stumbled a step forward. "Um . . . well . . . Baker's Treat is a gluten-free bakery."

"Isn't this whole gluten-free thing a fad?" a man shouted from the crowd.

I squinted at the crowd, trying to figure out who I was addressing. "Far from it," I said. "I mean, sure, some healthy people believe going gluten-free will help them live longer—"

"That's bullshit science. One barrel of good Kansas wheat feeds ten families."

I leaned toward Pete. "Who is that?" I whispered.

"George Meister," he said through his smiling teeth.

The Meisters were longtime farmers in the area and grew primarily wheat. George was a few years older than me. Since I hadn't lived in town for twenty years, I figured it was okay if I didn't recognize him.

"Hi, George." I hoped to defuse his obvious anger by being gentle. "My bakery's not trying to get rid of wheat or wheat products."

"You just said you were gluten-free."

"Well, right, some people—like myself—have wheat or gluten allergies. So what is good for the rest of the world could really harm us."

"So you're saying wheat is bad and what, rice is good? That's bull."

"No, I'm saying someone with allergies doesn't normally get to enjoy comfort food like bread. Or . . ." My thoughts scrambled as I tried to explain. "Or even a birthday cake on her birthday. Baker's Treat is here to change that."

"If you're anti-wheat, you're anti-Kansas. Why don't you go back to your Yankee Chicago?"

"George, Kansas was a free state, too," I pointed out, thinking I was being rational. "It means we can be all-inclusive."

"And the Bible says, 'Give us this day our daily bread.' If you're anti-wheat, you're anti-Christian."

"Now, now." Pete raised his hands. "Let's give the bakery

a chance, George. Like this little lady said, she ain't trying to take away from real bread."

I cringed at the "real bread" statement. "My baked goods *are* real," I stated. "They are made from all-natural ingredients."

"Like?" Lois asked, her eyes two sizes too big in her thick glasses.

"For example, we use sweet rice flour," I counted off on my fingers, "potato starch, tapioca, millet flour, flax, and cornstarch."

"Sounds nasty," Lois said.

My eyes grew wide. That wasn't the slogan I wanted associated with my business. I glanced at Pete, who had turned a bit red around the collar. He was no help. I gave the crowd my biggest smile while my brain scrambled for a way to undo potential damage. "Why don't you come in and give the pastries a try? After all, you can't beat free tarts and pastries."

"I'm for the pastries," Lois said.

"So am I," Pete added. "So, let's get this ribbon cut, shall we?"

The four of us with the big scissors slipped them over the ribbon.

"On the count of three," Pete said. "Smile for the camera. One . . . two . . ." Wham, something solid hit the top of the building and the sky was suddenly snowing white powder.

I choked and coughed. Pete coughed. Sherry desperately tried to wipe off the stuff when another missile hit the bricks above us and dumped more white from the sky.

"Damn it!" Pete shouted. "Somebody stop this nonsense. Where are the cops? Do we have a liaison officer present?"

It was then I realized the taste in my mouth was flour . . . of the wheat variety. The powder tickled my nose and I sneezed.

CHAPTER 2

I wiped the flour off my face with a warm, wet towel while Tasha graciously passed around platters of cookies. Everyone outside during the flour attack was currently inside the shop whispering about it—and me—and hopefully the cookies and tarts.

"And you didn't see who threw the flour bombs?" Hank Blaylock was Oiltop's chief of police and, as it turns out, happened to be attending the coffee. Too bad he'd arrived late. The Oiltop Police force was small, consisting of two patrols for day and one for night. There wasn't a lot of crime in town, except for around the college and they had their own security force twice the size of Oiltop's. Not that it mattered. Chief Blaylock liked to think he was in charge of anything police related in the city. His gruff demeanor let him get away with it.

"I didn't see a thing," I admitted. "I was looking down to cut the ribbon when the first one hit. My eyes were full of flour when the second one hit."

"Any idea who did it?" he asked, writing in his small notebook.

"George Meister made a fuss before the ribbon cutting, but I didn't actually see him do anything."

"What do you mean by 'made a fuss'?" Chief Blaylock frowned as if I spoke a foreign language.

"He was protesting the bakery." Tasha stepped in. "Cookie?" She passed a platter of the chocolate chip under his nose.

"They any good?" The chief's eyes narrowed.

"Better than your momma makes." Tasha winked.

"Now, that's saying something." He looked the cookies over. "I'm working . . ."

"Bag him up an assorted baker's dozen," I said. "And add a thermos of the good coffee."

"Will do." Tasha trailed off to play hostess with the rest of the cookies. The tarts were all gone. At least everyone was enjoying the food.

"I don't take bribes." The chief wrote something on his pad.

I sighed. "It's not a bribe. It's good business. No one will come in if they haven't tasted the product first. Besides, it's chamber-sponsored."

"In that case, I'll take it." He tapped his pencil against the notebook. "Okay, back to business. George Meister, in your words, 'made a fuss.'"

"Yes." I flattened my mouth and rolled my eyes. "There is always someone willing to protest something new, especially if they feel threatened."

"So you think George felt threatened?"

I took a deep breath. "He thought I said wheat was evil— I didn't. Then he got upset and said gluten-free living was anti-Christian, which is simply nuts."

"So, he had his panties in a twist." Chief Blaylock's brown eyes twinkled at me. The guy was five-foot-ten and what one would politely call husky. Still he wore his chief's uniform finely starched and with pride. His gray hair was thin. He was the same age as my father, which meant he'd pretty much seen it all over the years.

"I'm sure people will understand once they read my

interview in tonight's paper. Gluten-free food is a specialty niche for people with allergies and special-needs diets. I'm not trying to take away from the importance of wheat farmers."

"You said that in your interview?"

My mouth twitched slightly. "Not exactly. I hadn't fore-seen the need."

He scratched his head. "You're telling me you didn't think anything of setting up a wheat-free bakery in the heart of wheat country?"

"Come on, Chief Blaylock, I grew up here. The bakery was already doing well online when Mom left me the house. Where else but in town would I set up my storefront?"

"I see your point." He blew out a breath. "Look, I've inter-viewed pretty much everyone, and as far as we can tell no one saw anything. It was probably only a prank."

"A prank that could make me sicker than a dog," I mut-tered and realized that using the wet cloth to clean my face had had almost zero effect—on the cleaning, that is. Unless you counted the wet flour now hardening like papier-mâché paste on my nose. Which I didn't.

Hank narrowed his eyes. "Are you that allergic?"

"I have celiac disease. The gluten protein in grains like wheat makes me very ill. That's what I said when George got all defensive."

"Celiac disease? I've never heard of it."

"I'm sure you probably haven't, but it's not that rare. You should Google it."

"How many people know you have this disease?"

"Anyone who knows me or anyone who reads today's article. Why?"

He pursed his lips thoughtfully. "I was wondering if I should write this up as a prank or attempted murder."

His words rang in the small space. Suddenly, the crowd in the bakery was very, very quiet.

"I sincerely doubt it was attempted murder." I tried to wipe more of the flour paste off of my hands, but the towel had hardened as well.

"You said wheat makes you sick."

"It's not like a peanut allergy. It's more like food poisoning."

"Then we'll call it a prank." Chief Blaylock's gaze held concern. "But you let me know if you have any more trouble." He gave a quick nod.

"Okay." I gave up on the towel.

"Good. Any more questions?"

"No, I think that's it."

The chief raised his voice. "Fine, then you good people can enjoy your coffee. If anyone remembers anything, you have my number. Give me a call."

Tasha gave the chief a tan-and-white-striped box of cookies and a thermos with our name splashed across it.

"Thanks for your help." I waved at Pete Hamm, who'd asked me earlier to let him know when the chief was leaving. Pete was probably scared to walk out without the chief next to him for fear of more flour in the face.

The rest of the coffee klatch left soon after. I was happy to see that almost all the treats had been eaten. Some people bought rolls and breads and other pastries. Barring the fact that I looked like a grade-school art project gone wrong, it hadn't been a bad day.

"Hey, Tasha, thanks for your help."

Tasha finished washing the platters. "No sweat. You've always been there for me in a pinch."

I glanced at the mirror. My once perfectly styled and sprayed hair was now a sickly white. "Any suggestions for flour mixed with hairspray?"

Tasha giggled. "You look like a limestone statue."

"Great. I bet Rocky was excited to post the pictures of the flour-covered ribbon cutting on the newspaper website. Not exactly the kind of publicity I was hoping for."

Tasha rubbed my arm. "You'll be the talk of the town."

"I can't believe George Meister said I was anti-Christian for not cooking with wheat."

"He was upset. He thought you were robbing him of his family business."

"How?" I rested my elbow on the counter and my cheek on my fist. "Wheat is everywhere." I waved my hand.

"Including on your front stoop." Tasha grabbed the broom with a laugh.

I looked at the clock and sighed. "Get out of here. I can clean up on my own." It was nearly lunchtime and Tasha had her own cleaning and straightening to do at her B&B before she got Kip from school. She handed me the broom and headed for the door as I asked, "Do you need a ride?"

"Nope, I'm good. The walk will clear my head and make up for the cookies I ate."

"Hey, don't forget to take the box of cookies I fixed for Kip."

"Oh, right." She went back and rummaged around in the kitchen before pulling out the box. "Got it. Thanks! He loves your cookies."

We hugged and, as Tasha took off, I went out and sighed at the mess in front of my store. The brick building had round spots of white where the bags or balloons or whatever had first hit. The windows were coated in a fine dust. I frowned. There was nothing for it but to get an allergy mask and get to work.

CHAPTER 3

It took five separate washings with vinegar and water and two kinds of shampoo before my hair was clean of the gluten-filled glue. After using a deep conditioner, I rolled my hair in a towel, then heated a tub full of bubbles, poured a glass of red wine, and grabbed a copy of the *Oiltop Times*. The paper had gone to print after that day's ceremony so the ribbon-cutting story could be included. The paper had certainly got more news than it had bargained for.

The water was heaven. The wine, soothing. A picture of me and the highest-ranking members of the chamber of commerce covered in flour splashed across the front page, top of the fold, bigger than life.

"They say any publicity is good publicity," I muttered and took another sip of the wine. The story was interesting. Better yet, the name of the bakery had been used more than once.

Lois Striker was quoted. "It's such a shame to ruin a lovely ribbon cutting with a horrible prank."

Candy had covered the concerns of George and others about how the gluten-free trend put wheat farmers out of work. I shook my head and swallowed more wine. It was just nuts. Francy Bledsoe, president of the country club women's committee, suggested someone should open a "real" bakery across the street.

Thanks, Francy.

Interestingly enough, no one knew who threw the flour. Someone near the back said they thought they'd heard running. When they glanced over, they saw two people jogging around the corner but didn't know if they had anything to do with the vandalism or not. Everyone had simply stood and watched. Kind of like hanging around a bad accident, they were more curious to see the result than to prevent it from happening.

The phone rang and I glanced at the door. My brother Tim bunked in the bedroom down the hall. The phone kept ringing.

"Tim, get the phone, will you?" I called. There was no answer, of course. Tim was either ignoring the phone, although I had no idea how, or he was out. I sighed long and hard and waited for the ringing to stop. It did. Whoever it was could leave a message on the machine. Right?

Wrong.

The ringing started back up again. Of course, whoever it was wasn't going to let up. I climbed out of the tub and wrapped myself in a towel and got to the hall phone in time for it to stop. Crap. I dripped my way back to the bath, which was now lukewarm at best.

Pulling the stopper of the claw-foot tub, I watched with no little sadness as the bubbles disappeared down the drain. It was another five minutes of rinsing before my hair was soft and free of conditioner. The wine was gone. With the paper crumpled up on the bathroom floor, I felt better.

I shrugged into my fluffy robe, opened the door to the hall, and gave a short yelp of fright. Standing there was a short, round figure in men's dress pants and shirt. Orange-red hair stuck out from under a fedora.

"You were in the bathtub." My grandma Ruth pursed her lips. Her sparkling blue gaze took in my wet hair and robe. "Good. After reading the article, I feared you might be all alone and sick. When you didn't answer the house phone or your cell phone, I had your sister Joan keep calling until Bill and I could get over here."

Grandma Ruth Panken Nathers was the granddaughter of Richard and Lillian Panken, founders of Oiltop College. The pair had come to the wilds of Kansas as missionaries to start a college in the middle of the prairie. Grandma's dad, Charles, my great-grandfather, met her mom, another redhead, at a state college in Colorado. The two made a fetching pair, and it was rumored all the fun went out of the union when Grandma came along and they had to get married.

Grandma Ruth was a spunky sort. She lived through her parents' disputes, the loss of all their wealth in the 1920s stock market debacle, and soldiered on, marrying a car sales-man from Wichita. When her husband, Irving, asked for a divorce after thirty years so he could marry his mistress, she gave it to him. She and four of her eight kids moved back to Oiltop, where she went back to college. She got her degree in journalism and became Oiltop's first female reporter. They retired her at seventy-five, after which she took the Mensa test and became a lifetime member of the group where IQ score was a badge of honor.

Grandma never remarried. As a middle-aged single mom, she'd proudly earned her way into Oiltop's society, not caring a lick about how much she shocked the country club set. In fact, I suspected she liked shocking people with her outrageousness.

Some would call her a character. I must admit she certainly added color to my life.

"Good gracious, Grandma Ruth! You scared the wits out of me."

"You really should keep your doors locked," Grandma admonished, her voice rough from her three-pack-a-day smoking habit. How she could afford to smoke that much on her fixed income I had no idea. "Did you talk to your sister Rosa?"

"No." I shrugged. "The phone stopped ringing before I could pick up."

"Hmmph, the girl never did listen. Well, since you appear to be okay, what do you have for dessert?"

"Is Bill downstairs?" Bill was Grandma Ruth's longtime male companion. Sometime in my childhood, Bill had latched onto Grandma and she'd found him interesting enough to keep him around.

"Bill's waitin' in the den. He lit a fire in the fireplace. Hope it's all right."

"Let me get dressed." I wrapped my robe around me tighter. "There's pumpkin bread, apple coffee cake, and peach pie. You make the coffee and I'll be down to serve."

"Will do, kiddo." Grandma Ruth waved. "I'll have a small smoke break while you get dressed. Thank God your father had the good sense to install an elevator. Three floors of stairs are hard on an old woman's knees."

By the time I put on a tee shirt and pajama pants and got downstairs, my hair had frizzed. I passed the den to find Bill sitting next to the fireplace. Grandma came in, flung her fedora on the hat rack, and mussed her short, carrot-orange hair. At the age of ninety, she was proud to still have mostly red hair, even if the parts of it that framed her large, square face were white.

"Grandma, you smell like a honky-tonk." I waved my hand through the air to dissipate the scent.

"I see you left the butt can full of sand on the porch next to the swing. Just like your mother . . ." She settled down on the two-man settee next to Bill.

"Secondhand smoke kills," I tossed out into the air. It was an old argument. Grandma Ruth had taken up smoking on the advice of a doctor in the early 1940s. They'd told her it would help her lose weight. I shook my head at the thought. Grandma was two hundred pounds soaking wet, maybe more, and addicted to her beloved cancer sticks.

She laughed, thick and dark until she coughed. "At my age, everything kills, kiddo. Need any help getting that dessert out here before I get any older?"

"I've got it," I called on my way to the kitchen. "Hi, Bill."

I admit, the greeting was an afterthought, but my mama had taught me to be polite.

"Hey, Toni," Bill called. The man had a deep voice, which could carry nearly as far as Grandma Ruth's. Note, I said *nearly* as far. Grandma Ruth could yodel and was known for bringing the kids running from all corners of town once she started. She swore it was because they knew supper was ready.

Grandma considered opening a can of soup to be supper. She usually did it with her nose in a book. She did a lot of things with her nose in a book.

As for the kids coming running to eat whatever mystery thing Grandma had cooked up, I think they really just wanted to get home to make her stop yodeling before the neighbors called the police. Either way, it had been effective.

Grandma Ruth and Bill discussed the article in the paper. Grandma had bought several copies as family keepsakes. Meanwhile, I brought in two trays: one with pumpkin bread, coffee cake, and pie; the other with coffee, cups, and creamer. I had learned early how to serve with both hands full.

"It says no one saw anything," Bill pointed out and helped himself to the food I placed on the small table in front of them. You know, I might like Bill a bit better if he at least said thank you once in a while instead of acting as if I was supposed to wait on him hand and foot. It might be his age that led him to believe all women were there to see to his every comfort, but that didn't mean I had to like it. In my book he was a bit of a freeloader. I wouldn't tell Grandma this, of course. It would hurt her feelings. She actually liked Bill.

I curled up in the velvet-covered, wing-backed chair next to the fireplace. Mom had thought it would be fun to decorate the den in the Victorian manner with a 1970s twist. It sort of looked like a bordello on dope.

"It quotes the chief directly, 'No one saw a thing.'" Bill pushed his finger into his copy of the paper, crumpling it onto the tabletop.

"I don't believe it for a minute." Grandma Ruth picked up

a slice of coffee cake and took a bite. "Yum, good job, kiddo." She licked her fingers then lifted the crumbs, which landed on her ample bosom, with her wet fingertip and popped them in her mouth.

"I believe it. Everyone was watching the ribbon cutting," Bill pointed out. "Whoever tossed the flour bombs was behind the crowd."

"There were two bombs thrown," I pointed out as I sipped my coffee. "Seems like someone would have turned around after the first one hit."

"Have you seen the photo?" Grandma Ruth asked as she reached for the pumpkin bread. "Seriously. I would have been too busy laughing my fanny off at the sight of Pete Hamm covered in flour to notice another bomb coming or even who threw it."

"Laughing?" I drew my eyebrows together.

"Sure, this is a classic Charlie Chaplin prank." Grandma smiled like the Cheshire cat. "Did you look at the expression on your faces?"

I winced as she pushed the paper toward me. In the photo, my eyes were wide and dark against the white of my face and my mouth was in the shape of an *O*. Great. I looked like a deranged mime ready to go into battle with an oversized pair of scissors.

"It's a great picture," Bill had the audacity to say as he leaned back against the red brocade settee.

"Mike told me the story was so good that they had to print a third edition of the paper," Grandma added. Mike was a friend of Grandma and the editor of the *Oiltop Times*. She winked at me. "He also said to thank you for the boost in sales."

"I didn't have anything to do with that." I waved my hand at the offending shot. "The last thing I care about is selling papers."

"It's a great story," Bill said. "If interesting things happened more often in Oiltop, the paper would be making money instead of losing it." The man balanced a full plate of pastries on one fat knee, a mug of coffee on the other. He had stuffed a napkin in his shirtfront and currently carried an entire piece of peach pie toward his mouth using his bare hand. I swear I had silverware on the tray next to the plates.

His bushy white eyebrows wiggled above his bulbous nose and sparkling green eyes. His bald head shone in the light of the beaded shade beside him as he, too, licked his fingers.

My gaze was drawn back to the paper and the full color photo. I sighed. "I suppose someone in the family is blowing this picture up to couch size as we speak to use as a prop in the next family reunion."

"Wouldn't surprise me none," Grandma Ruth said. "We do love our practical jokes."

A terrible thought occurred to me. "You don't think someone in the family . . ."

"Oh, no, no." Grandma reached over and patted my knee. "Of course not, we're all proud of you. Besides, we know how sick gluten makes you. A stunt like that could put you in bed for days."

"Did you call Doctor Proctor?" Bill asked.

Doc Proctor had been the family physician since I was born and was currently approaching seventy years old himself. I kept my shudder to myself. "I'm fine, I promise. It's not like they could do anything. They don't have shots for gluten allergies."

"Great, you could die in your sleep." Grandma frowned. The freckles on her face formed a dark pattern when she got upset.

"Anyone could die in her sleep," I pointed out. "I'll be miserable for a while, but as long as I'm careful I'll get better."

"Maybe I should spend the night." Grandma's blue eyes danced. "Make sure you're okay. I could bring you tea and tummy medicine."

I love my grandma, but she could raise the roof with her snoring. Besides, she had no idea how to make tea and I had to get up early to start baking. I needed sleep. "I'll be fine. I promise." I made a point of looking at the grandfather clock in the corner. It was nearly eleven. "Really, guys, I have to go to bed. Four A.M. comes early."

"Wait, do you think this was an attempt to harm our little girl?" Bill asked, completely ignoring my strong hint to get lost. He stacked more slices of pumpkin bread on his plate. "I mean, lots of people know about her disease." He turned his laser green gaze on me. "Did you tell the chief this could harm your health?"

"He agreed it was a simple prank," I said impatiently.

"It won't be a simple prank if you end up in the hospital." Grandma Ruth nodded. She went into a coughing fit and Bill thwacked her on the back a couple of times. She recovered and choked out, "Thanks."

"You're most welcome." Bill went back to scarfing dessert.

I tilted my head. "Grandma, why weren't you at the ribbon cutting this morning?" I raised an eyebrow. Not that anyone could tell. Unlike Grandma, my hair was light enough you could barely see the red. Mostly it left a curly, frizzy mass of red-gold like a halo around my head. And my eyebrows had to be drawn in when I put on makeup. Grandma Ruth used to call me "the Golden Gollywog."

"Grandma?"

She hung her head slightly and played with the paper. "I had a Scrabble match."

"She's in the state semifinals," Bill said proudly.

"Grandma, it was my grand opening. You knew I needed all the help I could get. It's what a big family's for. . . ."

Grandma put down her plate and coffee mug. She took a moment to scratch her chin. Her nails against the five o'clock shadow sounded like sandpaper. For as long as I could remember, Grandma Ruth shaved her chin with an electric razor and cackled the whole time. With a happy glint in her eye, she would tell us kids that she bet we'd never seen that before.

I sighed internally. "What?"

"You know I love you, kiddo, right?"

Okay, I'd Play along. "Yes, I know you love me."

"And you know I'll always be there for you . . ."

"Grandma—"

"She hates Lois Striker with a passion," Bill interjected. He drained his coffee cup and set the empty dishes on the now empty trays. "Everybody knows it."

"The woman is a nosy busybody." Grandma stood, brushing the crumbs off her and onto the floor. "And worse, she spits."

"Oh, Grandma, you should have brought Bill to run interference for you."

"I had a rush job come in this morning." Bill stood and got Grandma's hat for her. "Avery Stuart's favorite cat died last night. He needed her stuffed for the memorial at the senior center on Friday. Which reminds me, I gave him your number. There are a lot of us old farts with special dietary needs." Bill patted his wide stomach. "Your gluten-free desserts would really help with the mourning process."

"Sure." I got up. Bill was a taxidermist. He and Grandma Ruth had met in art class in the early 1980s. In her mind, he was a sculptor who used skin and bones to create his vision. The thought made me shudder, but I suppressed it and plastered a wide smile on my face. "I'll make a note to send Avery a sympathy card."

I walked them to the front door.

"Want to know the best part?" Bill's eyes twinkled.

I kept my best poker face on. "Sure?"

"The cat was completely black with green eyes. It'll be perfect for the center's Halloween party at the end of the month. Avery picked the high-backed hissing pose. He said it most reminded him of her."

I swallowed and tried to think of something to say, but my mind had gone blank.

"I tell you what, kiddo." Grandma patted me on the arm as they stepped onto the porch. "I'll get a list of everyone who was at your coffee from Pete. He owes me. Then Bill and I'll see what we can find out. Seniors stick together. Maybe they'll tell us something they wouldn't tell Chief Blaylock."

"Hey, Ruthie, you can write a blog on this," Bill said.

"I'm sure it'll get people talking. You know how much they loved your column before Smith retired you."

Grandma lit a cigarette, held it in one hand, and smacked Bill on the arm with the other. "You are one smooth talker, my friend."

"That's what you like about me." Bill held out his arm and Grandma put hers through his.

"Take care, kiddo," Grandma said, squinting through a haze of smoke. "Lock your door."

"What about Tim?"

"He knows where the key is." Grandma leaned heavily on Bill as they walked down the ramp my responsible brother, Richard, had built on one side of the porch stairs.

I watched as they made their way slowly across the dying grass to Bill's big Lincoln. The giant elms in the small front yard were nearly bare, and the wind whipped the branches about in a good imitation of a scary movie.

I waved as Grandma got in the car and rolled down the window to stick her cigarette out.

"Lock the door!" she ordered before starting another coughing fit.

"Always," I called back and rubbed my arms against the sudden drop in temperature. I waited until they pulled away, then went inside and locked the door behind me. But it didn't matter much. Everyone in town either had a key or knew where we kept the spare. That was the joy and the curse of living in a small town. Everyone knew everything. So why didn't anyone know who the flour bomber was?

"It was a prank," I muttered and cleaned up the dishes. The clock chimed midnight and echoed through the big house. For the first time since I moved in, I was glad for the dead bolt I had put on my bedroom door.

CHAPTER 4

Tasha called me at ten the next morning. It was unusual for her to call during work time. I grabbed my cell phone at the sound of her ring tone. "Hey, you okay?"

"I'm fine," she said, sounding strangely breathless. "How are you?"

I glanced around at the small crowd in the bakery enjoying seconds on coffee and whispering about yesterday. I turned my back on them and dropped my voice. "Minimal health effects, nothing I can't handle. What's up?"

"I have a date."

Was that glee or terror in her voice? "That's good news, isn't it?"

"Yes . . . I think so . . . yes."

"Then that's really great—"

"I've been lying to you," she said quickly. I waited but she didn't elaborate.

"About what?" The mirror on the kitchen door told me people stared. I turned to face them and they all looked down. I reached over and turned up the peppy music, which was supposed to make them all buy more pastries.

"Do you have time for lunch?" Tasha asked.

"Carrie doesn't come in until 3:30 P.M.," I reminded her. Carrie Panken was a second cousin who was still in high school. She was a cute little thing with curly blonde hair—the pretty kind—and baby-doll blue eyes. She was also smart as a whip and more responsible than anyone else in the family. She worked in the bakery, as cashier and server, four hours every day after school, which gave me time to work on Internet orders.

"No problem. I'll bring lunch."

"Okay," I caved.

"Super! See you then." Tasha had gone out of her way yesterday to be helpful. Listening to her explain why she'd lied to me was the least I could do.

My therapist in Chicago would have said something about slipping boundaries. Thankfully she wasn't here, and I wasn't about to tell her.

Two hours later, most of the customers had decided nothing as exciting as yesterday's flour adventure was going to happen and had gone on to other things. The display counter was now half empty, proving I'd done a steady business. Maybe there was an upside to that awful picture.

"The only bad publicity is no publicity," I reminded myself as I wiped down the tables and refilled the remaining patrons' coffee cups. Someone asked why I didn't offer Cokes. The main reason was that soda of most varieties had gluten in it. Anything with artificial flavors usually meant malt or wheat or barley. Instead I offered coffees, sparkling and plain waters, and juices. I couldn't claim the bakery was gluten-free if I didn't really mean it.

By lunchtime, the shop was empty. The doorbells jingled, and I looked up from refilling the display case to see Tasha standing there with two bags marked with the GRANDMA'S DINER logo and a sheepish look on her face. The grandma in question was my cousin Lucy, who was only two years older than I was. In the family tradition, she had had her first babies very young and they had had their babies young, and now my forty-two-year-old cousin was a grandma. In between helping plan her children's weddings and baby showers, she'd opened the town's favorite place to share gossip and French fries.

"Hey."

"Hey," Tasha said back and looked around at the empty store. "Are you ready for lunch?"

"Sure. Do you want coffee, juice, or water?" I asked, breaking the slight tension.

Tasha's shoulders relaxed and she moved to the last table near the back. "Coffee, please. I think the weather is finally changing. It's like fifty degrees out there." She put the bags on the table and took off her jacket.

I handed her a mug of her favorite mocha with a dash of soy milk then took the chair across from her to keep my eye on the front door. I pulled out a heavy paper cup of the best gluten-free chili this side of the Mississippi, along with a spoon and napkin. Since celiac disease tends to run in families, Lucy knew enough not to thicken her diner chili with flour or use beans canned in sauce.

"I'm going to dive right in. . . ." Tasha's cheeks were bright pink and her eyes sparkled. "I've been dating Craig Kennedy for nearly a month now."

I froze partway through taking the recyclable cover off my soup. "You've been dating—as in seeing a man?"

"Yes."

"For over a month . . ."

"Yep." She nodded. Her mouth was in a straight line, but her eyes looked happy.

"Why didn't you tell me?" I let go of the lid and leaned forward. Tasha might have been nine hundred miles away when I lived in Chicago, but we'd talked and texted every day. In fact, she had been my sole source of comfort during my divorce. "I mean look at you, you look happy. How could I not have noticed?"

"You were busy with your big opening, and you're doing all the online order fulfillment work. . . ."

"But we've seen each other almost every day." I cringed

at the whine in my voice. "How come you didn't tell me? How could I not have known?"

Tasha leaned her elbows on the table and played with the noodle soup in front of her. Her eyes barely met mine as her bottom lip stuck out. "I didn't want you to know."

Oh, boy. I sat back. My feelings were hurt. Seriously hurt. Best friends shared everything . . . especially things like when they were worried or happy . . . or dating someone new. At least we had. "Why not?" The words came out in a whisper as I tried hard to keep the tears out of my throat.

"Oh, no, honey." Tasha reached up and patted my hand. "Not just you, I didn't want anyone to know."

I wrinkled my forehead and tilted my head. "Why? Is he an axe murderer? Oh my God"—my eyes grew wide—"did you find him in jail?"

"Oh, oh, no." Tasha giggled. "I found him at the bank."

I shook my head. "So he's a bank robber?"

"No silly, he's an adjunct professor at the college. He was at the bank because he works there part-time. It's Craig Kennedy."

Kennedy. Wait. "The younger or older Kennedy boy?" I had vaguely known both Kennedys since grade school, but they were both ahead of me and looked like bookends. I knew one of the dark, curly-haired guys was Ralph and the other was Craig, but I simply had never taken the time to figure out which was which.

"Craig is younger by a year. He was a couple grades ahead of us. Ralph is the older one who owns Walcott's Drug Emporium."

"I don't get it. I mean, he's a teacher at the college, right? He works part-time at the bank? Why all the secrecy?"

She looked down and stirred her soup. "I was afraid it might not work out."

I kind of understood her fear. Tasha didn't have as big a family as I did. In fact, it had only been her and her mom growing up. So, Tasha was a little naive when it came to men. Which may be why she'd been married three times,

each man more useless than the last. Her first husband, Al
Henly, was Kip's father. He'd run out on her the day Kip was
diagnosed, leaving her to raise a four-year-old with special
needs all by herself. Not that Tasha wasn't doing a bang-up
job without him, but it was tough when all she had was her
mom to lean on. Then there was Buck Giest, who lasted six
months before he ran off with a female trucker out at the
Trucker's Stop next to the turnpike exit. Last was Charlie
Jones, who was currently serving time for bigamy. At least
Charlie had been sorry enough to give her the money she
needed for the down payment on the Welcome Inn back when
getting mortgage financing was easy.

"I know you might be nervous, but this is a Kennedy
we're talking about. . . ."

"Exactly." Her eyes grew wide. "A nice guy, well educated, working two jobs, and a stand-up member of the community. I didn't think it would last." Tasha studied the wide,
fat noodles on her spoon. Her pretty blue gaze zeroed in on
me. "I didn't want to get anyone's hopes up . . . in case."

"In case he didn't like Kip," I finished.

"Exactly." Tasha appeared relieved.

I guess I could understand her worry. I did tend to push
when I thought something was good for a friend of mine. I
would have been all over this, telling her what she should
or should not do where Kip was concerned. The thought
made me blush a bit. "But you're telling me now because
it's working out?" I picked up my spoon and tried to appear
casual.

"Yes." Tasha waved her spoon, dropping the noodles back
into her soup. If it had been me, there would be noodles on
the wall by now. Not only was she pretty, but my friend had
excellent hand-eye coordination. "He's been stopping by a
few nights and getting to know Kip." Tasha appeared to glow.

My friend had been afraid to tell me. Boy, did I feel like
an idiot.

"Kip loves him. They've started this leaf collection.
Craig's a literature professor, but he was in 4-H in junior
high. He saw Kip was picking up leaves and showed him

how to press them. Then he brought over this big book and they've been identifying each one." She grew quiet. "You know how Kip obsesses with things."

I did. It was part of Asperger's. I patted her hand and didn't say anything.

Her eyes filled with tears. "Craig doesn't seem to mind at all."

I handed her a napkin, and she wiped her eyes. "In fact, he said he has a nephew in Louisiana with autism. Then he asked me how I felt about maybe going on a real date. Maybe taking Kip."

"Oh, sweetie, what did you say?"

"I said yes." Tasha nodded. "I wanted you to be the first to really meet him . . ." She turned and looked behind her and waved. The drugstore was across the street from my bakery, and a man leaned against one of the brass sculptures out front. The city had commissioned them from the college over the last two years, in preparation for the tourism boom the new lake would bring.

"Is that him?" I asked as he separated himself from the life-size brass figure of a cowboy. "Has he been standing there this whole time?"

"Gosh, no, he was in the drugstore talking to his brother. I asked him to give me ten minutes before he came out."

"Oh." I supposed that made me feel better. I didn't want to have been stared at this entire time without being aware of it. The door opened, and Craig Kennedy stepped inside. Tasha jumped up and took him by the arm, bringing him over to the table. I felt awkward sitting there looking up at the two of them, so I stood.

Craig Kennedy looked the same as he did in high school: about six foot with wide shoulders, a narrow waist, and nice jeans. He wore a blue dress shirt rolled up at the wrists tucked into his jeans. He had a thirtysomething male jawline that was just this side of soft from working a desk, but the mouth was the same; the nose, those eyes all held the stamp of Ireland on them. His curly hair was thinning now and cut short.

"Hey, Toni." He stuck out his hand. "Great to see you back in town."

"Hi, Craig." I shook his hand. "Have a seat." I waved at the other two chairs at the table. "Can I get you anything? Piece of pie? Coffee? Juice?"

"Tasha tells me you make a mean pecan pie." He sat down, scooting his chair next to hers. It kind of warmed my heart when he draped his arm across the back of her seat.

"Today's version has chocolate in it."

"Great."

I busied myself slicing pie and pouring coffee, but my attention was on Tasha. Her explanation for hiding her relationship sounded reasonable, so why did I feel slighted? I guess because I thought we were best friends, who shared everything. "Cream or sugar?" I asked as I brought the pie and coffee mug over.

"Black's fine, thanks." He waited for me to sit.

I did and stirred my now cold chili. I watched as he dug a fork into the pie and took a bite. His blue eyes lit up. "This is really very good."

"Thank you."

"Every bit as tasty as Tasha claims."

I smiled. "Tasha and Kip are my testers. Nothing goes on the menu that hasn't been approved by them." I took a swig from my bottled water.

"We were wondering . . ." Tasha began. Oh, boy, I should have seen this coming a mile off. First the guilt, now the payback. I tried not to sigh.

"We want to have a dinner party to get our friends together." Craig took hold of Tasha's hand and kissed it. "We'd love it if you could come."

Wow . . . okay. I'd expected them to ask me to take Kip for a while. Not that I wouldn't. I love the little guy and I knew Tasha never gets away, therefore I assumed . . . Darn it. I was not having a good day. Maybe I could blame the flour I'd snorted yesterday.

"I'd love to. When?"

"Friday night." Tasha rubbed Craig's arm. "I know it's

short notice, but I promise not to set you up with anyone. Unless you want to be set up. . . ."

"Or already have a date, then feel free to bring him."

I saw Tasha kick Craig under the table, and laughed. "I'll come, and no, I won't have a date. Do you need me to bake anything?"

"We do plan on going gluten-free, but I'm cooking this time. This is my dinner party and you deserve to come as a guest."

Oh, that was sweet. I was such an idiot. "I'm looking forward to it." I stood when they did. "What time?"

"Be at the house around 8 P.M." Before I could protest, she added, "I know the bakery is open until nine. Carrie said she could work then and close up for you."

"That sounds great." Huh. I couldn't decide if I was flattered Tasha had arranged for Carrie to stay or annoyed that Carrie had known about the relationship before me. I chose flattered since I'd been silly enough today. "Good to see you again, Craig."

I wanted to add, *If you hurt glowing Tasha and make her all un-glowing, I am going to have to hurt you.* But I kept it to myself. He didn't look like he was about to hurt her anytime soon; there was something about the sweet, smitten look in his eyes.

I hoped, for Tasha's and Kip's sake, this one really did work out. As for me, I wasn't going down that road again.

Ever. Eric had broken me. I doubted I would ever again believe that what I thought was love was real. You see, to fall in love, you had to trust more than just the man you were with. You had to trust that you weren't fooling yourself. And if I were to be brutally honest, I doubt I would ever trust myself again. I mean, if Eric could fool me for five years, what could someone else do? No. I couldn't trust that what I thought was love really was. I could never trust my own heart again.

CHAPTER 5

The online orders were prepped to ship, the sky was dark, and it was me and Bon Jovi on my mp3 player. Carrie had gone home a half hour before. I should have been ready to drop after a long day and the even longer ribbon cutting the day before, but I was ready to dance. The bakery store hours were technically seven A.M. until nine P.M., but I was being way too generous. In winter, the streets of a small town rolled up by eight. Now just past that hour, I was dancing to the music as I pulled the coffee carafes off the bar. Time to take them in the back and give them a good cleaning.

The door jangle startled me and I glanced over to see a gorgeous man of about six-foot-two step inside my shop. He wore a cowboy hat, which he promptly took off. His dark brown hair was thick and wavy with the right touch of gray at the temples. He had a square jaw, a generous mouth, a straight nose, and dark brown eyes that seemed to look right through me.

I swallowed and blinked. This must be a hallucination, another reaction to yesterday's flour bomb, because I'd never seen a man that handsome in real life. I mean, they didn't exist. Santa existed. Fairies existed, heck, unicorns existed, but not men who looked like this . . .

He stared at me. I stared back, my mouth dry. He wore a rancher's jacket made of denim outside and faux shearling inside, a dress shirt in some blue stripe, and jeans. Right. Jeans molded to him like a man who took care of his body and anything else he thought was his. Boy, did he take good care.

I refused to swoon. After all, I was hallucinating, right?

"Hey."

Well, hell, even his voice was nice. It had a dark sexy tone to it. "Hey," I replied like an idiot. I did a mental shake. If he was real, then he was a customer. "I mean, can I help you?"

"I certainly hope so."

I clutched the coffee carafes to my chest and retreated behind the nearly empty display case. He smiled at me. Not a sexy crooked smile. Not a flirty smile, but the smile of a man who was desperate. Hmm, maybe he was real. "I need something to serve at a party."

He walked up to the counter, hat in hand. In his dark eyes I saw intelligence, surrounded by crinkles from the sun and possibly laughter. A man who worked and laughed. Damn.

I put the carafes down and grabbed a pad and pen. "When's the party?"

He glanced at his watch. "Now." He looked back at me and ducked his head a bit, then turned on the sexy smile. "It's been one of those days."

I bet he'd practiced his smile from birth. "What kind of dessert did you have in mind?"

"I'm not picky and neither are my grandma and her friends."

"Your grandma?" The thought of this good-looking man bringing his grandma dessert had me melting.

"Yes, you see, my grandma fell on the steps of her porch today and twisted her ankle."

"Oh, no. . . ."

"She's fine. Doc says it was only a sprain, but her friends

came over and a poker game broke out and they sent me to get party food." He ran the rim of his hat through his fingers. "I was on my way to the Dillon's Grocery when I saw your sign and I stopped." He glanced at the nearly empty display case and winced. "I guess I'm too late. . . ."

"Oh, no, I have more in the back," the salesman in me piped up. In the back of my mind I was processing senior ladies playing poker and trying to figure out what kind of dessert to recommend. "Are there any food allergies I need to be aware of?"

"I'm sorry?" He pulled his thick brows together and looked at me as if I spoke a foreign language.

"My specialty is allergy-safe foods." I pointed to the gluten-free flours on the shelf.

"Oh." His face fell a little.

"No, no," I reassured him. "It's all really good." I reached down and grabbed a small cheesecake square out of the taster tray I kept filled. "Here, try."

He looked skeptical but desperate enough to try anything. Until he popped the small square in his mouth; his eyes grew wide and a seductive-as-hell smile broke out on his face. "Wow! That's good!"

"Thanks." I beamed. I couldn't help it. There was something heartwarming about having a hot guy taste your food and love it. "How many are at the party?"

"Let's see, there are four tables of four plus the dealers . . ."

"Dealers?"

His mouth went flat. "Gram's serious about her poker." The corner of his mouth twitched.

"We're talking approximately twenty people?"

"Give or take."

"Great, how about sample platters?"

"Will they have more of those cheesecake pieces?"

"Certainly, I have cheesecake, brownies, pumpkin tarts, and caramel apple tarts. How does that sound?"

"How fast can you put them together?" His eyes flashed and the corners of his mouth lifted.

"Less than five minutes." I poured him a complimentary cup of coffee. "Here, drink this while you wait." I scooted back into the kitchen and pulled together four platters, boxed them in thin pizza-shaped boxes, and brought them out to the front.

"You've saved the day." He paid me. "Do you take tips?"

"Oh, no," I said and handed him his change. "But it would really help me if you could put one of my cards by each platter." I handed him my fancy business cards. "Then the ladies will know where to come to buy more."

He picked up the cards. "Baker's Treat . . . wait, weren't you the one in the newspaper yesterday?"

I looked down and waited for the floor to swallow me whole. It didn't. "Um . . ."

"Oh, Gram is gonna love this. Thank you. Like I said, you made my day." He plopped his cowboy hat on his head, winked at me, and walked out into the darkness.

I crumpled against the back counter as I let my knees go weak at the memory of his wink. It was a fun and flirty little moment, and I enjoyed it. It didn't hurt to enjoy it. It wasn't like I was going to date him or anything. Still, he was pretty in a very rough-hewn way. I walked to the door to lock up, caught a whiff of his cologne, and tried not to think about how long it had been since I'd felt a little zing in my veins. No wonder Tasha glowed.

I was still thinking about the hot cowboy the next morning as I blasted Matchbox Twenty and Rob Thomas songs through the bakery and turned on the ovens in the back. At five-thirty A.M., I was filling the display cabinet when I thought I heard a noise outside. I went to the window and peered out, but Main Street was dead quiet. The sculpture of the cowboy across the street had his hand on his Stetson, his brass coat swirling around his boots. On the next block were a pair of Victorian ladies, their bronze heads tipped together, arms full of packages. On my side of the street was a horse sculpture, and in front of my store was a replica of a horse trough and a tying post. It gave Main Street a ghost-town feel at night. Every twenty feet were replica gaslights, the pools of light braving through the darkness, leaving too much in shadow.

Not seeing anything, I shrugged and went back to work. By seven, the sun had started to come up and I was ready for anyone wanting to stop by for breakfast or to grab a box of pastries for work. I opened the shades on the door, unlocked it, then stepped out to collect the bundle of Wichita newspapers I offered my early patrons.

It was then I noticed the horse trough had arms and legs dangling out of it. Weird. I glanced around, but only a single pickup rumbled down the street. Biting my bottom lip, I debated for a moment about getting out my cell phone. I mean, if the person snoozing in the horse trough were a drunk it might not be the smartest idea to approach him alone and unarmed . . . so to speak.

"Hello?" I called out. The sound of my voice echoed against the buildings. Nothing. I chewed on the inside of my mouth and glanced at my watch. Really, the last thing I needed was some liquored-up guy hanging out in front of my bakery door.

I got brave. After all, this was small-town Kansas, not downtown Chicago. I took a deep breath and marched over to the trough. The arms and legs belonged to a man, face-down in the trough. The trough wasn't filled, but it tended to catch rainwater, which meant face-first was probably not a great idea.

"You can't sleep here," I said stopping close enough to see he wore a long rancher's coat. His cowboy hat covered his face and there was a can of red spray paint on the ground next to his hand. "Hey!"

My gaze went from the can on the sidewalk to my front façade, where red spray paint scrawled across the bricks. It read, IN THE SWEAT OF THY FACE, THOU SHALT EAT BREAD . . .

"Damn it!"

I stormed inside the building, plopped the papers on the counter, and grabbed my cell phone.

"Nine-one-one, what is your emergency?"

"This is Toni Holmes, down at Baker's Treat on Main. I've got more vandalism and a drunk sleeping in the horse trough. Can you send out a patrol car?"

"One moment." There was a pause and I went to the door and glared at the drunk. Whether he liked it or not, he had been caught red-handed. "A patrol car is on its way, Ms. Holmes."

"Thank you." My heart pounded in my chest loud enough I could barely hear a thing.

"Where are you, Ms. Holmes?"

"I'm currently standing in the doorway to the bakery."

"Good, please stay there and stay on the phone until we get there," dispatch said. "It's for your own safety."

"You mean the safety of the drunk," I said. "Because this really pisses me off."

"Yes, ma'am," dispatch said.

A tan sedan parked in front of the bakery. My brother's school friend, John Emerson, got out. "Hey, Toni, what's going on?"

"I'm waiting for a patrol car." It took a lot of work not to stomp my foot. "I've got a bit of a thing . . ." I waved toward the trough. "Oiltop Police are on their way. Come on in and pour yourself some coffee. As soon as they get here, I'll come in and get you a pastry."

John stopped next to me and assessed the situation. "Darn fool vandals. You want me to rouse him out from the trough?" He nodded at the sleeping man.

"No thanks, dispatch says not to touch anything." I pointed at my cell phone.

John nodded his bald head and pulled the phone from my hand. "Hey, Sarah, how are you? Yep, that's what it looks like." His dark eyes twinkled at me. "Want me to bring you a couple of those apple turnovers? Will do. Here you go." He handed the cell back to me. "Sarah wants two of the apple turnovers to go."

"Sarah?"

"Hey, Toni." The dispatcher sounded less professional.

"It's Sarah Hogginboom. I was two grades down from you in school. John brought me some of your turnovers the other day. They were great."

"Um, thanks." I shook my head. Another car pulled up and two women dressed in nurse's uniforms got out. "Listen, I have customers . . ."

"Keep them away from the vandal," Sarah said. "You should be able to hear the sirens now."

In fact, now that she mentioned it, police sirens were echoing down Main Street as the car turned off of Central and onto Main.

"What's going on?" one of the two women asked.

"Nothing to worry about." I opened the door wider. "Come on in and help yourself to coffee. It's free this morning." Hopefully free coffee would keep people coming through the door instead of hanging around watching the cops haul away a drunk.

Both women smiled and went inside as the patrol cruiser screeched to a halt in front of the bakery.

"You can hang up now," Sarah said. "But don't let John forget the turnovers."

I pressed End on my phone and watched Barney Fife step out of the patrol car. I swear, the officer looked like the character on the old Andy Griffith show my mother used to love. He was a thin man in a blue uniform who sniffed and hitched up his heavy gun belt and walked over to me.

"What exactly is the problem here?" he asked, his voice cracking.

I tried to place him, to see if I knew him from school, but I couldn't get the Barney Fife thoughts out of my head. "Hi, I'm Toni Holmes. This is my bakery and that"—I pointed toward the arms and legs sticking out of the brass trough—"seems to be a drunk guy who was attempting to vandalize my shop."

I made an exaggerated motion toward the spray can on the ground and then the red paint on the brick front of my store.

"I see." The officer hitched up his pants and stared at the

drunk. Not that I blamed him. The guy appeared to be twice the size of the officer.

"Maybe you should call for backup?" I asked.

He shot me a look of disgust. "I'm a trained officer of the law. I can handle this." Then he hitched his gun belt again and took three steps toward the drunk. "All right," he said, "fun's over. Get out of the trough."

The wind blew and rustled the guy's coat, but the drunk didn't move.

Officer Fife, as I thought of him, had red creeping up his thin pale neck. His giant Adam's apple bobbed in his skinny neck. "I said, show's over, pal. Get out of the trough." He took out his nightstick and poked the drunk on the back. The guy didn't stir.

I pursed my lips. I could feel the customers behind me staring out the window. "Maybe if you removed his Stetson? Sun shining in his eyes might help."

Barney gave me another evil look, but he did what I said. He reached down and took the hat and we both gasped. The drunk was facedown in about an inch of water and the back of his head was covered in blood.

"That can't be good," I muttered. I dialed 911 again because Officer Fife stood frozen and stared at the guy.

"Nine-one-one dispatch, how can I help you?"

"Hello, Sarah, this is Toni again, down at the bakery. I think you need to send a second squad car and possibly an ambulance. I think the drunk guy might be dead."

CHAPTER 6

I stepped closer as the officer reached down and felt the drunk guy's neck for a pulse. He was a lot braver than me because I wasn't touching a possible dead body. I guess that's why they paid this guy the big bucks.

"Is there a pulse?" I asked. "Should we turn him faceup and start CPR or something?"

"No." The officer straightened. He was a couple inches shorter than me, and his face had gone white. His eyes were big and dark in his face. "There's nothing to revive. The man's colder than a witch's tit."

"Cold as in has been dead for a while?" The thought creeped me out. Had there been a dead body outside my bakery the whole time I was working this morning? I took an involuntary step back. "How long do you think he's been dead?"

The officer ignored me and hit the two-way radio on his shoulder. "Dispatch this is Officer Emry. I want to confirm the DB here on Main Street. Send backup and call the county ME and CSU."

I swallowed hard and stared at the dead man. Had he

died while I was in the bakery working? Had I been a mere few feet away when the murder took place? Or had it been a tragic drunk accident? Could I have saved him if I had seen him tumble into the trough?

"You need to step back, miss." Officer Emry put his arm in front of me. "As first responder, it's my duty to preserve the crime scene."

I took two steps back as a second cop car pulled up along with a small blue Toyota. Candy Cole stepped out of the Toyota and wormed her way around the cops to stand beside me.

"Hey, Toni," Candy stage whispered. She pulled out her small digital camera and snuck in a couple of photos while the cops huddled together discussing what to do with the crime scene.

"Hey, Candy," I whispered back. I'd known Candy since high school, when she'd worked on the *Oiltop High Gazette*. "Are you here for breakfast or the story?"

"I have a police scanner in my car. I heard the report as I was taking the kids to school."

"All right." Officer Emry strode toward us, hitching up his gun belt. He was thin enough that it probably would slip right off him if he didn't constantly hitch. He sniffed. "Looks like I need to keep you, Ms. Holmes, and everyone in your bakery for questioning."

"What? I have work to do."

"And we'll let you do it, ma'am, but first we have to tape off the crime scene and question the witnesses."

I noted a rotund policeman unrolling crime scene tape from the corner of my building, around the lamppost, across the front of the trough, then back to the other side of my building, completely blocking off the bakery. "What's he doing?" I asked, pointing at the giant "crime scene."

"As I said, ma'am, we need to process the area before it gets contaminated."

"But no one can get into my bakery."

"Looks like there are plenty of people inside now," Barney's voice broke. "Let's go inside, ladies. There's nothing to see here." He waved his thin arms and pushed us back into the bakery.

Inside, it was warm and smelled of coffee and sweets. The radio was on and, over the speakers, someone strummed a guitar and sang a lovely ballad about broken hearts. Meanwhile, Officer Emry closed the front door and threw the lock.

"Hey, you can't lock us all in here," John complained. "I've got to get to work, and I promised Sarah I'd bring her pastries."

"We have to get to the hospital," the nurses said in unison.

"I'm working in official press capacity." Candy flashed her newspaper ID. "You need to help these people out, Officer Emry, or there might be a nice sidebar on police brutality in tonight's paper."

I did love Candy. She'd worked with Grandma Ruth for years and now was the lead reporter. She knew how to manipulate things in a small town.

"All right, all right, calm down." Officer Emry took a notebook from his coat pocket. "I promise not to take too long. First off, I need a place to question each of you individually." He looked at me expectantly.

The man had just touched a dead person and had yet to wash his hands. There was no way I was letting him into my kitchen. "You can take the small table in the corner." I motioned toward the corner farthest from the windows.

"Good, I'll start with the first customer you had this morning."

"That's me." John's mouth went flat and turned down at the corners. The men moved toward the table.

"Everyone, pour yourself some coffee and pick out a free roll." I went behind the counter and grabbed plates and tissue squares. After I got everyone settled with breakfast, I studied the full display, dismayed that it might remain full.

A glance out the window showed someone had placed a tarp over the trough and the dead guy; at least there were no longer arms and legs showing. The cops stood around waiting for the coroner.

Another car pulled up nearby and Rocky Rhode stepped out with his giant digital camera. He snapped a few pictures of the cops, the crime scene, and my storefront. Great, another less-than-flattering photo of my business. I stepped back from the window to ensure I wouldn't show up in the shot.

"Did you get a look at the guy's face?" Candy asked me, sipping her coffee and drawing my attention back into the room.

"What? No." I shook my head. "His cowboy hat covered his head. I thought he was blocking out the sun."

"Hey," Officer Emry shouted. "No talking until you're interviewed."

I rolled my eyes at Candy. She grinned.

Outside, the crime lab guys showed up. They wore dark jackets with CSU on them in white letters. They took pictures and got out fingerprint dust and dusted the trough and the bakery windows. I could have told them they were wasting their time. I mean, it was pretty clear the guy had been spray painting. Why would he have touched anything?

"You know, you'll have to go down to the station and get fingerprinted," Candy said low, her eyes sparkling. Her golden-brown hair was the color of soft caramel. Her heart-shaped face held fine features and a smattering of freckles across the nose. A little shorter than me, Candy was thin but curvy and had married a doctor. They had the perfect marriage and the perfect family of two kids, a boy and a girl. I would have loved to hate her, but she was such a sweetheart she kind of deserved what she had.

"Why would I need to do that?"

"They'll need your fingerprints to determine which ones are yours and which ones belong to the victim and the killer."

"Fabulous," I muttered. My prints would be on file for all the world to see. Now, I know I sound paranoid, but if they took your fingerprints, wouldn't they run all future crimes against your prints? I mean, there's something creepy about the idea that you could be innocently opening a door to a bank one day and suspected of being a robber the next. I shuddered and knew I had Grandma Ruth to thank for my morbid imagination.

Speaking of which, a crowd had formed around the cops outside my bakery. Rocky continued to eat up the photo opportunity and snapped shots right and left. Grandma Ruth was front and center in her scooter. Her brown fedora smashed down wisps of orange-and-white hair. She took careful notes of the action.

"Hey," I said to Candy, "looks like you have competition." I pointed to Grandma, who was currently grilling a young kid in a cop uniform.

"She may have the outside scoop," Candy winked, "but I have the insider info. Right?"

I did a quick head count of the crowd. There must be twenty people out there. It would be great if I could get them in here to buy baked goods or a cup of coffee at the least. I was certain the police wouldn't mind. In a small town everyone knew everyone. It might even be better to have a wall between the crowd and their crime scene. I grabbed my cell phone off the counter and speed-dialed Grandma.

"Hey, kiddo, I'm kind of busy here," Grandma Ruth said.

"I know, I can see. Listen, could you do me a favor?"

"Will it interfere with my story?"

"I don't think it will," I said.

"Then name it."

"Could you mention to the crowd of lookie-loos that the view is better from inside the bakery? It's also warmer in here and there's coffee and baked goods?"

"Oh, you're inside?" Grandma scanned the windows. I waved when she spotted me. "Is that Candy with you?"

"Yes, Candy got here when the police did."

Candy gave Grandma a thumbs-up.

"Darn it," Grandma muttered. "Okay. How do you plan on getting these folks inside?"

"Tell them to come around back. I'll have the door open."

"Will do, kiddo." Grandma hung up and used her megaphone voice to announce the bakery was open for anyone who wanted coffee and a better view. All they had to do was go around to the back entrance.

People surged toward the alley. I felt success bloom in my heart. "Candy can you watch the front for me while I open the back door?"

"Sure." Candy settled in on the stool behind the counter. I rushed to the back and opened the door, letting everyone in.

By the time Officer Emry got done with John, the bakery was standing room only. I sold at least twenty coffees and several muffins and pastries.

"You shouldn't have let these people in," Officer Emry chided while I boxed up a baker's dozen apple cinnamon turnovers for John. "I've got no place quiet to question the remaining witnesses."

"This is a business," I replied. "My bills don't go away because you have to investigate a crime scene."

"Looks like my crime scene has brought you some good business. Sounds like motive to me."

I rolled my eyes for the second time that morning and handed John his change. "Thanks, John. Tell Sarah hi for me. The door to the back is through here." John made his way through the kitchen. I turned my attention back to Officer Emry, who currently had narrowed eyes.

"I'm sorry. Listen, you can take the nurses into my office. It's the small alcove next to the back door." I showed him the way. "Will this do?" I turned on the light of what used to be a utility closet but now held a tiny desk, two chairs, and my computer.

"Fine. But don't say anything about this morning until I talk to you," Officer Emry said. "Or I'll have to cite you for obstructing justice."

"No problem." I closed the door on him and the first nurse, Judy, and smiled as Grandma Ruth came through the back door on her scooter.

"How's the coffee?" she asked as she scooted through the kitchen. "It's cold out there, and the cops are slow as molasses in January."

"The coffee's fresh, Grandma, come on in. Good luck getting a seat by the window."

"No worries." Grandma grinned. "One of the advantages of being old is you can push your way through the crowd. If that doesn't work, I'll whack them with my cane." She pulled the cane out of the back of the scooter and waved it.

It was certainly going to be an interesting day.

CHAPTER 7

It seems death can be profitable.

I had nearly sold out by the time they hauled the body off to the medical examiner's office. But I had to close down when Officer Emry wanted to question me. Candy had left to file her story, muttering how circulation was going to soar and that she deserved a raise. Grandma had left to practice for her next Scrabble match and now there was no one to watch the front.

Luckily, most people lost interest the moment the body was put in the black bag and onto a gurney. Morbid, I know, but even I tried to get a look at the guy's face. The cops covered it so only they knew what he looked like and who he was.

"All right, Ms. Holmes." Officer Emry cleared his throat. "Why don't you start at the beginning?"

I sat in my office chair, happy to be off my feet for a moment. Then my stomach started to clench. Funny, but you wouldn't think a person could be nervous if they innocently spotted a dead body, but I was. "What beginning?" I asked. "Like I was born at Oiltop Mercy or when I opened my shop door and noticed a drunk guy sleeping it off in the horse trough?"

From his expression, Officer Emry was not amused. "Let's begin with what time you came to work this morning?"

"I got to work at four. I take Central and pull into the back-alley parking." Interestingly enough, for the first time, I really noticed my office was painted closet white and with no windows. It looked a bit stark, and it smelled like a combination of pine cleaner and printer toner.

"You didn't see anything?" He wrote something in his notebook.

"I didn't see anything." I craned my neck to see if I could read his writing upside down. He tipped the notebook up and raised an eyebrow at me, and I continued. "I'm sure you know the streets are pretty much empty at four in the morning. You do patrol at that time, right?"

"I've been known to take that shift." His protruding Adam's apple bobbed up and down. "Then what happened?"

"I parked in the lot and didn't hear anything. I mean, I'm a girl alone at four in the morning, I listen."

"You opened the back door . . ."

"I unlocked the back, turned on the kitchen lights and locked the door behind me. The rest was the usual stuff."

"Like what, exactly?"

I sighed. The metal office chair was not as comfortable as I remember. Maybe it was my nerves getting to me or maybe I didn't want everyone in town to know how boring my life was. "I pulled out the dough I made the night before to get it warmed up. Then I came in here, turned on my computer, and did about thirty minutes of paperwork. Wait, I went out and made some coffee after I turned on my computer. Then I came back and did paperwork and checked my online orders."

"Let me see if I have this straight. You got here around four and were in your office until four-thirty."

"Yes." I nodded. "I worked in the kitchen from four-thirty until six. There's actually a schedule hanging up on the kitchen wall if you want to look at it."

"A schedule?"

"Sure, I plan out what I'm making the night before based on Internet orders and sales. Sometimes it changes if I get a rush online order but not this morning."

"Sounds exceedingly organized."

I narrowed my eyes and pursed my lips. Was he suspicious of my lists? Geez. "I not only bake but run the front. I need to know exactly how much time I can devote to each recipe."

"And while you were back here, you didn't hear a thing . . ."

I sent him a quick, closed-mouth smile. "I like to blast my music. It keeps me awake and from worrying about being alone."

"You Play loud music?"

"It's not like I'm bothering the neighbors."

"I see." He wrote more things in his notepad. I tried not to roll my eyes. I hate it when people judge me. In a small town, everyone judges you. It was one of the reasons I had left. Right now I was having second thoughts about coming back.

He brought his gaze up. "Then what happened?"

"I filled the display case around five-thirty. Made fresh coffee around six forty-five, and, at seven, I opened the shades, turned the sign around, and unlocked the front door. That's when I noticed the guy in the horse trough."

"And all that time you heard nothing."

I scrunched my forehead and frowned. "Wait, no, I did hear something. It had to have been around five-thirty because I went out to get the display trays. I heard like a thump or something."

"A thump?" He sat up straighter.

"I don't know . . . it was like something hit the store window. I looked out but didn't see anything. It was pretty dark. The streetlamps don't exactly shine bright."

"Did you call 911?"

My eyes widened for a second and I shrugged. "Why? It was only a thud. It certainly didn't sound like a gun going off or a car backfiring. It could have been anything."

"What did you think it was?"

"I don't know, that a bird or something hit the front window. Like I said, I looked out and didn't see anything. I went back to work."

"Did you hear anything else?"

"Nothing. Seriously, I opened the front door and spotted the guy in the trough at seven. I might have said something like, 'Hey, get off the sculpture.' But he didn't move. Then I noticed the paint can."

"The paint can?"

"Yes, there was a can of spray paint on the ground next to the guy's hand. That's when I noticed the paint on the front of my store."

"How did that make you feel?" He looked down his long, thin nose at me.

"What are you, a therapist?"

"Answer the question."

It was hard not to get snarky. Seriously, what did it matter how I felt? "I guess I was mad someone would do that to my storefront." He wrote my words down. My nerves picked up. Did he think I had killed the guy over spray paint? Crazy, I lived in Chicago. People tag stuff all the time. It's expensive to clean up, but you don't kill people over it.

"Then what did you do?"

"I called 911 and reported the drunk guy with the spray can." I took a deep breath and let it out slow. "Sarah kept me on the line until you showed up."

"Did you touch the DB?"

I sat up straight. "What's a DB?"

Officer Emry frowned. "The dead body . . ." He waved his hand dismissing my ignorance. "Did you touch it or anything near it?"

"No and no. I wasn't about to confront a drunk all by myself. Like I said, as soon as I saw the spray can I took a step back and called 911."

"You're telling me you didn't know he was dead?" Officer Emry's eyes gleamed. I bet he was having fun with this.

"How could I know? This is Oiltop; people don't die on Main Street."

"Did you identify the body?"

A queasy feeling washed over me. There had been an actual dead person in front of my store—as in smelly, squishy, creepy dead. "No, I didn't see his face. The hat covered his face. You saw that. In fact, I thought he had his head turned to the side, like someone who sleeps on his stomach. Seriously, I figured he was a drunk sleeping off his bender."

Officer Emry stood and hitched up his gun belt. "We'll need you to come down to the station and let us take your fingerprints. It's procedure."

I rested my elbow on my desk and the side of my face in my hand and closed my eyes. "Candy told me."

"When can we expect you?" His tone was pushy—real pushy and grating on my last nerve.

"When my help gets here, after school." His pause and narrow-eyed stare caused me to be more precise. "I'll be there at 3:30 P.M." I stood, pushed in my chair, and glanced at my watch. It was nearly noon. "When will they take down the crime scene tape?"

"In a day or two."

Really? They were going to block off the entrance to my bakery for a day or two? "Why so long?"

Officer Emry stepped out into the kitchen. It smelled better here, like rising yeast dough and sugar. "Depending on what the county ME finds, we may need to come back and look for more evidence."

"Like what kind of evidence?" I went over to the sink and washed my hands.

"Bullets and the like."

"Bullets?" I leaned back against the deep stainless steel and felt the blood rush from my head. "Are you telling me the guy was *shot* outside my bakery?" Thoughts of bullets flying through the windows and walls had me shaking. I'd heard of plenty of innocent people shot in the safety of their own living rooms. My gaze went to the front wall. The storefront was brick, but there was no way of telling if it was decorative or real.

"I can't say if the victim was shot or not." Officer Emry shrugged. "But it's a possibility."

"A possibility? There was a possibility I could have been killed by a stray bullet in my own shop in Nowhere, Kansas?" I grabbed a work stool and sat down, hoping the action of drying my hands on a clean white towel would distract from my distress. I guess it worked because Officer Emry didn't seem to notice.

"Is there anyone who can verify you were inside the bakery all morning?"

My eyes widened. "Um, no. I told you, I work alone." Just me and Bon Jovi. "Why does it matter if I work alone or not?"

"The way I see it, Ms. Holmes, you'd better hope you don't have a motive, because your alibi is a bit thin."

My right eye started to twitch as Officer Emry jangled his way toward the front door of the bakery.

"You'd better lock this behind me," he said. "If anyone comes through the taped off area and goes through this door we might have to charge you with aidin' and abettin' the destruction of a crime scene."

I got up and locked the door behind him. I almost stuck out my tongue at the skinny runt of a man, but then I realized my mama was probably looking down at me from heaven and would disapprove. I leaned my back against the glass door and stared at my empty bakery. I wasn't going to ask if the day could get any worse. That would be asking for trouble, now wouldn't it?

CHAPTER 8

"Oh, my God, are you all right?" Tasha's eyes were wide as she rushed into the back of the store. It was close to six P.M. and I hadn't had a new customer since I came back from the police station. "I got here as soon as I could. Kip had two doctor's appointments today."

I kneaded dough. It was great to have something to slap around. It had taken me fifteen minutes of hard scrubbing to get the ink off my fingertips. "You know, I don't know." I rolled the yeasty dough and pushed in with all my strength, turned, rolled, pushed. "A man died outside my door." I waved toward the front of the store. "The front door is locked because it's taped off with crime scene tape and I have exactly no customers coming in through the back. Even though I posted a big sign in the window announcing I was open."

Tasha hugged me tight. I couldn't hug her back because my hands were covered in sweet rice flour. "You must have been very scared."

My shoulder muscles relaxed. Here was someone who cared about me and what I had gone through. Tears sprang to my eyes and I fought them back. "It's silly to feel sorry for myself." I sniffed. "I mean, the poor man died. His family will be devastated. What if he left little kids behind?"

Tasha stepped back, straightened her arms while keeping her hands on my upper arms and studied me. "Of course you get to feel sorry for yourself. First the flour vandalism the other day and now this." She shook her head. Today she wore a long sleeved tee shirt, stylish jeans, and a smart tweed jacket. Her hair was pulled back but looked like a movie star's hair, not tumbled about in a messy ponytail like mine. "I saw the paint on the front of the building. The sight of it scared the tar out of me. He vandalized you while you were alone in the building."

I slumped down onto a nearby kitchen stool. "You make it sound as if he might have hurt me."

Her generous mouth thinned. "He could have. Then I would have had to kill him myself."

I blinked back the tears. I guess I was more emotional than I thought. Or maybe I was tired. I'd used today's free time to tear apart and clean my kitchen. I was currently on my fourth batch of backup dough. "Officer Emry told me my alibi was weak and I'd better hope the ME declared this an accident."

"What?" Tasha was aghast. "What an idiot. Don't let him get to you. He's a bumbling fool. Reminds me of Barney Fife from the old *Andy Griffith Show*. Don't you think?" She pulled another stool around and sat down, then reached out to rub my arm. "Now, really, how are you doing?"

"The kitchen is clean." I waved my hand at the spotless, sparkling tiles and countertops. Even the sink shone to within an inch of its life. Tasha knew me long enough to know I worked when I was upset.

"Darn it, I tried to get here sooner." She frowned at me. "How many extra batches of cookies have you made?"

"Not too many." I shrugged. "I had to go down to the police station and get my fingerprints taken." It had been a bit humiliating. Half the guys at the station had gone to school with me. I had no idea what they were thinking, but

I'd felt their gaze on my back when I walked through the building.

"Why on Earth . . ." Tasha's blue eyes flashed.

"They said it was to rule me out." I stared at my fingers.

"That's it. Come on." She grabbed my arm and stood.

"What?"

"I'm going to buy you dinner and a drink. A really big drink." She tugged me toward the door.

"But I've got work to do—"

"There isn't anything you can't do later." Her expression was stern. "I'll bet you haven't eaten all day. . . ."

Huh, I couldn't remember eating. But then again, who would want to eat knowing there'd been a dead body a few feet from your table.

"Wash up and grab your coat. We're going to your cousin's diner for dinner."

I threw a clean cotton cloth over the dough I had been working and washed my hands. "But you bought me lunch yesterday."

"And now I'm buying you dinner, but only so you can have a couple of drinks without passing out. Trust me, honey, you need a drink."

"Carrie isn't here. Who'll watch the store?"

"Do you have any customers?"

"No."

"Then lock up and put a 'be-back-in-an-hour' sign up."

She was right, of course. Besides, there weren't any customers. Not now and probably not until the crime scene tape came down. Between that and finding a dead guy in the horse trough, I needed a drink. Any sane person would. I grabbed my jacket and tugged it on, then locked up, slapped a handwritten note on the door, slipped my arm through Tasha's, and we walked the four blocks to Grandma's Diner.

When we stepped inside, the entire dining room went quiet. Everyone stared. I looked at Tasha. She looked at me and shrugged. Then we both grinned and grabbed the booth in the farthest corner.

The diner's interior was rustic. The walls were paneled wood. There were booths along the outer walls and tables on the inside and along the wide front window. The window curtains matched the checkered tablecloths. Every table had a red glass candleholder with a lighted candle inside. Then there was a stainless napkin holder, glass-and-stainless salt and pepper shakers, and a small bottle of ketchup. It could have been one of many diners across America, but to me it looked and smelled like home.

My cousin Lucy came out of the back room. "What are ya'll staring at? Eat something." She shamed them into turning away, then walked up and gave me a big hug.

Lucy was a little shorter than me with generous curves and bouncy blonde hair. I swear, not a strand of gray in sight. She had a turned-up nose, sparkling blue eyes, and the cute look that made men's heads turn. "I was wondering if you'd come. You need to be around family after a day like today. I made gluten-free chicken-and-rice casserole." She brushed at imaginary crumbs on the checkered tablecloth. Everything in her diner was pristine. "Tasha, how are you? How's Kip?"

"I'm good," Tasha said. "I came as soon as I could get away. Kip's with his developmental tutor for the next two hours and I stole Toni from her work. We're here for a drink. What do you have?"

"Honey, the bar is open." Lucy's eyes sparkled. "What's your desire? It's on the house."

"No, I can't . . ." I protested. I know Lucy worked hard for any profit the little diner made. Happily married to her husband, Robert Brockway, for twenty-five years, Lucy laughed when I called her a child bride, but had been only seventeen when she and Robert got married. They had their share of ups and downs, but managed to still keep love in their relationship.

I asked her once how she did it. She said they had made a promise to be brutally honest with each other always. Then she winked and said a good love life softened the blow. Robert was a local truck driver and worked long hours, but he was home on weekends and that was all that mattered. Right now I envied them their connection, their long-term partnership. It would be nice to have someone to lean on when a dead body showed up outside your door.

"I'm buying," Tasha said firmly. "We'll have two gin and tonics, some of those great tortilla chips you make, and salsa."

"Coming right up," Lucy said. "Toni, you call me if you need me. Emmi will be your waitress tonight, and the tab is on me. No protesting—" Lucy raised her hand to cut off Tasha. "We'll settle things next book club." She gave me another hug and was gone, checking on customers and urging her waitstaff to keep on its toes.

Our waitress, Emmi, was a tall college student in her early twenties. She had long brown hair, which she wore in a ponytail at the back of her neck. The drinks in her hands were in tall glasses with ice and a lime slice hanging off the edge. She placed them down in front of us. "Chips and salsa will be right out. Lucy said you wanted the GF chicken casserole, right?"

I nodded and wrapped my hand around the drink.

"What are you having?" Emmi asked Tasha.

"I'll have a club sandwich with fries, thanks."

I sipped the tall, cold drink and enjoyed the tang on my taste buds. The drink was light on the tonic and heavy on the gin. Lucy made it medicinal strength.

"Oh, my, this is good," Tasha said. "Drink up. I want to see the color come back into your face."

"I didn't know the color had left my face."

She patted my hand. "Of course you didn't. I bet you've been pushing yourself to work so you don't have to think. Right?"

Thankfully, at that moment Emmi brought over a large bowl of hot, fresh chips and two small bowls of salsa so I didn't have to answer Tasha's question. The second and third sips of gin and tonic went down easy and I relaxed a bit.

"Now." Tasha dipped a chip and popped it into her mouth. "Tell me everything. Don't leave out the juicy parts."

I sighed and grabbed a chip. Munching, I realized I was hungrier than I thought. Armed with liquor and snacks, I told Tasha the whole sordid tale, adding how I'd had to give away coffee the first hour until Grandma Ruth showed up and helped move the crowd inside.

I was halfway through my drink when Tasha stopped me with a hand to my wrist.

"Oh, my, look who came in for dinner."

I looked over my shoulder to see the handsome rancher from the other night.

"Yum!" Tasha whispered.

"Hey, I thought you were dating Craig."

"I am but Sam Greenbaum can put his shoes under my bed any day."

"Sam Greenbaum," I repeated. Huh, the handsome guy had a name. I watched him settle an old woman into a chair at a table next to the window. He noticed me and waved.

I waved back. He moved in our direction and I ducked back into the booth. Tasha's mouth hung open and her eyes went wide. "Do you know him? You must know him, you waved, and now he's heading our way."

Discretion was not one of Tasha's best qualities. The heat of a blush rushed up my cheeks. Being a redhead, I'm certain it showed like a glowing fire. Why could I never look calm, cool, and collected?

"Hey," he said, approaching the table. The man had a way of walking that could bring a tear to your eye.

I swallowed hard. "Hi." My drink was in my hand before I knew it and I sipped in a poor attempt to cool off. I might have even pressed it against my heated cheek.

"You're the bakery lady from last night, aren't you?" His eyes twinkled—actually twinkled, mind you. I tried to keep from drooling.

"Yes. How did your grandma and her friends like the sample platters?" Hooray for me for being able to make conversation when I was face to waist with the hand-some hunk who was probably married . . . or gay.

"She and her friends loved it. They took several of the

cards to call you for catering jobs. I'd say that made it a success. I'm Sam, by the way." He held out his hand.

"Toni." I shook. Darn it, his hand was big and warm and callused in all the right places. "Toni Holmes."

"Nice to meet you, Toni." He squeezed my hand gently. His gaze made the blush on my cheeks that much hotter.

"I'm Tasha," Tasha said, breaking the silent admiration in his gaze. Or was that my gaze? Anyway, thank goodness for Tasha. "Tasha Wilkes, Toni's best friend since grade school. But then you didn't go to school with us, did you?"

"Hello, Tasha. No, I'm from Towanda, originally. I went to school there my whole life. It's probably why we haven't met." He shook her hand as well, then turned his attention back on me. "I'm here with my grandma." He turned to Tasha. "Grams moved into Oiltop to live in the assisted living center. I brought her here for some comfort food after being poked and prodded by her doctor." He pointed his hand toward a table near the front door. Grandma peered at me through her thick lenses and I smiled and waved. I wondered if she knew Grandma Ruth. I almost asked Sam if she did, but thought better of it. Grandma Ruth was cool and quirky, smart and loyal, but her independent streak gave her a reputation some elderly ladies didn't like much.

Not that I wanted to make a good impression or anything. Or could, even if I tried. I tried not to sigh. My family always made the impression first. There was no way around it. Sooner or later, Sam would figure it out.

"I wanted to stop by and introduce myself and thank you again for saving me." Sam's smile had my cheeks glowing.

"Hey, anytime." I watched him walk back to his table, admiring the way he wore his Levi's.

Emmi arrived to block the view and put china plates with generous servings of steaming food down on the table.

"You've been holding out on me," Tasha said as she grabbed a French fry from her plate and dipped it in ketchup.

"There's nothing to hold out." I peppered my casserole. "He came into the bakery and needed some platters for his grandma's poker tables. I set him up with several dessert sample platters."

"And gave him your card . . ."

"It was purely business." I lifted my empty glass at Emmi and she nodded and turned toward the bar. "I told you, I'm never going there again." No matter how much my heart went pitter-patter. It's what got me in trouble with Eric, and I was never trusting that feeling again. "You enjoy yourself with Craig."

"Oh, no, Sam Greenbaum is not easily ignored." Tasha waved her glass Emmi's way as well, jangling the remaining ice.

"He's probably married with five kids." I refused to look at him again no matter how much I wanted to. It would be too obvious.

"I happen to know he's a widower with no kids." Tasha wiggled an eyebrow at me. "You should ask him to come to the dinner party on Friday."

"What? No."

Emmi set down fresh drinks and took away the empty glasses. Now we wouldn't look like lushes, although I was starting to feel like one as the gin buzzed in my head. "No. No. No."

"Why not?"

"Well, for one, I don't ask guys out. It's a rule of mine because it sets a bad tone for the entire relationship. And B, I can't date now, not with the dead guy and all. It seems kind of disrespectful. And three, I don't have time. I have a business to get up and running, which takes every minute of my day and most of my nights, planning and baking and such."

Tasha narrowed her eyes and pursed her mouth. "We'll see about that."

"And don't you ask him either," I said. "You promised not to set me up."

"Hell, why did I go and make such a fool promise, anyway?"

"Because you're my BFF. Cheers." I toasted her and we clinked glasses. I took a sip of my drink and took a peek at

Sam. His head was bent over the menu and he pointed out
something to his grandma. His dark hair curled a bit around
his collar and his smile was filled with love for the older
lady. And yeah, I might have sighed a little.

My divorce was less than a year old and it had been ugly.
I don't know how Grandma had done it after thirty years. Eric
and I were married only five. Of course, I later found out he'd
been sleeping with everyone and possibly their brother the
entire time we were married. First I'd discovered he'd run
through all our savings with his drinking. Then I found out
about Mercy, his best friend's wife. It'd been ugly, really. I'd
left something at home and went back to get it only to find
them knocking boots on the living room couch.

I burned the couch, of course, after I tossed them both out
on their asses. The hardest part was discovering my entire
marriage had been a lie. While I thought Eric and I were soul
mates, working partners moving toward future goals, Eric
figured I was an easy paycheck and a dupe he could string
along with his pretty eyes and to-die-for ass. When everything
crumbles, when all your dreams are nothing but dust, it takes
a lot more than a handsome face to make you want to date
again.

I sipped my gin and took one last glance at Sam. Eric
had a grandma, too. It turned out his grandma and his mom
came first. His wife, well, I was good for keeping the house
clean, his clothes washed, and the checking account full. It
would be a long time before I fell into that trap again. Happy
hormones or no, I'd learned my lesson well.

CHAPTER 9

I couldn't sleep. Even after Lucy's dinner and Tasha's company and three large gins with almost no tonic, I was a head case. I stared at the ceiling in my bedroom. Officer Emry's words echoed through my head.

". . . Your alibi is a bit thin."

The identity of the man in the horse trough was pending notification of his family. No one had said a word about how he was killed.

It had to be an accident. Right? I mean, he was probably drunker than a skunk, fell into the trough, cracked his head, and had a heart attack. All the chief would say was that it was an ongoing investigation. I'd even sicced Grandma Ruth on him, but, if he knew more, he wasn't telling.

To top it off, Carrie quit. I turned onto my side, pulling the pale blue-and-white checked comforter with me. When I asked why, she explained it was because her mother had said she couldn't work where it wasn't safe. She offered to let me talk to her mom, my cousin Liz, personally, but I turned down the offer. When Liz's mind was made up there was no changing it, no matter how much Carrie loved the bakery.

I'd lost my extra help. The thought made me punch my pillow. Punching didn't make the pillow any more comfortable or stop my mind from racing. Even the lavender scent I spritzed in an attempt to create a calm environment didn't calm the panic in my gut. How was I supposed to run a bakery without even part-time help? I didn't suppose putting a HELP WANTED sign in the window would work either—at least not until the crime scene tape was taken down.

Ugh.

I flipped onto my other side, getting my legs tangled in the sheets in the process. Great. I straightened out the blankets and wished my life were so easy to set right. I needed to find a way to get people back into the bakery. Well, it *was* October. People put crime scene tape up as decorations all the time for Halloween, right? Maybe I could somehow leverage that.

I tossed to my other side. The sheets tangled, again, and I comforted my frayed nerves with the reminder that I still had the online orders. They were the real bread and butter of my shop. Thank goodness the shipping guy wasn't afraid to come to the bakery. I could count on those lovely brown boxes going out on time.

Maybe I could contact Pete at the chamber and get him to rustle me up a catering job or two. After all, Halloween parties were coming up. Nursing homes and schools were great places for gluten-free goodies. I'd even said so in the newspaper interview.

That was it then. I decided to make up some fliers in the morning presenting holiday party options. Now if I could get some sleep . . .

Yeah, right. Sleep was highly unlikely. Let's face it: the only thing more terrifying than the possibility of being an out-of-work murder suspect was the idea of going back to work in the early morning . . . alone . . . with a killer on the loose.

* * *

"**G**ood morning."
    "What are you doing here?" I tried to blink the grit from my eyes without disturbing the makeup I'd troweled on, and for a brief moment wondered if I was still in bed dreaming.

Nope. Grandma Ruth stood in my kitchen making coffee at 3:45 A.M. "You know us old people." She poured cream into her espresso and then put the pint container back into the refrigerator. "We're up at the butt crack of dawn. By the way, you've got like twelve messages on your answering machine."

I glanced at the offending device as I grabbed a thick mug from the cupboard beside the sink. "It's probably Rosa and Joan checking on me." Tim and I were the only two who still lived in Oiltop. My sister Joan lived in Kansas City and Rosa lived in Wichita in fancy houses with fancy friends.

Eleanor wouldn't call. Between the family vacation at Disneyland and the fact that she lived in San Francisco, it would take a week before she found out. And by then the murder would be solved. As for my oldest brother, Richard, he would only get involved if Rosa bugged him and then he was more likely to e-mail than call.

I shrugged off the messages. Most likely Rosa and Joan wanted nothing more than the inside scoop so they could gossip with their friends. I didn't have time for that right now.

"Tell me the truth, Grandma, you're here because you didn't want me in the bakery alone, did you?" I added cream to my coffee and took a sip.

Grandma shrugged. "Like I said, I was up."

I glanced out the window. My van was the only vehicle in the driveway. "Did Bill drive you?"

"I drove myself."

The state had taken away Grandma Ruth's driver's license last year after she totaled a car for the third time. She was angry at the time, but had gotten over it and bought herself a scooter. Now she drove the scooter down the middle of the road. Tim had equipped it with lights and a large orange flag on a pole tall enough so that drivers could see her when she came around corners.

"You drove the scooter? You know, one day the police are going to give you a ticket for driving an unauthorized vehicle down the street."

Grandma shrugged. "This time of night, no one's around to complain. I have my cell phone should I get into trouble."

I made a face. "Even if you think you can afford to pay the fine, I don't want to have to attend your funeral when some drunk runs you over."

"Kiddo, either way one of these days you'll be attending my funeral. Besides, freedom of movement is a constitutional right."

"Humph." It'd been a while since I took American Government, but I highly doubted our forefathers had Grandma Ruth's scooter in mind when they wrote it. "Come on. I'll load the scooter into the van and we'll get going."

"Great!" Grandma hefted her bulk out of the kitchen chair. Cane in one hand, coffee mug in the other, she let me hold the back door as she ambled out. "I needed a cigarette. You certainly take your sweet time getting dressed for work. I've been dying for a smoke for thirty minutes."

"What time did you get here?"

"Right before your alarm went off. Tim let me in. Did you know he got a job at FedEx filling trucks?"

"No, I didn't." Tim was older than me, but he'd never settled down. Richard's responsible streak had sent Tim in the opposite direction. While Richard worked hard, Tim glided through life. His tall, lanky body and scruffy dirty blond hair made him a favorite at the bar scene. Needless to say, Tim only came home to change clothes or to sleep. We might live in the same house, but we ran in different circles. "I haven't seen Tim in days."

I loaded Grandma's scooter into the van. Lucky for me, I had a ramp for the van and it was simply a matter of driving the scooter up into the back.

"Probably because he sleeps while you work and vice

versa." Grandma took a long drag on her cigarette. "Like I said, he let me in. Told me he had just come in from work. You might know that if you answered your machine." I took her chiding in stride and opened the van door for her. She frowned, then twisted the ash off the end of the butt and stuffed it into her coat pocket. "Waste not, want not."

I coughed and waved away the cloud of smoke as she settled into the passenger seat. "Someday you're going to start a fire in your pocket from doing that."

Grandma grinned. "I'll go down in the *Guinness Book* as spontaneous human combustion. Getting my name in there has always been a dream of mine, you know."

I rolled my eyes and closed her door. The walk around to my side was brisk. The air had the crisp scent of fall. People around town had already started putting out decorations of cornstalks, pumpkins, and scarecrows. Still it wasn't Halloween until Mr. Peters, who lived two doors down, put up his annual graveyard display. A tiny shudder streaked down my back. Graveyards and skeletons hit a little too close to home at the moment.

Grandma Ruth made a regular pest of herself for the rest of the morning. She poked and prodded into everything I made. And she went out to smoke every five minutes, letting the cold air blow into the kitchen. I had to put my yeast goods in a proofer to prevent them from falling. Then there were the ashes, which fell off her every time she moved. I had to check each batch of dough to make sure nothing got into the food. I finally sat her down in my office and turned on the computer. She found a Scrabble game and I was home free.

Until seven A.M., when I opened the front door to put up a go-around-back sign only to find Candy ducking under the crime scene tape. Rocky was right behind her with his camera in hand.

"Hey." I smiled at them and held the door open. "Come in, want some coffee?"

"Oh, we're not here for the coffee." She took out her little recorder. "We came for your reaction."

"My reaction? To what? To the fact they haven't taken down the crime scene tape yet?" I put the sign down and made my way around the counter to get coffee mugs. "Let me tell you, crime tape certainly isn't good for business."

"Oh, no, dear." Candy's smile was darn right predatory as she leaned across the display case. "I take it you haven't heard."

"Heard what?" I put two oversized coffee cups and saucers on the counter in front of them. "That my misfortunes are selling newspaper subscriptions? Yes, I've heard."

"No, not that." Candy waved her hand. "I'm not talking about the increase in newspaper sales or my negotiations for a bonus."

"Then why are you here, Candy?" I stuck my hands in my apron pockets.

"For your reaction, silly." Candy picked up the cup. Her eyes sparkled.

"Like I said, what reaction?" I felt like I was doing an Abbott and Costello routine.

"She doesn't listen to the local radio." Grandma Ruth came out from the kitchen, moving quick for an old woman with a cane. She snagged the cup out of Candy's hand, made a beeline for the coffee, and helped herself. "Let me guess," Grandma said as she added generous amounts of cream and sugar. She drank her coffee beige. "They announced the dead guy's identity."

"That's right." Candy was nearly breathless. Her lovely caramel-colored curls trembled with excitement.

"Get on with it." Grandma waved.

"It's George Meister." Candy's eyes were wide. She stuck the microphone under my nose to capture my thoughts.

Only, I didn't have any. Not intelligent ones, anyway. "George Meister?" I wrinkled my forehead, trying to place the name as Rocky snapped photos. "I know that name. Who was he, again?"

"The protester," Grandma informed me.

"Oh." I felt my expression freeze. My thoughts raced. Candy's mic followed my every motion while Rocky caught every nuance of my expression on film. All I could think was oh, crap, but I didn't expect those words would make a good caught-on-tape moment and I certainly hope it didn't show on my face. I said the next thing that came to mind. "I guess that explains the paint can."

"Put that camera down," Grandma ordered and shifted her weight onto the stool behind the counter. "How'd he die?" She took a sip of her coffee, but I could see the reporter in her thinking and thinking hard.

I personally had my fingers crossed that he'd drowned. You know, drunk, accidental drowning. Or heart attack. Yeah, heart attack would be even better. Case solved. Crime scene tape gone. I looked at Rocky. His eyes gleamed. His hands were ready on his camera.

"They're calling it a homicide." Candy's eyes were alight with intent. "Toni, did you kill George Meister?"

My mouth went dry. My jaw went slack. The camera's flash kept popping, blinding me. "What?" I glanced toward Grandma for some help.

"Don't answer," Grandma said sharply. She narrowed her blue eyes at Rocky. "I said, put that camera down or I'll put it down for you."

He lowered the camera and held out his free hand. "Okay. I'm putting it away."

Grandma gave him her best evil eye until he tucked the camera into the bag strapped across his shoulder. Then she turned her attention to Candy. "What made you ask that question?"

"Everyone knows George Meister was behind the flour bombing of your grand opening."

"They do?" I was confused. "I thought the chief said it was two joggers."

"Add the fact that George was vandalizing your store when he was killed," Candy pushed on. "Then you yourself told everyone you were inside the store at the time he was murdered."

"I was? You mean he wasn't killed before I got here?"

"What time was he killed?" Grandma asked. She studied her coffee cup as if the pattern in the cream would give her the answer she wanted.

"The county medical examiner estimates George's time of death to be around 5:30 A.M."

The hairs on the back of my neck rose. "Oh, no, the noise I heard was a man being murdered?"

"What noise?" Grandma asked, her fierce, intelligent gaze intent on my face.

"There was a thud around 5:30 that morning. I thought maybe a bird had flown into the window or something. I looked out but it was too dark to see anything." I tried not to imagine what would have happened had I actually stepped out to see what the noise was.

"Honey," Candy pushed, "noise or no noise, you had motive and opportunity. Did you do it?"

"Seriously?" I asked her. Here I'd been ready to give her a free cup of coffee. Not anymore. I stepped back.

"Did you?" Her hand wafted under my nose.

"Of course not." I pushed the mic away. "I wouldn't kill anyone."

"Are you telling me it's a coincidence you're new in town and a man who attacked you at your ribbon-cutting ceremony gets murdered outside your bakery?" Candy's eyes glittered like a snake's. Rocky glanced at Grandma and stayed out of the fray.

"Are you kidding me? I'm not new in town." I crossed my arms in front of me. "I grew up here. Are you saying any murders that happened while I lived here as a kid were my fault?"

"No," Candy said thoughtfully. "But it's a good angle. I can check and see how the murder rate was when you lived here and what happened after you left."

"Stop it." Grandma slapped her big square hand on the counter. "Toni wouldn't kill anyone."

"Oh, really? Then why is the chief at the courthouse right now getting a warrant signed to search your home and your bakery for evidence?"

I sat down hard at the word *warrant*. I think I wanted to throw up. No, I wanted to faint.

"Put your head between your knees." Grandma was beside me. Her sharp tone of voice combined with her palm on the back of my head had me doing exactly what she said. I had to admit, staring at the black-and-white tile floor was a bit more calming than looking at Candy. Her delight at my distress was unnerving.

"I thought we were friends, Candy," I muttered to the floor.

"We are friends, honey." Candy came around the counter and squatted down to peer at me. "That's why I came here before the chief did."

I turned my head in uncertainty. "You came to warn me?"

"Good friends hide the body, honey, remember?" Her gaze took on a warm and concerned look. I wasn't sure if I should believe it.

"I don't have anything to hide," I insisted.

"Don't talk to her," Grandma chided. "She might be your friend, but she's also a reporter. Everything you say is on the record."

"Is it?" I sat up and narrowed my eyes at them both. Grandma nodded and did a half wink. Candy tried to look innocent. Good lord, they both wanted the story.

I covered my face with my hands. Crap.

The door opened, jingling the bells. I peeked between my fingers to see John and the nurses come in. Thank God, customers. Yes! The crime scene tape wasn't stopping people from shopping. I glanced at the sign I'd made to tell people to go around back and shrugged. Too late now, I thought and ignored the echo of Officer Emry's warning that people crossing the crime scene tape could get me into trouble with the law. At this point, what's a little more trouble?

"Hi guys, what can I get you?"

"Oh, I'll take a blueberry muffin and a coffee," Kay said. Today she wore light blue scrubs and a navy blue jacket

"Make mine a pumpkin muffin and coffee," Judy said. She had on matching scrubs but a pale pink sweater instead of a jacket

"Customers," I hissed and waved Candy and Grandma out from behind the counter. I filled the nurses' orders and went to bag them when Kay spoke up.

"Oh, we don't need them in a bag." She tilted her head and batted her brown eyes at me.

"No?" I wrinkled my forehead.

"We don't want them to go. . . ." Judy stated.

I felt confused, but went ahead and took out plates and ceramic coffee mugs. "Don't you have to work today?" I placed their muffins on the plates and handed them off. I mean, they had their uniforms on, why wear them if they didn't have to work?

"Oh, yes, we have to work, but we got permission to hang around." Judy pulled her muffin-filled plate and cup and saucer toward her.

"You got permission?" I rang up the bill. My thoughts whirling. "Why?"

"We're here to see them serve the warrant." Kay and Judy sent each other looks as they reached into their purses and paid. "Everyone at work wants to know what happens when the police come."

Crap. Really? They walked off and settled into a nearby table facing the door.

"Gawkers should have to buy more than a muffin and coffee to get the good seats," Grandma muttered from her seat on the stool near the coffee bar. I sent her a look. She returned it with a smile.

"John?" I asked, waiting for him to change his usual order and goggle at me and the cops like everyone else.

"Make mine the usual," he said. "Sarah's waiting." He leaned against the counter and seemed uninterested in gossip.

I blew out a breath. "Thank you." One sane person in the whole town . . .

The doorbell jangled again and I jumped.

It wasn't the police. It was half the town coming in for coffee and a pastry. Crap. The crime scene was trampled. I glanced at the sign and wondered if it wasn't too late to put it up and lock the door before Officer Emry got here.

CHAPTER 10

Apparently humiliation was profitable, too.

My small shop was standing room only. I'd refilled the coffee twice and sold nearly all the breakfast baked goods before the police car showed up. The blue-and-red lights reflected in the shop window and everything grew still. People held their breath for what they clearly hoped would be a good show.

I took the bull by the horns, pushed through the crowd, and met Officer Emry at the door. "Hello," I said as he walked up. "Did you come to take down the crime scene tape?" It was silly to have it still up since everyone had ducked under to come inside, including Officer Emry. I'd be sure to point that out should he decide I'd somehow been ruining his crime scene.

"Ms. Toni Holmes, I have a warrant to search the premises." Officer Emry's voice cracked. He hitched up his gun belt then sniffed and handed me a piece of paper folded in thirds.

"I thought Chief Blaylock would be here."

"What gave you that idea?"

"Never mind, come on in . . ." I waved him toward the door and held it wide, exposing the crowd inside.

"I'm afraid I have to ask you to step out while we search," he said, unmoving.

"Really? The place is full of customers." I pointed at the crowd in case he hadn't noticed.

"I'll man the registers," Grandma Ruth piped up.

"Works for me," Officer Emry said, his head bobbing up and down.

"Fine." I stepped out into the brisk fall air. "Can I at least take a cup of coffee with me?"

"I'll bring one out," Candy called from inside.

"And a jacket?" I rubbed my forearms. It was probably fifty degrees, but fifty degrees could get cold if this took any length of time. Thankfully, my storefront was small.

"You got it, honey," Candy called then disappeared into the crowd.

Two of yesterday's crime scene techs went inside the bakery with Officer Emry. They carried dark, fat briefcases full of who knew what. Candy came out with my jacket and a tall cup of coffee. The small smatter of freckles across her pert nose glistened in the morning light.

"I gave you a generous amount of cream."

"Thanks." I put on my coat, then took the coffee and gave it a sip. "Perfect. Now what? Am I the only person not allowed inside?" I studied the small crowd as they watched the cops check out the front of the shop before disappearing in the back.

"You see, if you're guilty, you know what to hide. Therefore, yes, you're the only one not allowed." Candy put her hand on the door.

"This is nuts."

"But it makes for great news copy." She smiled her dazzling smile and scooted inside where it was warm.

I leaned against the wall, wishing I'd put the café tables and chairs out on the walk like I'd intended to do in the spring. Then I'd have someplace to sit and put up my feet. As it was I was left huddling next to the door like the Little

Match Girl. I looked around. Cars drove by slowly. There were two cop cruisers with lights flashing in front of the store. The street was fully packed. Yellow crime scene tape blocked off my business. The trough itself still held slimy water. I shuddered at the thought that it was the last thing George Meister breathed in.

I turned my back on the trough sculpture. Maybe when this was done I'd petition the city council to have it removed— out of respect for George, of course. I watched through the glass as the crime scene guys dusted the door and countertops for fingerprints. Every single customer must have touched something. Did they plan on fingerprinting the entire town? What were they looking for?

Evidence George had been inside the shop, I figured. But he hadn't, so good luck to them on that. I shifted my weight from one foot to the other and sipped nervously at my coffee until the cup was empty. I wanted more, but I wasn't allowed to refill my own mug.

Sighing, I set the empty cup on the ground and prayed Officer Emry wouldn't fine me for ruining his beloved crime scene. With nothing to do but wait, I decided to kill time by reading the warrant. After all, they had to have probable cause to issue a warrant, right? What was their cause?

The legalese made my brain go numb. Well, crap. I was a baker and a businesswoman. I didn't know very much about law. Why did they think I could read this? I should probably call a lawyer or Grandma Ruth. She'd know what the heck the document said. I peered through the window and tried to catch her eye. No dice. She was busy chatting up the cops.

I frowned. The only attorney I knew was a corporate lawyer who had helped me set up my business and ensured I had all the proper licenses and inspections. My only other option was my wild brother, Tim. He had had a few run-ins with the law as a teen. If anyone knew the county law system it was him. I pulled my cell out of my pocket and punched his number. He picked up on the first ring . . . not a good sign.

"Hey." Tim sounded put out. "What the hell did you do to have the cops issue a search warrant?"

"I didn't do anything." I rolled my eyes. Brothers—they always assumed the worse. "What did *you* do?" There, that would get him.

"My name isn't on the search warrant."

Right. I jiggled from foot to foot in an attempt to keep warm. My nose was red and starting to run. "They have one of those warrants for the house, too?" I knew Candy said they did, but I didn't believe her. After all, she would say anything to get a story. I sniffled.

"They most certainly do," Tim said. "You need a lawyer, little sis." He sounded sincere. Tim was rarely sincere. He had always been the laid-back party guy who ran just this side of the law.

"I don't know any lawyers besides the one in Chicago who helped me set up the business." It was an explanation, not a whine. At least, that was what I was telling myself.

"For something like a search warrant, you need someone local," Tim advised. "Someone who knows the county judges and the district attorney."

"You sound like you have some experience in this kind of thing." I had to get my digs in where I could. No matter how lame they sounded at the moment. He was my brother, after all.

"Look, do you want advice from me or not?" I'd hit a sore spot. Huh, I'd have to ask him about that someday when my life wasn't on the line.

"Yes, please." I decided it was best to ask nicely or he might send me to someone who would torture me. Which could be just about everyone in town.

"Call Brad Ridgeway. He's the best in the county."

"Brad Ridgeway?" My brain perked up. Memories flashed through it. "As in Brad Ridgeway star basketball player two years ahead of me in high school? Mr. all-star-jock-voted-most-popular-male-student-of-the-decade?"

"One and the same." Tim sounded pretty sure he knew what he was talking about.

"I thought he was in like Houston or New York or

somewhere." I sniffed again. Darn it. Did I even have a tissue in my pocket? I did. I pulled out a wadded-up but clean one and wiped my nose.

"Brad went to KU, got his BA, his MBA, and went on to law school. He came back five years ago when his dad wasn't doing well. Bought a house out by the country club and settled in."

"Huh." Brad Ridgeway had been every teenage girl's dream—tall, blond, gorgeous with sculpted jock muscles that went on forever. I sighed, remembering the huge crush I, and every girl within a five-year range and fifty-mile radius, had had on him.

I did a mental shake. That was what, twenty years ago? He was probably bald, married with four kids, and fat. Right? "Text me his number."

"When you call him, ask him if there is any way he can get the cops to hurry up on their search of the house. I need to sleep before my shift tonight."

"Oh, yeah, Grandma told me you got a job at FedEx. Congrats."

"Thanks." Tim sounded tired. "I hope to save up enough to move out in about a month."

"Really?" I did a silent happy dance at the news until I noticed people watching. I turned my back on the windows. "Text me the number, then go over to Grandma's for some sleep. She's here with me at the store. I doubt she'll be home for a few hours."

"You are brilliant," Tim said. "Tell Brad I said hello."

He hung up. I glanced inside the shop. Grandma Ruth was still hounding the CSU guys. Candy was gone—probably in the kitchen keeping an eye on Officer Emry. They might be doing it for selfish reasons, but I know neither Grandma nor Candy would let anything happen to my stuff. That at least was a relief. The crowd seemed content to eat pastries and drink coffee. Maybe they'd decide the food was great and make it a habit to stop in for a bite. A girl could hope.

My phone vibrated. And there it was, Brad Ridgeway's number. I did a quick check on the time: 9:05 A.M. His office should be open. I dialed the number, shivering a little while doing so, before I could chicken out. Yes, the idea of having his number made me feel fifteen years old all over again.

"Ridgeway and Harrington Attorneys-at-Law, this is Amy, how can I help you?"

The secretary's voice was nice. I bet Brad was dating her on the side. No, wait, that wasn't fair. As far as I knew he never ran around on his high school girlfriend, head cheerleader Sheila Hamm. "Um, yes, hi, this is Toni Holmes. I own Baker's Treat."

"Oh, the new gluten-free bakery?"

"Yes—"

"I heard good things about your food. Can I ask, do you use peanuts in any of your baked goods? My son's allergic."

"Oh, no. I am very careful not to use any peanut ingredients at the shop. I offer some peanut cookies online, but I bake those in my home kitchen. Cross contamination is such a big issue with allergies." I watched a couple of cars crawl by the store. I waved at the drivers, who stared. That got them to speed up a bit.

"Perfect. How do you feel about kid's birthday parties?"

"I love to cater kid's birthday parties." Which was true. You could be much more inventive with kid food. It brought out the artist in me. "In fact, I have several birthday selections including cake, cupcakes, giant cookies, you name it."

"Awesome, are you free to cater on November fifth?"

Okay, weird, right? I mean, I'd called her and she was acting like she'd called me. Who was this chick? "Um, I don't have access to my datebook right now. I'm kind of in a bit of a bind what with the murder and all. But I can get back to you as soon as I'm able." The wind picked up and brought along the scent of fallen leaves and oil refinery. Had to love Oiltop; it was the only town boasting an oil rig behind the Pizza Hut.

"Oh, oh, my, I'm terribly sorry." Amy did sound sorry and perhaps a bit embarrassed. "Does this mean you can't cater on that day?"

If anyone had been watching I'm sure my astonished expression was hilarious. Whoever Amy was, she simply

wasn't understanding that this call was about me, not her.
"I'm sure I can cater. I would love to cater your son's birthday party. Can I call you back once I have access to my
calendar?"

"Oh, certainly, but I'll need to know soon. It's only three
weeks away, you know."

"Yes, I know."

"Let me give you a tip . . . a good smartphone would give
you access to your calendar right from your cell. All the
new technology these days is great, don't you think?"

"Right." My head had started to hurt a little. "Um, before
you hang up, could I speak to Brad Ridgeway, please?"

"Oh, oh, did you call me?" There was a small pause and
I didn't know quite how to fill it. "You did call me. Sorry, one
moment and I'll send you over to Brad." She must have put
me on hold because I heard soft rock tunes playing in the
background.

I pinched the bridge of my nose. My head started to
pound. I couldn't tell if it was from standing out in the cold
or from Amy's crazy conversation. Still, a sale was a sale,
and I shouldn't complain but . . . really?

"This is Brad Ridgeway, how can I help you?"

Oh man, his voice was still sexy. Good thing I'd sworn
off of men or I might be more breathless than I was already
finding myself.

"Hello?"

"Yes, I'm here," I said weakly as I forced myself to
breathe. "I'm sorry. I'm Toni Holmes. My brother is Tim
Keene. He said I should call you."

"I see, Ms. Holmes, how can I help you?"

"Well." I glanced at the police cars and tried to sound
rational and coherent as I explained, "I own Baker's Treat,
the gluten-free bakery here in town. George Meister was
murdered in front of my store yesterday and now I've been
handed a search warrant for my business. Tim says they are
also searching my home."

"You need a lawyer." Brad was the master of understate-
ment.

"I know. They kicked me out of my own business and I'm hanging out on the street."

"I'll be right there. You're at the bakery on Main?"

"One and the same. You'll know it by the surrounding crime scene tape. And the cop cars."

"Don't say a word to anyone until I get there." I heard him get up and put on his coat. "And most important, don't worry. I'll see you're fully protected."

I bet he got a lot of girls with that line.

CHAPTER 11

"I came as soon as I heard." Tasha scooted under the tape. She wore a jazzy sweater set, tailored pants, wool trench coat, and shoes to die for. I envied her a little. I was dressed in my standard chef gear of black pants, white shirt, white apron, and my blue jacket. My hair whipped around in the wind while hers looked naturally gorgeous. I didn't want to even think about my red nose and the tissues I needed to blot it every two seconds.

I gave her a quick hug. She smelled of expensive perfume. "You can join the crowd. Everyone in town's here." I motioned toward the standing-room-only group assembled in the bakery.

"Yikes." She rubbed my arm. "Maybe you should tell them all to go home."

"Oh, no, after yesterday, I'm serving every customer I can get. Grandma Ruth is inside manning the register. Hopefully the coffee won't run out. Apparently I'm not allowed inside while they search."

"I can go in and take care of that." Her gaze was filled with concern. "Are you all right?"

"Truth? I'm not sure. I called Tim and he said they also had a warrant for the house." I rubbed my arms to ward off a shiver. The reality of what was happening was sinking in.

"This is ridiculous. I'm going to go in there and give those cops a piece of my mind."

"I wouldn't." Brad's deep voice shocked us both into whiplash-evoking head turns.

"Oh, hi, Brad." Tasha smiled and did a little hand wave.

"Hi, Tasha, how's Kip doing?"

"He's good. Great, in fact." Tasha flipped her hair and I think my jaw fell open. I elbowed her. "What?" she hissed.

"Hi." I held out my hand and pretended to be a professional. "I'm Toni Holmes."

Brad encased my icy hand in his warm one. "Yes, I remember. You were two years behind me in high school, weren't you?"

"You remember me?"

"I remember Tim." Brad pulled his hand away. "He played on the basketball team with me."

Of course he did. Sigh. I pushed the stray hair out of my eyes and wiped my nose with the tissue.

Brad looked into the windows. His handsome face and square jaw held interest. Thick blond eyebrows raised a fraction. He still had a full head of wavy, blond hair. "Did they give you a copy of the search warrant?"

"Yes." I held up the paper. "Although I don't know why. They didn't need it. I'd have let them look at anything if they'd asked."

"That's not a real good idea," Brad's tone chided me.

I stuck my chin out in response. I hated to be chided.

"May I see it?" he asked and held out his hand.

I handed him the paper and shoved my hands in my pockets to warm them. While Brad perused the paper, I took the time to peruse him. He was still extremely tall, maybe six-foot-five. I was five-foot-seven and had to look pretty far up to see his electric blue eyes. His broad shoulders were encased in a standard black wool trench coat, which hung open to reveal a smart suit in some dark pinstripe, a dress shirt in a coordinating blue-and-white stripe, and a red silk tie. The man was a walking *GQ* billboard. What was he doing in Oiltop, Kansas?

"I can't figure out what they are looking for," I said. "They have to have probable cause, right?"

"It lists you as a person of interest." Brad turned his electric-blue gaze on me. In high school, the rumor was he wore contacts to make his eyes that particular color, which was fine by me. "The warrant says you had motive because George assaulted you at your grand opening. When his body was found, there was a paint can nearby and evidence he'd started to paint something on your storefront."

"And they got a warrant because of that? That shouldn't be enough of a reason." I stomped my foot, which tingled from the cold. "For one, I didn't know he was behind the flour bombs. Last I heard, the chief said it was a prank. Two, I didn't even know George was out here until I opened my door at seven A.M., nearly two hours after he . . . died."

Brad glanced at the papers. "It says here you admitted to being in your shop at the time of the murder."

"Behind a locked door." I waved my hand at the glass door now covered with fingerprint dust. "Who knows who was on the street at the time? It could have been anybody."

"I agree," Brad said after studying me for a full breathless moment. "Their cause is weak. You should have called me the minute they asked you to go in to be fingerprinted."

"Which, by the way, was humiliating." I pursed my lips and frowned. "And should have ruled me out as I hadn't touched anything at the crime scene."

I saw movement in the window and noted the CSU guys were carrying my computer out of the back room. "Hey, is that my computer? They can't take that. More than half my business is online." I grabbed the door handle to storm in but Brad's hand covered mine and stopped me.

"They can take anything they deem evidence." His deep voice soothed me but his words frustrated me.

I was even too mad to notice how long it took him to remove his hand from mine. "I have customers who depend on me." I glanced at Tasha. "People with kids who require routine." I grabbed Brad's coat sleeve. "My baked goods are part of their routine. I have to have my computer."

"I'll go in and see what's what. You stay out here." He pulled open the door and went inside.

"Wow, if I didn't have Craig in my life I would totally want to be you," Tasha said watching him move toward the cops on my behalf.

"What?" All I could think about was how much I hated to be told what to do. Plus, my life was disintegrating before my eyes. Why would Tasha want to be me? I mean, look at me.

"Between Sam Greenbaum and Brad Ridgeway, you've got a whole lot of hot testosterone in your life."

I could not believe her mind had gone there. My life was falling apart, and she was busy playing matchmaker? I shook my head. "I told you, I'm not interested. Besides, my hands are full with my own problems. I don't have time to add someone else's to the mix." I blew my nose. "And I need my computer."

"Brad'll get it back for you." Tasha had awe in her eyes.

"What if he can't?"

"You have a library card, right?"

I frowned. "Yes . . . why?"

Tasha shrugged, her attention on the men inside. "Go to the library and use its computers."

"Wait, what? No! Some rush orders come in late at night."

She looked at me funny. "You check your orders late at night?"

I tilted my head, my eyes wide. "It's how I get things shipped on time."

Tasha pursed her lips. "Point taken. Okay, the library is out." She looked down at her watch and sucked in air. "I have to run and check on the maid. We've had a few issues." She slipped a key off her key ring and handed it to me. "Brad'll fix everything eventually. Until he does, you know where my office is. Feel free to use my computer anytime, day or night."

"Thanks!" I clenched the key in my hand and hugged her tight. "I think you just saved my life."

"That's what friends are for." One more long look at Brad through the window and Tasha took off for work.

The police finished their search right after noon. Candy and Rocky left to file yet another front-page story. The crowd dwindled off, and I was left with a shop covered in black fingerprint dust. Grandma Ruth left to write her blog about the oppressions of a police state and to go see Mike Smith, the *Oiltop Times* editor, to see if the increase in sales meant he would hire her back.

Without my computer, which Brad said they could keep for at least forty-eight hours, there was little I could do but clean up.

Fingerprint dust was difficult to get off. It took all afternoon scrubbing to get the place clean. I washed the windows three times before the streaks went away. Then I took pictures of the spray paint and set to work scrubbing the bricks with a wire brush and soap.

"Oh, you shouldn't do that," Sherry Williams warned me as she stepped under the crime scene tape. Her perky Miss Kansas hair and put-together outfit made my back teeth ache.

"The marks are bad for business," I said, pointedly looking toward the empty shop. "Something about graffiti scares people away. I thought you, being convention and tourism bureau manager, would know that."

"Au contraire," she said with a perfect French accent. "This outdoor crime scene is just the thing for tourism. People love all that CSI stuff. And later, we can do walking ghost tours. People will pay to simply walk by your shop and touch the trough."

I tossed the wire brush into the bucket of suds and stared at her. "It's morbid." My hands were cold even wearing thick pink rubber gloves.

"That's the tourism business." She smiled. "So stop what you're doing. Besides, I think the only way to really get it off is to paint over the bricks."

"That's a job for my landlord." I stood and brushed off my knees.

"Exactly." Sherry took my arm. "Come on, I'll buy you a cup of coffee. I want to talk tourism and ghost tours."

I let her drag me inside especially since she was going to buy coffee.

"You see," Sherry said, as she sat across from me at a table, "the whole thing requires you to sign a waiver allowing me to use your bakery's name and image. But here's the good part—it's great publicity. People will stop by to see if they can see George's ghost and then we'll file inside for warm drinks and tasty treats. What do you think?"

"I think I'd be profiting from a man's death." I made a face. "Is that legal?"

"Very legal." Sherry nodded, her eyes wide, her plaid wool jacket complementing her skin tone. "Pete's talking about adding brass crime scene tape to the trough." She leaned in until her dark green silk top fluttered above her coffee cup. "People love a juicy murder."

"I don't know." I sat back and warmed my fingertips on the sides of my cup. "It sounds creepy. . . ." I wondered what the police would think about me actively using the murder to drive sales. They'd probably think it added to my motive. Not good.

"We'll start with a memorial service this Friday. We want you to cater, of course. People can leave flowers near the trough, and we'll get a whole crowd into your bakery."

"Wait, do you think my catering is a good idea? I'm already a person of interest. What if the police think my profiting on George's memorial is more motive on my part?"

"That would be great!" Sherry's enthusiasm nearly bowled me over. "People will really want to come out then."

Her words took me aback. "More people will come out if I'm moved up from person of interest to suspect?"

"That's right."

"Why?"

"They'll want to be here if the police arrest you. Just the idea that they ate your food and were here for the arrest will get them talking."

My jaw dropped open. "What if I say no?" Seriously, it was bad enough people went to see a person hanged. I didn't want to experience what it was like to be the hangee.

Sherry merely shrugged and dismissed my threat with a wave of one perfectly groomed hand. "The memorial notice will be in tonight's paper. People will come to see if the killer shows up. It doesn't matter if you cater or not." Her gaze grew hard. "As for the ghost and murder tour, the mockups for the tourism brochure are already being designed. It's your loss if you don't sign the waiver." She pushed the paper toward me and eyed me over the top of her cup. "Haven't you lost enough business because of George Meister?"

I stared at the paper as Grandma Ruth's voice went through my head. *"Remember, in business, you can't care what people say. What's important is they talk about you."*

Saying a small prayer that I wasn't giving the chief more reason to hang me, I signed on the line. Sherry smiled her pageant smile and left with a baker's dozen GF chocolate chip cookies for the office.

I returned to scrubbing and hoped I hadn't made the worst mistake of my life.

CHAPTER 12

"This is serious." Grandma Ruth took a long drag on her cigarette and closed the newspaper. She turned it so that I could see a photo of me once again on the front page above the fold. This time I looked shocked and almost guilty. The headline screamed, "Dead man identified as George Meister, bakery protestor. Baker possible suspect."

I grabbed the paper from her. "I should have kept the front door locked like Officer Emry said."

Grandma puffed on her cigarette and gave me a stern look while her wild cap of carrot-colored hair rustled in the breeze. "Mike says sales of the *Oiltop Times* have tripled."

"I know. I heard." I crumpled the paper so I couldn't see the headline. It was nine P.M. and I was sitting with Grandma out on the wide front porch of Mom's house.

"The whole town thinks you did it." Grandma Ruth had changed clothes from this morning and was now sporting a yellow blouse, a butterfly-patterned vest, and a paisley skirt with knee-high hose. The outfit was topped off with blue-and-white men's running shoes.

"You know I didn't." I wanted to throw the paper away

but with my luck I'd get arrested for littering. "I don't think
the cops are looking at anyone else. The worst thing is, the
longer they take to look at me, the farther away the real killer
gets."

"Plus it's killing your business." Blue smoke rose up over
Grandma's head. "No pun intended."

"Especially since they took my computer away." I sat back
and closed my eyes at the weirdness of it all. "Now I can't do
any online fulfillment without going to Tasha's."

"As far as I see it, there is only one thing to do." Grandma
paused for dramatic effect.

I opened my eyes. "What's that?"

Her eyes narrowed. "We have to solve this murder our-
selves and clear your name—the sooner, the better."

Crap. Was that determination I saw on her face? "What
do you mean, solve this murder?"

"I mean, we should investigate this crime and find the
real killer before he gets away." It was determination. Her
steely-eyed look always meant trouble for someone.

"The last time I checked, neither you nor I had a private
investigator license. I know neither one of us is on the police
force. We are not equipped to solve crimes. Besides, my
superhero cape is at the dry cleaners."

Grandma snorted. "I don't need a cape. I was an inves-
tigative reporter for years. I know a thing or two. You're as
smart as me. Together we can figure this thing out faster
than those bumbling idiots in the police station."

I stared out into the darkness. She had a point. Officer
Emry was lavishing all his attention on me and I was innocent.

"Listen, kiddo, police procedure is going to kill your
business. How long do you think you'll last with your store
taped off and your computer gone?"

"Not long," I mumbled, my shoulders slumping at the
reality.

"Then you have no choice. Now, do you want my help or
not?" Grandma's eyes sparkled in the low light coming from
the front parlor window. She could be fierce when she

wanted, and from the look in her eyes I could tell she was going to do this thing with or without me. Like Sherry Williams and her ghost/murder tours.

"Fine, I'm in," I said weakly.

"Good." Grandma slapped me on the thigh. "Good." She took a long drag on her cigarette.

"Where do we start?" I hoped she had an idea because I hadn't a clue. In truth, I'd been away from Oiltop too long. I didn't know much of what went on in town. Least of all what George's life was like and who would want to kill him.

"We start by finding out who—besides you—wanted George Meister dead," Grandma Ruth answered as she twisted the ash out of the butt of her cigarette then shoved it in her pocket.

"Wait a minute. I didn't want him dead. I barely knew who he was," I protested.

"That's beside the point." Grandma waved her square hand in the air, then slapped her hands together and rubbed them in delight. "Tomorrow I'm going to do some digging in the newsroom archives and public records. George was up to something. We simply have to figure out what."

"What do you want me to do?"

"You can interview witnesses, in between work and keeping up your orders." Grandma reached inside her jacket pocket and pulled out her pack of cigarettes. She tapped it across the side of her hand then pulled out one long white stick. Putting it in her mouth, she slipped the pack back in her pocket and took out an old steel lighter.

"Witnesses?" I asked, not sure what she meant. I mean there were no witnesses, right? Or the cops wouldn't be looking at me as their main suspect.

"Yes, kiddo, anyone and everyone with a business on Main and Central could have been on that street or driving by that morning and seen something." She said the last bit between her teeth, as she lit her cigarette.

"Got it." I liked the way Grandma thought. Really, had the cops asked everyone on Main if they were in their shops?

"I'll take a bunch of business cards with me and introduce myself to all the business owners and offer a free pastry."

"There you go, that's the spirit." Grandma patted me on the thigh again. "With the introductions you can kill two birds with one stone. Drum up new business and help solve the case."

I scrunched up my nose and scratched my forehead. "Let's not use the word *kill* at the moment, okay? Someone might take it wrong."

Grandma laughed real hard, and she started coughing. I pounded her on the back. "You really should stop smoking."

"I know . . . it'll kill me." She grinned and we both laughed.

The next morning, Tim rode to work with me. I thought it was a sweet gesture until he mentioned Grandma Ruth had put the fear of God in him. She said there was no way she was letting me go to work alone with a killer on the loose and told Tim if he didn't act as my bodyguard she'd make sure he never got a good night's sleep again. Grandma Ruth didn't make idle threats, and Tim liked to sleep, which meant I now had an extra pair of eyes to help me start looking for clues on the streets of Oiltop.

As we drove, I asked Tim to look out for cars and trucks on Main and Central. Whoever had killed George might have done so on his or her way to work. It was a couple of hours earlier than George's time of death, but it was a place to start. We saw exactly one cop car, one pickup with a handyman graphic on the side, and an oil truck heading toward the Quickmart. Small towns don't have a lot of traffic at 4 A.M.

There wasn't a single vehicle in the parking lot when I arrived behind the bakery. But then there rarely was. Next to me was a bookstore, an antique store, and a fabric store that boasted all the quilt-making supplies you could ever need.

I parked and Tim jumped out of the van. He wore beat-up

jeans and a heavy-duty denim shirt with the sleeves rolled up. He didn't wear a jacket because forty degrees was nothing to the guy.

I zipped up my jacket against the chill, got out, and unlocked the back of the van. "Thanks for riding in with me," I said as he reached in and pulled out his bike. It was then I noticed the ink on his forearm.

I grabbed his arm and pulled up his sleeve. "Is that a tattoo?"

"Yeah, so?" His eyes twinkled in the lamplight.

"When did you get that?"

"Right after mom died," he said. "It's a daisy."

"Her favorite flower."

"Yeah," he said and pulled away from me.

I looked at him for the first time in months. "Thanks for helping me."

"No problem." Tim shrugged and swiped a lock of his mop-like hair out of his eyes. The hair, combined with the lean muscle from his wide shoulders to the tips of his steel-toed boots, never failed to make women take notice. If he hadn't spent his twenties and thirties "looking for himself," he might have been married by now with at least one kid. He was a few inches taller than me, which made him about six foot. "I forgot to ask, did you hire Brad Ridgeway?"

"I did." I shoved my hands in my pockets to keep them warm. "He's working to get my computer back and some other stuff Officer Emry confiscated."

Tim narrowed his eyes. "Emry needs a good, swift kick in the pants."

I had to agree with him there.

"Give me your key." Tim held out his hand.

"What? Why?" I tightened my fist around the keys in my pocket. No way was I giving them up to my brother.

"I promised Grandma I'd open up the place and check it out before I left you."

"I'm good, really. I'm a big girl." I slammed the van door and pushed past him.

"Yeah, a big girl who had a glass door between her and

a murderer not three days ago," he said, walking with me to the back door. Tim hit the kickstand and rested his bike along the side of the building. "Hand it over."

"Fine." I gave him the key and watched him unlock the door and flick on the light. "I don't know what you think you can do that I can't."

Tim grinned and raised his arm, forming a bicep. "I can squash the measly killer."

"Riiiight. Maybe when you were twenty, old man, but not as much when you're forty-two." I grabbed my keys out of his hand and strode through the bakery, turning on all the lights in the place. My poor office looked lonely without a computer. They'd left the various cords dangling. The kitchen was sparkling clean, as was the front. Both were empty of any living being.

"It's clear." I patted my brother on the shoulder. "You're good to go. Thanks." I buzzed a kiss on his five o'clock shadowed cheek and pushed him toward the door. "Good night and remember, take note of anyone you see driving around town on your way home."

"Are you sure you don't want me to bunk here?" He studied me over his shoulder.

I tried to disguise the horror I felt at the idea. "No, no. I'm good. I promise I'll even lock the doors behind you." I pushed him the last foot out the door and half closed it so he wouldn't get any ideas. "Text me when you get home so I know you're safe." I closed the door and threw back the bolt. Finally, I had the place all to myself. This was the part I loved the most.

I took off my jacket and hung it on the coat hook. Then I grabbed a big apron, slung it over my head, and hit the button on the mp3 player letting Nickelback scream into the air.

I took out dough to proof then put out a HELP WANTED sign. Hiring real help would be very hard on my budget, but there was no way I could investigate a murder if I was stuck in the store all day.

While I baked up the goodies for the display case, I made

a mental list of stores in the area I needed to visit. I figured I could do a block at a time on my lunch breaks. At that rate, it would take about two weeks to investigate the entire downtown.

I blew out a breath and attacked the dough. Well, it couldn't be any slower than the police department. Sad but true. I remember reading somewhere you needed to catch a killer in the first forty-eight hours or the evidence would grow cold. I glanced at the clock. They had two hours left and right now the only suspect they had was me.

CHAPTER 13

By the time I closed up for my lunch break at one P.M., I'd sold only a few baked goods to a handful of regulars. Thank God for John Emerson. My guess was he worked out at the oil refinery. I didn't think to ask because it really wasn't any of my business. But he was in every morning at 7 A.M. and bought apple turnovers for Sarah and coffee and pastries for himself. Then Tasha'd been kind enough to order two platters of assorted Danish, turnovers, muffins, and cake donuts for the Welcome Inn. She'd stopped by around eight to pick them up.

Setting the clock sign to let everyone know we would reopen at two, I grabbed my jacket, locked the door, and headed across the street with business cards in hand. First stop was Walcott's Drug Emporium. I stepped into the warmth and paused a moment to take in the scent of perfume, the canned shopper's music, and the general layout. It looked the same as it had when I was a kid. I had a paper route and delivered on this part of Main. Every time I entered the pharmacy, I had a flashback to tromping through the ice and slush, a canvas bag full of rolled papers on my shoulder and the sound of Christmas music. For the Christmas season, Walcott's always blared music out onto Main Street. It sounded tinny, but it gave the street a festive air.

"Hi, can I help you?"

I came back to the here and now and saw Craig working behind the counter. "Hey, I didn't know you worked here. I thought you were a part-time banker/part-time college adjunct."

"The college doesn't offer insurance benefits, so I worked at the bank for a while, but in this economy the bank had to downsize. Now I'm here with my brother, making ends meet." Craig was dressed in dark blue Dockers and a light blue dress shirt with the sleeves rolled up. "The bank was a little too stuffy for my taste, anyhow."

"Huh." Working at the bank would have probably driven me crazy, too, although the hours were better than the ones I kept.

I wandered over to the glass counter with the most expensive items locked inside. The cash register sat on top of the glass. Behind Craig were stacks of goods such as cigarettes and aftershaves and colognes. "How come you don't teach full-time at the college?" I realized it was probably too nosey a question and cringed, waiting for him to tell me it was none of my business.

Instead he smiled. "This is my first teaching gig at the college level. You usually have to have a few years of adjunct under your belt before they hire you full-time."

"Oh." The silence was awkward and I shoved my hands in my pockets, trying to come up with something else to say.

Thankfully, I didn't have to because Craig added, "I know, it's crazy. You have to jump through a lot of hoops for forty grand a year. What brings you in today?"

"Oh, I'm passing around my cards to businesses in the area." I pulled out my stack of rubber-banded cards and tugged one free. "If you bring it in, it's good for a free cookie with a purchase of coffee." I handed him the card. "I have one for your brother, too, if he's in."

"Hold on." Craig got on the phone. "Hey, Ralph, come down here a minute. There's someone I want you to meet." He hung up the phone. "He'll be right down."

Craig looked my card over. "It's a nice place you have over there. Too bad about George, though."

I crinkled my face. "I agree." Raising an eyebrow, I asked, "Did you know him?"

"Not all that well." Craig leaned his arm across the top of the register. "George pretty much kept to himself. I understand he was a hard worker, but wheat futures aren't what they used to be. I think perhaps he'd fallen on hard times."

I tilted my head and moved in closer. "Really?"

"Sure, happens a lot." Craig tapped my card along the edge of the register. "Farming's a gamble no matter what you grow or raise. I think it's why George was all fired up about your business being wheat-free. He must have felt his livelihood was at stake."

"It wasn't." I crossed my arms. "You'd have to be pretty scared to think my little store would make or break your farm. Do you think he owed anyone money?"

"I don't know. Ed at the bank could tell you." He tilted his head and gave a slight shrug. "It's a small town. Everyone knows everyone else's business."

Another man walked down the aisle toward us. He looked a lot like Craig only he was older and had darker hair. His brown eyes were gentle.

"Hello," he said. "You're the gal who opened the new bakery, aren't you?"

"That's me." I pulled a second card out of my pocket and handed it to him. "I'm Toni Holmes."

"I've heard great things about your bakery," Ralph said. He was a big man with brown hair, a soft jaw, and the hands of a man who worked in an office his whole life. "My son, Tommy, has autism. He's sensitive to a lot of things. I've read gluten-free foods might help some of those kids."

That made me smile. I loved to talk to people who understood GF. "A lot of people dismiss it as a fad, but if you're sensitive to your environment or have bad allergies, then sometimes GF can help. I have celiac disease, which makes me more than sensitive."

"I've been meaning to stop in and buy a few things to send to my son, but things have been a bit crazy here at the pharmacy."

"It didn't help that the police had the front of my store roped off." I tilted my head. "Did you know George Meister?"

"Yes, we went to school together." Ralph's mouth twitched. "His family patronized the pharmacy since it first went into business."

"I was surprised I haven't heard anything about his family."

"His mom died a few years ago." Ralph shrugged. "And George was real mean. He pushed everyone away."

"Sounds like you knew him well."

"Only a bit," Ralph said. "Like I said, we went to school together and I'd run into him here sometimes or at the Grey Goose. He was even meaner drunk, if you can believe that. Man's brain was all in his seat."

"He hated the idea of my bakery," I mentioned. "The police believe he was in the process of spray painting the front of my building with graffiti when he died."

"Idiot. No wonder there aren't too many people missing him. I bet there are even a few who are happy he's gone."

"I didn't know him well enough to be one of them," I said for the record.

"What's it like being a person of interest?" Craig leaned in closer. "Did they stick you in an interrogation room and question you for hours?"

My eyes widened in horror. I grabbed on to the cool glass top of the counter to balance myself. "Not yet. God, I hope never." I tried not to shiver.

"Tasha tells me they took your computer."

"Yes, but she's letting me use hers until I get mine back."

"Tasha is a great woman, isn't she?" His eyes glistened. The guy had it bad.

"One of the best. Um, listen, one more thing." I straightened.

"Sure. . . ."

"Did either of you guys happen to be in the store around 5:30 A.M. the other morning?"

"Are you asking if we saw the murder?" Craig rested his elbow on the counter and placed his chin on his fist. "No. We were here, though."

"Yes," Ralph said. "I came in early to work on the quarterly taxes."

"And I came with him to set up the store for the Halloween season." Craig waved his free hand and I noted the two aisles of costumes and decorations. "Need anything?"

"Um, no, but thanks for the info. And it was so nice to meet you." I shook Ralph's hand.

"I'll make it a priority to come by your shop sometime soon."

"Great," I said. "Don't forget, you get a free cookie with coffee purchase. Oh, and I do ship if you think there's anything your son might like."

"Thanks," Ralph said, his eyes shining. "That's good to know."

I headed to the door when Craig stopped me.

"We'll see you Friday, right?"

I froze, my hand on the door, and made a face. Crap. "I forgot. I was asked to cater George's memorial service on Friday."

"What time?" Craig straightened. His dark eyebrows went up.

"I think it's at seven."

He visibly relaxed. "Then we'll have dinner after the service. Dinner was at eight, we'll push it to nine in case anyone else wants to attend the memorial."

"That's awesome. Thanks." I left the pharmacy thinking how nice the two brothers were. Plus they liked my business. It was also good to know other people were on Main Street early in case I felt threatened. I had their number. I just might give them a call.

* * *

The men's clothing store was next door to the pharmacy. The manager's eyes narrowed as I walked in the door. "May I help you?"

He was a slight man of about five-foot-eight. It was difficult for him to look down at me but he managed. He was also dressed in a suit that cost more than my entire wardrobe. I tried not to think about it as I handed him my card. "Hi, I'm Toni Holmes. I opened up the gluten-free bakery across the street."

He took the card and carefully read it. I was suddenly thankful for the high-quality paper and embossed gold lettering. "Baker's Treat . . ." he muttered.

"It's a Play on words."

"Oh, I understand the reference, Ms. Holmes." He held the card between two fingers as if it were contaminated or something. "What can I do for you?"

"I'm going around introducing myself to my neighbors. Sort of a hi, I'm here, maybe we can share customers kind of thing." I gave him my best hello-neighbor smile.

His right cheek twitched and he crossed his arms. "I don't see a lot of donut-eaters in my shop."

"Right." I looked around. He had some really nice stuff. I mean, if I were a guy I'd shop there. "If you bring the card in, it's good for a free cookie with coffee purchase."

He held the card out. "I don't eat cookies."

I had to admit, he looked like he didn't eat cookies or much of anything at all. "I have a wide variety of free trade gourmet coffees and espresso. Come on over and your first cup is on me."

His thin lips went thinner. "I don't know . . ."

"Is it because of the murder? Because I really had nothing to do with George ending up in the horse trough." I was getting desperate.

His dark eyes narrowed. "George Meister was an egotistical bastard. The last thing I care about is his murder."

"Wow, sounds to me like George was not your favorite person." Maybe I still had a chance to connect with this guy.

"The man had the gall to complain that I rented tuxedos for too much money. He called them cheap monkey suits. I'll have you know they are Armani and Hugo Boss." He sniffed and tugged on his jacket.

"Clearly all of George's taste was in his mouth," I said. "Seriously, you'll love the coffee. You won't get coffee this good anywhere else in town. Come over sometime and enjoy a cup on me."

He pursed his lips. "Perhaps I will."

I did a mental "Yes!" and fist pump when he slid the card into his jacket pocket. "Thank you very much. I look forward to seeing you, Mister . . ."

"Todd, Todd Woles."

"Nice to meet you, Mr. Woles." I headed toward the door and then paused. "You wouldn't have been here at work when George was killed, would you?"

"Oh, God no, my store opens at ten. I usually get here at nine-thirty. I'm not a morning person."

Not being a morning person was one thing I understood. "I don't think of it as morning." I gave him a half shrug. "I think of it as very late at night. See you soon." I waved. It appeared as if George wasn't well liked, which was interesting considering Sherry had set up a memorial.

The last business on this side of the street was an office supply store. The manager wasn't in so I left my card with the clerk. The young guy had no clue who George was and, like the men's clothing store, the office supply store didn't open until ten.

I crossed the street and stopped at the antique store. It was dark and stuffed with all kinds of things, very few of which might be considered real antiques. But I'd learned from my mom a long time ago that antiquing was an art. It wasn't about buying real antiques in an antique store; it was about finding a treasure in a pile of junk.

The bells on the door jangled and I heard a muffled,

"Hello, be right with you," from somewhere in the back. The place smelled of dust and old people, and the floor creaked under my feet as I navigated the tiny isle between "displays."

"Hey," I called.

"Oh, hi!" A little old woman with white hair, which was teased and sprayed within an inch of its life, popped out from behind a chest of drawers. When I said little, I meant little. She might have come up to my shoulder. She wore a simple sweater set and pair of synthetic slacks with the crease sewn down the front.

"Hi, are you the manager?" I asked.

"Owner slash manager, Celia Warren." She held out her hand. "That's me."

I shook her dry hand and grabbed my business cards out of my jacket pocket. "I'm Toni Holmes. I own the new gluten-free bakery down the block." I handed her a card. "I'm simply going store to store to say hi to my new neighbors and let everyone know if they come in they can get a free cookie with coffee purchase."

"Isn't that nice." She looked at the card. "I do like to take tea in the afternoons." Her eyes were some odd color of gray, but they twinkled. "Isn't your store where that young fellow died?"

"Yes." I nodded. "That's my store."

"Terrible thing to happen, just terrible."

"I agree. I hope it won't keep you from coming in and trying out the free cookie. I have tea as well as coffee."

"At my age, I'm not about to let some silly crime scene tape keep me from my afternoon snack." Her smile was positively radiant.

"Wonderful." I couldn't help but smile back. "Say, you wouldn't have happened to be at work the morning George was killed, would you have?"

"Oh no, dear, I was at my Zumba class at the Y from 6 to 7 A.M. By the time I got down here, the police were already cutting off all traffic to the store. I had to spend the day doing inventory. Absolutely no one came shopping. Such a waste of a lovely day, wasn't it?"

"Yes, ma'am," I agreed. "It was."

The fabric store was run by Mrs. Becher and her daughter Amy. Mrs. Becher had been my 4-H sewing project teacher and such a stickler for details that I now had a sewing phobia. In fact, the fabric store made me sneeze . . . several times. I claimed an allergy and simply handed my card, asked my questions, and got the heck out of there.

It appeared only the pharmacy and the bakery were open early in the morning. Everyone else opened at ten, which meant they didn't have a reason to be around at 5:30 A.M. Most hadn't seen anything until they came in, and then all they saw was my place crawling with cops and people in CSU jackets.

Hopefully, Grandma Ruth had been able to get further with the investigation than I did or I was doomed.

CHAPTER 14

"Thanks for letting me use your computer." I was in Tasha's office printing out orders for the next day's shipment. So far my online customers were still buying.

"Mom's computer is for work only," Kip said without looking up. Tasha's office had a corner especially for Kip. He had his own desk with a small computer and computer games to occupy him while Tasha worked. His hands were currently full of controller as he swung and jerked and hit the buttons necessary to keep the game going.

"That's right," Tasha said gently. "Aunt Toni is using it for her work at the moment."

"Mom's computer is only for Mom's work," Kip said and continued with his game.

"Aunt Toni doesn't have her computer right now so I am letting her do her work on mine." Tasha leaned against her desk. Today she wore chic jeans and a sweater set made out of something incredibly soft looking.

"How come Aunt Toni doesn't have her computer? Did she lose it?"

Tasha met my gaze. "My computer is being worked on," I said. It wasn't entirely a lie.

"You should have Craig look at it," Kip said. "Craig's good with computers."

"I bet he is." I hit Print.

"I saw your help wanted sign," Tasha said quietly. "What happened to Carrie? Is she not coming back?"

I twisted my curly mass of hair into a sloppy knot to get it out of my way. "Her mom won't let her come back to work . . ." I glanced over to ensure Kip was deep in his game. "Not until the killer is caught, anyway," I said low. "Not that I blame her. It's a little spooky working not more than twenty feet from a crime scene . . . so much for small-town safety." I logged out of my website.

"Craig tells me you're catering George Meister's memorial on Friday."

"Weird, right?" I grabbed my orders from the printer and slipped them into a binder. I'd brought in a ream of paper to help offset the cost of my printing. "Sherry Williams came by, bought me a coffee, and told me they were having a memorial, and that she wanted me to cater. I told her I thought it was in poor taste considering the fact . . ." I leaned over to keep my words from Kip's ears. "I'm a person of interest, who had been served with a search warrant and all. But she said my catering showed I had no hard feelings toward George for the flour incident."

"And you bought that?" Tasha tilted her head and looked at me all too knowingly.

"She said if I didn't cater, they'd find someone else." I clutched my binder. "But I'm the most conveniently located."

"Now that sounds like the real Sherry Williams."

I tucked the binder into my leather bag and contemplated Tasha. "Did you know Sherry is setting up ghost tours now? She asked me to sign a waiver to allow participants to tour the bakery."

"Did you?" Tasha's eyes went wide.

I winced. "Yes, but, if it makes any difference, I told her

I thought it was in poor taste considering George isn't even buried yet."

"Not to mention any profits you make on George's death don't look good to the police." Tasha put her hands on her hips to emphasize how stupid she thought I was being. Maybe I was.

"See, that's what I told Sherry." I tossed my hands wide in supplication. "But she said the tours would happen with or without me. I felt like it was either sign on and earn something from the misfortune, or don't and become a look-but-not-touch bakery."

"Well, that's pretty convenient for her." Tasha crossed her arms.

"I know. The whole encounter felt a little like a mob threat. You know, pay us for protection or take the consequences . . ."

"Did you tell Brad?"

I felt the heat of a blush rush up my cheeks. "No. Do you think I should?"

"Well, he is your lawyer. He could advise you on whether it's a good idea or not, plus you get to call him." Tasha smiled. "I almost wish I had a reason to call him."

"Trade ya," I teased.

"No way." She held out her hands to ward me off. "No murders at my inn, thank you very much."

"What? You don't want to be part of the ghost tours? Why not? Think of the extra income you could gain." I was being sarcastic and Tasha knew it.

"There's no such thing as ghosts," Kip said loudly, still not looking up from his game. "They are products of people's imagination."

"Yes, honey." Tasha ruffled his blond hair. "Yes, they are. I'm going to walk Aunt Toni out. Are you going to be all right?"

"It's Mario, Mom," he said with a dramatic sigh. "Of course I'll be all right."

Tasha and I walked out into the hall. "Hmm, you know being part of a ghost tour might be a great idea." She narrowed her eyes and tapped her index finger to her lips. "I'm going to do some research. This house is over a hundred years old. Someone must want to haunt it."

I shook my head. "Well, I'll leave you to it. I've got to call my lawyer and prep for these orders."

"You mean you have other people to question about George's murder."

I froze. "What?"

She pulled me aside, out of range of the office door and the lobby. "Oh, please, Craig totally caught on that you were looking for the real killer. It was kind of nice and sneaky though, giving away free cookies to find out who was around."

My cheeks grew hot again. "I told Grandma Ruth I wasn't any good at this detective thing." I moved down the hall.

Tasha matched her stride to mine. "I don't blame you. If it were me under suspicion, I'd try to figure out who did it, too. So, who did you talk to?"

"Well, Craig and Ralph, plus the owner of the men's store."

"Todd Woles?" Tasha raised an eyebrow

"Yeah, why?"

"He might be a good suspect." Tasha's eyes glittered.

I stopped, drew my eyebrows together, and pursed my mouth. "Why?"

She pushed her hair behind her ear. "Last year, Todd and George got into a big fight. I heard Todd called the cops to force George to leave the store. In fact, he might even have a restraining order out on him. You should check that."

I guess I could see Todd calling the cops on George if George were half as mean to Todd as he had been to me. "Wow, I will. Crazy. Do you know what the fight was about?"

Tasha shrugged. "There are a couple of theories but no one really knows."

"Todd did call George a bastard."

"Really?"

"Yeah, something about George protesting the cost of Todd's tuxedo rentals."

"Sounds like George." Tasha shook her head. "He was a farmer through and through."

I headed for the door, my mind whirling.

"Oh, and be sure to pay attention to who all shows up at the memorial," Tasha said as I opened the door.

"Why?" I scrunched my eyebrows.

"Because, silly, everyone knows the killer always returns to the scene of the crime. The memorial is the perfect time."

"Oh, right." The thought of the killer returning to my bakery made my stomach clench. My feelings must have shown on my face.

"Don't worry." Tasha patted me on the shoulder. "Craig and I will be there to make sure nothing happens."

"What do you mean? Why would something happen?" I narrowed my eyes.

"Because you're looking for the killer, silly. After today, everyone knows you're nosing around, which means who-ever did it might see you as a threat. But . . . no worries. Your friends will keep you safe."

"Gee, thanks." I stepped out into the dark night and tried to brush off the warning. "Go do your ghost research." Tasha yelled good-bye and headed inside. I stopped on the side-walk and studied the star-filled sky. Well, Mom, I thought, if ever I needed a guardian angel, it's now.

I checked around the van before I hopped in. I locked the doors quickly, started it up, and looked over my shoulder. The van was empty and I was simply being silly. But Tasha had spooked me with her whole everyone-knows-you're-looking-into-the-murder statement.

I tried to think of something else. Anything else. I rolled down my window a crack and sniffed the fresh, crisp air of October. It brought back memories of high school.

At that time, Main and Central were the streets the kids drove at night. In small towns like Oiltop, that's all the kids had to do on a school night, cruise up and down and wave at friends. Turn around in the McDonald's and drive the street again. If you were lucky, cute boys would follow you and you could meet up in an empty parking lot. Meanwhile you played your music too loud and flirted through windows.

Maybe the kids didn't do it as much anymore, what with the price of gas and the ease of the Internet. Maybe instead of fresh air and bad music, kids stayed home in their bedrooms and talked via webcam.

I suddenly felt ancient.

Checking out the cars around me when I drove was an old habit born out of my cruising years. One had to be ready in case the cutest guy in school—like Brad Ridgeway—happened to be driving in the car behind you. Maybe memories made me check tonight. Maybe I was paranoid. Either way, I noticed the small dark sedan that trailed behind my van at a steady pace. It was too far back for me to see who was driving. I stopped at a light, but the car let some kids cut him off so they were between me and him. The bass of their music boomed through the windows.

I went through the light and turned down Pine Street with one eye on the rearview mirror. Sure enough, the sedan turned down Pine as well. I turned left onto Third Street, left again onto Maple, and headed back toward Central. The car still followed.

A creepy-crawly feeling went down my back. Now what? Do I call 911? What would I say was my emergency? Someone is following me? I swallowed hard. The police station was two blocks behind Main down from the county fairgrounds. I decided I'd drive by there and see if the car followed.

The problem with the streets behind Main was they were dark, with a streetlight only every half mile. People didn't usually flock to the fairgrounds or the baseball stadium this late at night in October. I sped up a little, figuring if I got a ticket I could at least talk to the cop about the car staying two lengths behind me.

I'd never been followed before; it was unnerving. The only thing I could think to do was to pull into the police station parking area. The sedan drove down the street, but pulled over and turned off its lights about a block away.

"I can still see you," I muttered. I was pissed off. I had work to do. It was bad enough this mess had scared away my customers, but now scaring me prevented me from working. I should have been able to go back to the bakery and work. I shouldn't have to worry about stalkers, damn it. I had bills.

I worked myself up to a good tizzy, got out of the van, and slammed the door behind me. A quick click of the key and I locked the doors with a comforting honk. I was only a few feet from the door to the police station. Maybe that's what emboldened me. Instead of going inside like an intelligent woman and letting the big, strong policemen with guns take care of my stalker, I went all redhead and stormed over to the little sedan and knocked on the driver side window. "Hello. Open up."

The window rolled down slow. I could see the green lights of the dashboard. The driver wore a tweed suit coat with patches on the elbows He moved his face out of the shadows and a sense of relief went through me.

"Hi, Toni." Craig had the good grace to look a little embarrassed.

"Craig, why are you following me?" I waved my hands. "You scared the daylights out of me."

"Um, I saw you leaving the inn and I thought I'd make sure you got to where you were going safely." He ducked back into the shadows. It was hard to see his face but his tone of voice sounded sincere.

"How did you know I wasn't going to the police station?" My voice rose. Like I said, when I get scared, I get mad. Right now I trembled from head to toe. I had to put my hands on my hips to stabilize myself.

"Well." He ran his finger around his collar as if his tie was choking him. Or maybe he was worried *I* would choke him. "I figured you might be running in to see about your computer, but then you'd still have to go home."

"What? You thought you'd hang out here until I did whatever and then you'd keep following me?"

He looked like a kid caught with their hand in a cookie jar. "Yes."

"No." I stomped my foot. "I don't need to be followed. I'm an adult who lived in Chicago. I think I can handle myself."

Craig leaned forward. "Toni, look—"

"No, you look." I pointed at him. "If I catch you following me again I'm going to do something you aren't going to like. I mean it."

"Yes, ma'am." I think I got through to him. He did sort of look contrite.

"Good, now go home."

"Good night, Toni."

I turned on my heel and stormed off toward my van. I was aware enough of my surroundings to notice that Craig rolled his window back up and took off down the street. My heart beat like a freight train and my hands shook a little. I still had a lot of pent-up energy. I glanced at the police station. Maybe I should put the energy to good use. Since I was already there, it couldn't hurt to go bug them about returning my computer. Could it?

CHAPTER 15

Grandma Ruth was in my kitchen when I got up the next morning. She sipped espresso and snagged two cookies out of the cookie jar on the counter. It was day three of having a drive-to-work babysitter, and after last night's encounter with Craig, I wasn't in the best of moods. It didn't help that the blinking answering machine now had twenty messages on it.

"I don't need you to come to work with me, Grandma," I stressed as I worked the machine and made my own espresso. Then I dumped the thick brew into a large cup and added steamed milk until the lovely smell filled the air.

"I'm not here to be your bodyguard, kiddo," Grandma said. She sipped her coffee and then licked her index finger and swiped up the cookie crumbs from off her bosom. "I have news."

"What'd you find out?" I leaned against the counter. While I wore my usual white shirt, black slacks, thick socks, and black walker shoes, Grandma wore men's brown corduroy slacks, a maroon butterfly-patterned waffle weave undershirt, and a flannel lumberjack shirt. She wore a thick denim rancher's jacket over that.

With the right hat, you wouldn't be able to tell what gender she was. Grandma liked that.

"I spent the day in the public records department at the county courthouse." Grandma loved public records and, more important, she loved research. "Seems George Meister inherited his father's farm a few years back. Did you know ever since he took it over, the place has been leaking money like a sieve? He asked for an extension on his property taxes three times last year. I talked to Roger Payne at the county extension office. Turns out George had taken a risk on a new genetically modified wheat seed."

"What happened?"

"Last year, we had a rainy spring and a very dry summer. The wheat rose quickly then got spindly and died off from the lack of water. George had to till under more than half his crop." Grandma's blue eyes sparkled. She loved a good disaster story.

"What was the seed supposed to do? I mean, why gamble if there wasn't the promise of a big payoff?" I took a sip of my latte and let the caffeine go to work on my brain.

"The seed was supposed to withstand drought, but the rainy spring ruined it." Grandma shook her head. "The good news is he wasn't the only farmer trying the seed and a lot of people lost their crops."

"How's the fact that people lost their crops good news?" It might be early but even my sleep-addled brain didn't like the idea of farmers losing crops.

"Those with traditional wheat got more per acre for their harvest. George tried to sue the seed company, but a judge dismissed the case as frivolous and ordered George to pay for the company's lawyer fees. Mr. Meister filed for bankruptcy two weeks ago."

I leaned against my counter and digested the news. "No wonder he was mad. It really had nothing to do with me or my bakery." I grabbed up my keys and my leather bag. "Are you coming?"

"Since I'm here." Grandma shrugged and hauled herself out the door after me. She stopped at the top of the steps and lit up a cigarette. "I heard you didn't have any luck interviewing the business owners on your block."

"Well, yes and no." I blew out a breath. It steamed out in the early morning air. There was frost on the ground for the first time. Fall was well and truly here.

"Okay, spill."

I tried to form my thoughts as the sound of my footsteps on the bricks echoed through the cold air. I opened the back of the van, let down the ramp, and drove Grandma's scooter inside. "I learned that most of the businesses open at ten," I informed her. "Only my bakery and the pharmacy open early. Craig and Ralph were in the pharmacy working on the books and the Halloween displays but they didn't hear or see anything."

"So we're mostly clueless as to who did this." Grandma frowned and puffed on her cigarette while she watched me work. I closed the back doors and got into the driver seat.

"Not really," I said as Grandma put out her cigarette butt and climbed into the passenger seat. "Todd Woles, the men's store owner, really didn't like George. He told me so himself."

"But you said he wasn't downtown at the time."

"That's what he said." I chewed on my bottom lip. "But Tasha told me that Todd and George got into a fight last year. I guess the cops were called to force George to leave the store. Tasha thinks there might even be a restraining order on George."

"Huh." Grandma narrowed her eyes thoughtfully. "I can check on that. Todd might be a good suspect after all."

"What I want to know is how George was killed." I started up the van and waited for Grandma to buckle her seat belt. "It could make a difference in suspects." I noted the small burn mark on the knee of her pants and sighed.

"You're right. It could make a difference." Grandma snapped the buckle in place. "Not to worry. I have an in with the ME. I'm taking her to lunch today."

"Of course you do." I shook my head and backed the van out of the driveway. "What about friends? Did George have any? Did he go to church, Play poker, anything?"

Grandma squinted a second. "I don't know . . . Do you think a friend would kill him?"

I frowned. "Well, I can't imagine a seed company executive standing out on Main Street at 5:30 in the morning. Can you?"

"Hmm, probably not."

"What if he talked one of his friends into planting the seed and their farm went belly-up along with George's? I saw George's anger. Can you imagine how angry his friends would be?"

"Good point," Grandma said. "Effy Anderson did tell Eloise Blake that her son Bob was mad enough to choke a heifer over crop loss. But I have no idea if he was around that morning. I'll tug on a few of my community strings and see what I find out."

"Community strings?"

"Old folks, kiddo." She reached over and patted me. "Oil-top is a small town. Not much goes on here that someone, somewhere, doesn't know about. When I worked for the paper, I had a lot of tipsters. You know, friends who would call in and tip me off on something new coming down the pike. Like those ghost tours Sherry Williams talked you into being a part of. . . ."

"Drat," I mumbled, embarrassed again. "It's your fault I signed up for them."

"My fault?" Grandma tried to look innocent by placing a hand on her bosom.

"Sure, you're the one who always told me there's no such thing as bad publicity. Do you think the chief knows?"

"Of course the chief knows."

My stomach turned over. I was going to have to call Brad. There was no way Chief Blaylock would give up his suspicions without prodding. I didn't want to think about that and changed the subject. "Tasha thinks we should pay close attention to who attends the memorial. You know, because the killer always comes back to the scene of the crime to either gloat or because he or she feels guilty or something."

"That's a great idea." Grandma clapped her hands and rubbed them together. "I'll have Bill bring me. What're you serving?"

"I'm offering petit fours and cheese tarts. I suppose it is ironic for George to have a gluten-free memorial."

"I understand the bank's going to auction off his ranch in two weeks. Maybe Bill and I'll go. Who knows? Perhaps he was killed for a fast sell."

"Now you're reaching." I pulled into the parking lot behind the bakery. "The auction was set up two weeks ago. If someone wanted the land, why kill him now? And speaking of the bank, don't let me forget that I have to make a deposit."

"Don't you usually do that at night?" Grandma asked as she heaved herself out of the van.

"Yes, but I had a few things on my mind last night and forgot." I opened up the shop and turned on the lights. As was my new habit, I checked the office, the pantry, then the front and bathrooms for any hidden dangers . . . like murderers.

Then I unlocked the safe and took out the deposit bag. Most people paid electronically these days, but you still had people who carried cash, especially in a farming town. As much as Oiltop liked to think it was a progressive county seat—we had the county courthouse, the fairgrounds, and the semipro baseball stadium—we were still a very small town. A town surrounded by farm fields, ranches, and what Pete and the rest of the chamber of commerce hoped would soon be a tourist Mecca of a slowly filling lake created by damming the river, which tended to flood certain parts of town every spring.

I don't know about tourists, but farmers and ranchers dealt in cold, hard cash. Also, bankers and farmers didn't have a good history with one another. Not when you considered how many small farms were repossessed every year.

I filled out the deposit slip and stuck it in the bag, which had quite a heft to it. Bankers and ranchers . . . hmmm. I walked over to Grandma Ruth, who was currently in the office reading the *New York Times*. She had a weekend subscription and prided herself on being "in the know."

"We really need to find out how George was killed." I leaned on the door frame and tossed the bag up and down. "I think we can rule out bullets, right? I mean, I didn't hear a shot and they haven't dug around for bullets in the wall."

"What do you think killed him?" Grandma kept her eyes on the paper. Her fingers were pinched as if she held a cigarette. She probably would have if I didn't have a strict no-smoking policy in the bakery.

"I don't know." I eyed the bag. "It's why I want to know what the coroner's report says."

"We'll get it today. Then our investigation will really start going places."

I hoped she was right, because right now it was going nowhere.

CHAPTER 16

By mid-morning, Grandma and the breakfast crowd had left. The mirror on the door to the bakery allowed me to see the front door from the kitchen while I worked. Tomorrow was George Meister's memorial and I was hard at work on the menu. Sherry had picked out a variety of fancy cookies such as ladyfingers, date pinwheels, and pistachio thumbprints. Also finger foods with protein, which included cheesecake bites and cheese tarts. Finally there was a wide selection of petit fours. I made them out of gluten-free white sheet cakes and filled them with chocolate, raspberry and, in keeping with the season, pumpkin filling. These were then cut into one-inch squares and topped with pourable fondant. Then there were gluten-free chocolate cakes filled with chocolate, cannoli, and cherry filling. The chocolate petit fours were decorated with a green leaf and the white with a white cross.

It was a lot of work, but the chamber of commerce paid well, and I wasn't about to complain. Saturday was also Amy's son's birthday party and the bowling league's monthly meeting. Both of those parties had Halloween themes.

The doorbells jingled and I glanced up to see a young woman walk in. She looked a bit ragged with dyed black hair and a worn coat. She had her eyebrow pierced, which was an interesting contrast to her thick black cat-eyed eyeliner and what had to be false eyelashes. The combination made it hard to guess her age. Anywhere from sixteen to twenty-six might apply.

"Hi, can I help you?" I came into the front room, wiping my hands on a towel.

"Yes, um . . . you have a help wanted sign?" She pointed at my hand-printed bit of desperation.

"Yes, I do." I smiled at her because she didn't seem too sure of herself.

"Well, um, my uncle Sam—Sam Greenbaum—said you might be hiring."

Ah, handsome Sam must have seen my sign. I leaned on the counter and studied her. "I'm looking for help who can work whatever hours I need, but the pay is barely above minimum wage."

She brushed her bangs out of her eyes. "I graduated high school last May. I can work when you need me. That means anytime." She glanced around. "Nice bakery."

"Thanks, we're gluten-free. Do you know what that is?"

"No wheat or malt." Her gaze came back to mine and I noticed her eyes were a lovely shade of blue, deep enough they were almost lavender. "I, um, have a friend with celiac."

"I see."

"Oh, sorry." She stuck out her hand. "I'm Meghan."

I shook her hand. It was clean and firm. Her nails were appropriately short with no polish. "Well, Meghan, do you think you might want to be a baker?"

"Actually, yeah." Her eyes lit up. "I love the Food Network. All those baking challenges. I thought, I want to learn how to do that. Problem is, my mom and dad kicked me out and there's no money for school."

I frowned. "Why'd they kick you out?"

"You know." She shrugged. "Eighteen and done. My dad always said we would get a suitcase and a twenty-dollar bill on our eighteenth birthday. We all knew he meant it and that we'd better be prepared."

I swallowed hard. It seemed very wrong. My feelings must have shown on my face.

"I know." She gave a soft smile. "It's kind of old school. Anyway, I need a job. Right now I'm working three nights a week at the Quickmart and bunking with my girlfriend. When Uncle Sam told me about your sign I thought, cool. I thought I could maybe learn a thing or two while I save up to go to school."

"Well, Meghan, let me scrounge up an application. Do you want to fill it out now or bring it back in?"

"I can fill it out now, if that's okay." She pulled a pen out of her purse. "I'm prepared."

"Great." I reached under the cash register counter and pulled out one of the five applications I'd downloaded from the Internet. "Here you go." I handed her the form. "Take a table."

"Thanks." I watched her walk to a small table and place the form and her pen on top. She took off her dark gray wool coat and draped it on the chair behind her. She wore a clean tee shirt, which was a size too small, and a pair of jeans finished off by thick-soled black boots.

She looked hungry. I decided to bring her a small coffee and a piece of cherry pie. "Here." I placed them on the table beside her. "You need to know what the food tastes like before you decide to work here. I need employees with a passion for gluten-free foods."

"Oh, thanks." She picked the fork up off the plate and took a bite of the pie. "Oh." Her eyes grew wide. "This is fab."

"Thanks." It warmed my heart to see her enjoy the pie. "I'm working in the back. Bring me the form when you're done and, if you have time, we'll do a little interview."

"Thank you," she said and took a sip of coffee.

"There are creamers and natural sugars at the counter." I pointed out the coffee bar.

"I like it black. Thanks."

I'd done what I could and went back to the kitchen. My

opinion of Sam had lowered when she said her parents tossed her out and she was now living with a friend. If he were her uncle, why hadn't he done something to help her out? I was pouring fondant over the last of the petit fours when Meghan knocked on the doorjamb to the kitchen. "I'll be right with you," I said. She walked in and watched intently.

"Is that glaze?" Meghan asked.

"Pourable fondant," I answered as I tipped the pan, then took a knife and smoothed out the tops. "It hardens and creates the petit four shell."

"Huh, I didn't know they had a pourable kind. I thought you had to knead and roll it."

"It's hard to cover inch-size cakes by rolling," I said and finished the smoothing with a flourish. "Therefore we pour."

"Makes sense." She waited for me to wash and dry my hands and then handed me the application. "I've listed three references. One is Uncle Sam; well, he's not my real uncle. He's my uncle Steve's best friend. That was, until Uncle Steve died. Then Uncle Sam stepped in and sort of took his place. There's also my home ec teacher. I put her down because she's seen me cook. Last is my current boss, Harold Mooney. He manages the Quickmart."

"Will he be okay with me hiring you?" I kept my gaze on her face. Most bosses didn't like it when you stole their employees. The last thing I needed was to piss off another guy in town.

She shrugged. "I think he'll be fine. His son dropped out of college last week and he's been talking like Joe'll need my job, anyway."

I studied the application. Meghan had very neat handwriting. Everything was properly filled out. She was willing to work whatever hours I needed. "I'll need to call your references before I can hire you."

"That's fine." She stuck her hands in her coat pockets. "I listed my roommate's phone number. I don't have a phone yet. If you want, I can come by another time."

I rubbed my chin. "If I hire you, you'll need black slacks, a white shirt, and good black tennis shoes. Can you do that?"

"I'll figure it out."

"You'll also have to wear your hair back all the time. We have food safety rules."

"Great."

"And I may need you to clean bathrooms before you leave at night."

Her mouth turned up. Her blue eyes twinkled. "I'm willing to do whatever it takes to learn the bakery business. If that means cleaning floors with a toothbrush, I'm there."

"Great. There's a memorial service for George Meister at seven tomorrow. Come in a couple hours before and I'll let you know what I've decided."

"Thank you." She held out her hand and I shook it. "I hope you'll consider my enthusiasm. I really mean it when I say I want to be a chef."

"I believe you do." I watched her walk out. She was eighteen and willing. To top it off, I was desperate. I glanced at the neatly printed form and picked up the phone.

I left Sam for last. Harold Mooney gave Meghan a glowing review. He mentioned he was sorry to have to let her go but his kid needed the work and family came first, right? I thought about the girl forced out on her own and then I thought of my own huge family that came and went at will, crashing in my big house. It was pretty clear Meghan's family had a different idea of what family meant. Even if I did sometimes wish I didn't have to see so many of them quite so often.

I rang Sam's number. Why was I nervous? It was his voice, I decided. His voice was mellow enough to melt a woman's knees.

"Hello?"

Oh, boy. "Is this Sam Greenbaum?"

"Yes."

"Hi, this is Toni Holmes from the Baker's Treat. I'm calling about a reference for Meghan Moore."

"Oh, hello, Toni."

I smiled involuntarily at the way he said my name and the warmth that blossomed in my chest.

"I'm glad you called," Sam said. "I sent Meghan over when I saw your help wanted sign."

"Thanks for thinking of me." I pretended to be professional. "Do you think her family would be upset about her working for me?"

"No, why would they?"

It was like we were cocooned together and he was talking into my ear and my ear only. I turned away from the front and faced the wall. "My last helper's parents feared for her safety, what with George being murdered in front of the store and my being the police's number one person of interest."

"How's that going?"

"If you're asking if I did it, no, I didn't. If you're wondering if the cops are closing in on me, gosh, I hope not."

He chuckled. It was a deep rumble that made me smile again. "I know you didn't do it. I was wondering how your own investigation was going."

"Oh." I blew out a long breath. "How did you know I was looking into the murder?"

"Word gets around." I swear I heard him shrug. "It's a small town, and my grandma's pretty tuned in. She thinks you're innocent, by the way."

"Thanks, Grandma," I muttered.

"And speaking for Meghan's parents, they'll be happy she has a good job."

"Are you saying they wouldn't care if I were a killer as long as I paid well?"

"They want to see their child succeed on her own. It's a family tradition. One that'd been practiced for over one hundred years."

"Well, it's a bad tradition if you ask me." I took a deep breath. Meghan had told me Sam was not her real uncle. Still . . . "What about you? Do you think it's right to abandon a child as soon as they turn eighteen years old?"

There was a long pause.

"Look," he said, "I'm not going to argue one way or the other whether their choice is right. Meghan is a great kid and a hard worker. She wants to be a chef. You need help and I think she'll work hard for you."

"Okay." I supposed that was fair. It was a good reference and all I could realistically expect from him. I barely knew him and he had so far been nice to me.

"Are you going to hire her?"

I leaned on the doorjamb and sneered at myself in the mirror. "I think so, yes."

"Good."

"Thanks for sending her my way." Professional. Keep it professional, Holmes, no matter how badly you wanted to pry. It is none of your business.

"You're welcome, but I did it for selfish reasons."

That caught my attention. I scrunched my forehead. "Why?"

"I thought that maybe if you had help, you would have time to get a coffee with me and we could get to know each other better."

My stomach did a little jig. "Oh."

"You sound funny. Is coffee a bad idea?"

His voice was low again. I rubbed my arms and turned away from my reflection. "Coffee isn't bad. But I have the best coffee in town right here."

"Then how about a cocktail? Beer? Wine?"

I scratched the back of my neck. I should not be this excited. "I've sworn off dating and men." Oh, wait, crap did I say that part out loud?

"Are you saying it's not personal?"

"Oh, God, no. . . ." I tended to talk with my hands; the one not holding the phone flailed about. As if he could see it from the phone.

"Let me guess, bad relationship?"

I winced mentally. "Divorce."

"Oh." There was a slight pause. "Then how about lunch. You do eat lunch, right? I'll even let you buy your own lunch. That way it won't be a date."

"It won't be a date?" I chewed on my lip.

"No."

"Then what is it?"

"It'll be two people buying lunch and eating it at the same table."

I stared out the window into the evening darkness. "I don't know. . . ."

"Good, how about tomorrow at one P.M.?"

I cringed inside. He was a nice guy but I was still having serious rebound issues from my divorce. Nice guy or not, did I want to go out?

"Toni?"

"Hold on, let me check my calendar." Maybe there would be a good reason why I could put off this whole lunch thing without ruining my chances if I changed my mind. I popped into the kitchen and consulted the big calendar next to the baking schedule. "I don't know. I'm catering George Meister's memorial tomorrow and Saturday I have two events."

"I promise it won't take more than an hour and it's mostly business."

"Fine." I didn't want to be a poor sport after he'd been so kind as to send an employee my way. "Tomorrow it is."

"Good, I'll come by the store around 12:30. We'll walk down to the deli."

"Oh." I felt my chest fall. "I can't eat bread. I have celiac disease."

"Right, well, then we'll walk down to the deli and convince them to let you supply them with gluten-free bread."

"Huh, now why hadn't I thought of that?"

"You would have, but you've been a bit busy lately."

I laughed. "Busy isn't the half of it. Taking gluten-free sub rolls to the deli sounds great, but then it really would be a business lunch."

"Great." I could hear the smile in his voice. "We'll do the thank-you lunch another day."

"Oh, you are sneaky."

"Only when it comes to getting something I want."

Smooth. He was smooth, but I wasn't falling for that line. "Thanks for the reference, Sam."

"See you later, Toni."

I hung up thinking I was a crazy woman, but what the heck. If Meghan worked out, I would owe the guy big. Besides, his deli idea was a good one. I could take a few twelve-inch sub rolls for them to try. If everything worked out I could have a new customer and Tasha would have another place she could take Kip for lunch. What could be wrong with that?

CHAPTER 17

"George Meister died of blunt-force trauma and drowning." Grandma Ruth had driven her scooter down to the bakery in the dark to let me know.

"Blunt-force trauma, as in someone hit him in the head with something heavy and he fell into the trough and drowned?"

"Precisely." Grandma smelled of cigarette smoke. There was a burn mark on her coat sleeve. She wore a corduroy coat, a shearling-lined plaid trapper hat, and overalls.

"Did they say what they thought he was hit with?"

This had been the longest day ever. It was 9:15 P.M. and I was closing up. All the prep work for the morning was complete. Most everything was done for the memorial. I locked the door behind Grandma's scooter and turned the sign to CLOSED. Then I went to the register and pulled out the bank deposit bag for my second trip to the bank's drop slot. I needed to go twice in one day if I was going to get back on track.

"They aren't sure. His skull was smashed in, but there wasn't a definitive wound mark."

I juggled the bag and pursed my lips. "You mean they can't tell if it was a pipe or a shovel or something?"

"Can't tell, but whatever it was, was heavy enough to kill. It's why they are calling it murder and not accidental drowning." Grandma followed me through the kitchen, her scooter wheels soft on the tile floor.

"I didn't see anything left behind." I held the back door for Grandma and turned on the security system, hit the lights, and locked the door.

"Maybe they took it with them."

"Maybe." I hit the Unlock button on my car key and the van's door locks popped open. I went to the back, opened the door, stuffed the bank bag under my arm, and lowered the ramp. "Maybe they threw the weapon in the gutter."

"Oh, yes!" Grandma was so excited she almost drove off the ramp. Thankfully, she turned her scooter at the last minute and got safely into the back of the van. "Bill and I could check the sewers tomorrow."

"Grandma, you and Bill should not be looking in the gutters." I made a face.

"No worries," she said as I climbed into the driver's seat. She had settled herself into the passenger seat and opened the window to light up. "I know someone in the city sewer department. He'll help us."

"No smoking in the van," I reminded her. "I transport food in here."

Grandma rolled her eyes and closed the window. "Fine."

"How will the sewer guy help you?" I asked as I backed out.

"He can stop traffic and put out those orange caution signs."

I blew out a deep breath. There was no point in arguing with Grandma Ruth. She could always out-argue.

"What do you think you'll find in the gutter?"

"Oh, I don't know." Grandma rubbed her chin. "It was probably a weapon of convenience. I mean, there's very little chance a killer premeditated smacking George in the head and letting him drown in the trough. It's too complicated."

"Any idea what would be a weapon of convenience?" I turned onto Main.

Grandma shrugged. "I don't know, perhaps a rock or a brick?"

"And if you find a rock or a brick down in the sewer, how will you know it's a murder weapon?" I raised an eyebrow at her. She didn't seem the least bit fazed by my reasoning.

"We'll have it tested, of course. You know, they can test for blood very easily these days. I see it on TV all the time."

I pulled into the bank parking lot and parked. "I'll be right back."

I grabbed the bank bag and jumped out. It was a short walk to the deposit drawer. The bag was not as heavy as this morning, but it was close. I tossed it in my hand and a thought occurred to me. What if the killer had used a full bank bag?

I swung the bag in the air simulating hitting someone upside the head. It didn't seem to be enough force to kill someone . . .

"What are you doing?" Grandma leaned against the van, cigarette in hand. She had gotten out to sneak a quick drag.

"I was wondering if a bank bag could have been the murder weapon." I frowned and pretended to hit someone with a downward stroke. That felt like it held more force. Was it enough to kill a guy? I didn't have one of those cool CSI dummies to check it on.

"Oh, you mean like in *The Postman Always Rings Twice*?" Grandma took a drag and squinted through the smoke.

"I'm sorry?" My attention was on Grandma Ruth.

Grandma shook her head. "You need to read more. I keep saying you could be in Mensa like me if you read more. I swear you could pass the test."

"Thanks for the compliment, Grandma." I'd heard this line most of my life. I'd never considered myself a brainiac, but it was nice Grandma thought I was. She usually called it how she saw it. At least in her mind I had a high IQ. My cousin Emma on the other hand, well Grandma Ruth had

told her to make a good marriage while she was young
because looks were all she had.

I would have been horrified. Emma took it all in stride
and was happily married to a doctor and had two kids.
Meanwhile I was up to my eyeballs in debt while under
suspicion for murder. I think it might be a toss-up as to who
had the higher IQ.

"But you have no idea what the murder weapon in the
Postman was because you never read the book."

I winced. "I think I saw the movie once . . . a long time
ago . . ."

Grandma wagged a finger at me. "Read, kiddo. It's how
you learn."

I waited but she merely stood there taking more puffs off
her smoke. "Fine." I tried not to roll my eyes. "I'll check the
book out tomorrow. Now, what was the murder weapon?"

"Ingenious, really. They put rocks in a sock, struck the
guy over the head, and left him to drown in the bathtub."

"Rocks in a sock?"

"Yes. Afterward they dumped the rocks and washed the
sock. Evidence was all gone."

I studied the soft money bag. "Sort of like this, only filled
with coins. Smash George upside the head, then deposit the
bag and voilà. No murder weapon."

"It could work." Grandma squinted through the smoke.
"How many bags do you have?"

"I get a new set of six every Saturday. A delivery guy
brings them by. I use a new bag a day, fill it up, put in a deposit
slip, and stick it in the night depository chute."

"Do they clean the bags?"

"I have no idea." I pursed my lips and studied the bag,
narrowing my eyes. "I guess if the murder weapon was a
bag, it would still be inside the bank. New bags aren't delivered for another two days."

"Do you have a flashlight?" Grandma asked.

"Sure, in the glove box," I said. "Why?"

"Hold on." Grandma twirled the fire and ash off the end

of her smoke and shoved the butt into her pocket. Then she grabbed the flashlight out of the glove box and carefully hobbled her way over to me. "Let's see if there's any blood on the depository chute."

"Great idea." I turned and opened the shiny metal door. Grandma shone the light inside. We checked for bloody drag marks and were disappointed to find nothing but clean, shiny metal.

"So much for that," Grandma Ruth said. "Make the deposit. Let's go home."

I gave the bank bag one more look over, tossed it into the chute, and dumped it. Then I sighed and got back into the van.

"It was a good idea," Grandma said.

"Suppose we can speculate all we want." I shrugged. "But what we really need is evidence. Unless you found out more about Todd Woles. . . ."

"Oh, right, Todd did have a restraining order against George. Meister couldn't come inside the men's store or within fifty feet of Todd's home. You might want to ask Todd about that."

"I will." I put the van into gear and rolled through the bank parking lot. "But does a nearly two-year-old restraining order give Todd motive? I mean, George was vandalizing my shop, not his."

"Guess we'll have to find out more tomorrow. Take me home. I need my rest if Bill and I are going to search the gutters and sewers."

I turned back onto Central and took Grandma home.

Tasha called me later. "Hey, stranger, what are you doing?"

"I'm making peanut butter cookies. I had an order for three dozen." I put the phone on speaker and went back to measuring ingredients.

"I haven't heard from you in a couple of days. I thought maybe you'd run away with Brad."

I laughed at Tasha's wild imagination. "Honey, the man hasn't looked at me twice, except maybe to calculate his bill."

"I'm disappointed in you, Toni," Tasha muttered. "I'd have thought you were smart enough to have jumped on the guy. I mean, you're single with a reason to call. Forget your rules and ask him to dinner."

"And be billed two hundred dollars an hour? No, thank you."

Since I wasn't up to more dating advice, I changed the subject. "Are you and Craig still coming to the memorial service? I mean, I know you're having your dinner party after. Do you have time to traipse over to the bakery?"

"Of course! I want to come see if I can identify the killer."

"How can you identify a killer when you weren't anywhere near the murder scene?" I turned on the mixer and let it cream the butter, peanut butter, and sugars.

"I know, silly, right? You probably think it's best if we skip out on the freezing-cold fun. I mean, it's not like I knew George at all." She sounded like she really wanted an excuse to attend. "Unless you need me to help you serve . . ."

Bingo. "I'll be fine, either way," I said. "I'm prepared and I think I'm going to hire a girl tomorrow. She can help me serve."

"Really? Who?" Tasha did sound disappointed.

"Meghan Moore, she's eighteen and wants to be a pastry chef. She seemed pretty sincere about working whenever and doing whatever I asked. It doesn't mean you can't come." I threw Tasha a bone. "You know I can always use your support."

"I'll talk to Craig and see."

"Sounds good." I added the dry ingredients to the mixer after carefully weighing them. In baking—gluten or no gluten—it was all about proper proportion.

"I'm not sure I know the Moores," Tasha said.

"I know I don't." I had the mixer on low for thirty seconds then moved it up to medium. "The parents kicked Meghan out the day after she turned eighteen."

"What?"

"I know, crazy, right? But apparently they figured they did their job raising the kids and at age eighteen, it's time to grow up. They literally give each of them a suitcase and a twenty-dollar bill for their birthday and put their stuff on the lawn the next day."

"That's crap."

"I completely agree. But I heard the family's been doing this for over one hundred years."

"That doesn't make it any less barbaric."

"No kidding. Anyway, she had great references so I'm going to give her a shot. Besides, I'm desperate for help. If she works out, I can do a lot more work and stuff—like errands."

"And come over and visit your best friend?"

"Hey, how's the inn?" I asked to distract her. "How's Kip?"

"Kip's good. He's talking about going trick-or-treating this year."

"Really? I thought he didn't like scary stuff."

"His tutor suggested it and that he would earn a reward if he went, therefore he said yes."

I couldn't tell if I detected terror or pride in her voice, perhaps both. "Does he have a costume in mind?"

"He wants to go as a third grader."

I laughed. "But he is a third grader."

"I know. I tried explaining it to him, but he insists since he is a third grader then he should go as a third grader."

"How are you going to pull that off?"

"The tutor has some ideas, but we're both working on explaining the costume part of Halloween."

I finished mixing the dough and pulled the bowl off the big mixer and set it on the counter. Then I rolled one-inch balls and placed them on the cookie sheets. "Thanks for letting me use your computer the last couple of days. I'm calling Brad in the morning and demanding mine back."

"How's the investigation going?" Tasha asked. I heard her eating on her side of the phone. It was after ten P.M. She must have had a busy evening if she was eating after Kip went to bed.

"Grandma learned that George died of blunt-force trauma." I picked up a fork and began to make the traditional crisscross pattern on the cookies.

"Which means?"

"He was hit in the head by something and fell into the trough and drowned." I picked up the cookie sheets and placed them in the oven, then set the timer.

"Wow, what kind of object?"

"They don't know. Grandma Ruth said she was going to look in the sewer tomorrow to see if maybe something was thrown down there. Anything that doesn't have my fingerprints on it would be good."

"You mean like a pipe or a bat?"

"Or a brick or a big rock." I sipped on the glass of red wine I had poured myself. "Who knows? For a while I thought maybe it was a bank deposit bag full of money. You know how heavy they get."

"That's a great idea," Tasha said. "Smash George in the head, walk down, and toss the bag in the depository."

"Exactly, but then Grandma and I looked in the depository chute and it was clean as a whistle. If someone had used a bank bag it should have left at least a streak of blood, don't you think?"

"Maybe," Tasha said. "Or maybe the chute was cleaned."

"Really? They clean that?"

"Every Wednesday. Remember, I used to work at the bank. Hey, by the way, I heard Ed Bruner had foreclosed on George's farm. Has anyone asked the banker where he was at 5:30 A.M. that morning?"

"Why? That would only make sense if George had killed Ed, right?" I sipped wine, thinking about the topsy-turvy world.

"No, I heard after Ed set up the auction and put the place up for sale, he had a couple of interested buyers. Then George got a lawyer involved and threatened to draw out the foreclosure as long as possible. It was a big stink. The buyers picked up their briefcases and walked out. They weren't interested in waiting. They wanted the farm now."

"Why?"

"Who knows," Tasha said. "Word is they were taking their money and going home."

"Wow. Then Ed did have motive to kill George."

"Motive and, if you can prove your bank-deposit-bag theory, he had means. What we need to do is prove he had opportunity."

"Right." I stared out the window. The kitchen was warm and cozy and styled like the rest of the late-Victorian house with black-and-white tiles, white cabinets, and tiled countertops and backsplash. It was the most recently remodeled room and felt like home.

"Maybe he'll be at the memorial service," Tasha said. "You could ask him then."

"You did say the killer might be at the service."

" I did, because I'm smart like that. So, did you find out more about Todd Woles's fight with George?"

"Yes, you were right. He did have a restraining order out on George."

"So you have two good suspects."

"Maybe," I said, scooping cheese tarts off their baking sheets and onto a cooling rack. "The restraining order is two years old. Why kill George now?"

"Something must have happened," Tasha declared. "I'll see what I can find out. In the meantime, if I were you, I'd keep an eye on Ed."

The timer buzzed softly. "I will. Listen, I have to go. See you tomorrow around nine?"

"Or earlier if I can have everything ready in time to let me attend the memorial and help out."

After I hung up, I pulled the cookies out of the oven. Of the two suspects, the banker had stronger means and motive. All I needed to do now was place him at the scene. That was going to be the hardest part of all.

CHAPTER 18

Tim went into work with me. I kept my eye on the bank, but it was dark and had no cars in the parking lot.

"Do you know of any reason for Ed Bruner to be at the bank early in the morning?" I asked a sleepy Tim.

My brother looked at me and drew his eyebrows together in a *V*. "Hell, no, banker's hours remember? The guy gets to work six hours a day, like from ten to four or something. I swear, if Dad had been a banker we'd all be set."

"Dad was a good professor at the school."

"And lived on a professor's income with six kids, for God's sake. We had nothing."

"Nothing but love." Mom's words rolled off my tongue. My brother growled at me. I shrugged and continued to drive. It was going to be a big day. I was nearly done with the catering platters for the memorial. A few more little details and they would be ready.

I still had the children's birthday cakes to finish today as well. "Do you know any of the Moores?"

"Rob Moore was two years ahead of me in school, why?"

"Does he have a daughter Meghan?"

Tim shrugged then yawned. "Beats me, why?"

"I'm going to hire her. Things have been crazy since Carrie left. I really need more help."

"Huh. Good for you."

Brothers are so helpful. I rolled into the parking lot. The light next to the bakery's back door was out.

"Light's out." Tim perked up.

I parked the van. "I see. Hand me the flashlight."

"What flashlight?" My brother was dense as a cornfield when he was tired.

"The one in the glove box." I held out my hand while he opened the glove box, riffled through, and slapped the flashlight at me. "Thanks."

I got out of the van and turned the flashlight on. The light had been broken. I got up under it.

"Wow, BB gun or rock?" Tim offered, his hands in his coat pockets.

I looked around. I didn't see any rocks out of place. There was a small mark in the back siding. Definitely a BB gun. I shone the flashlight around but there wasn't anyone hiding in the shadows.

That's when I noticed it: a giant mass of spray paint on the back door. The flashlight hit the metallic paint and reflected the light back at me.

"What's it say?"

I swallowed and read out loud. "Stop nosing around or you'll regret it."

"That's a threat." Tim turned to me. "What did you do to make someone do this?"

"Nothing." I half shrugged.

"Toni . . ."

"Grandma Ruth and I might be looking into the murder."

"Oh, man, sis, are you nuts? Whoever killed George has to know you're trying to figure out who he is."

I unlocked the back door and opened it. "I must be getting close," I pointed out, "or he wouldn't feel threatened."

"Let me go first." Tim hit the lights and stepped inside.

I was right behind him and turned off the alarm as he checked the office. "It's clear."

I locked the door behind us and held on to Tim's shirt as we checked out the rest of the bakery. "No one's here," I said with some relief. "The alarm didn't go off."

"Do you have a camera on your rear entrance?"

I pursed my lips and cracked my knuckles. "No. I didn't think I needed it."

"This is crazy." Tim's face grew red. "What if you'd come here alone? What if whoever killed George was waiting for you? Geez, Toni, you're not safe here."

"Oh, come on." I could feel my anger rising. Someone was scaring me and I didn't take kindly to it, so I took it out on my brother. "This is Oiltop, for God's sake, population ten thousand when the college isn't in session and fifteen thousand when the school is in. It's a heck of a lot safer than Chicago."

"If it's so safe, how come some guy was murdered a few feet from your front door? And why are we so worried about you we're not letting you go to work alone?" Tim flapped his hand around, his voice rising.

I raised my voice and stood toe to toe, nose to nose with him. "I didn't kill the guy. And I have no idea who would vandalize my place or why. Plus, I never asked you or Grandma Ruth to take me to work. So you can go home and forget worrying about me." I had my hands on my hips, and I could feel my temperature rise.

"I'm here because you need a keeper." Tim pointed at the back door. "I don't want to wake up one day and find the cops at my door telling me they found your body in the street."

"Technically, it's my door."

"What?" Tim jerked back at the low blow. I was too angry and scared to be ashamed as his face flushed. "Fine. Do whatever you want. You're a grown woman and I can't worry about you. Just make sure you make a will or something, will you? I don't want Mom's house stuck in probate for fifteen years."

"Great. Fine. I'll have Brad get right on it. I suppose you think I should leave the house to you."

"Damn it, Toni, I don't want the house. I want you safe. Why the hell do you think I stay up late every other day and see you safely here? I'm doing it because I care about you and, from the looks of your back door, someone needs to be here."

I rubbed my temples. "I have a security company."

"You need to have them put an outside camera in the back."

"Fine."

"Good. Now call 911. When the cops get here, I'll head home."

I wanted to stick my tongue out at him for making me mad and for being right. I hated it when my brother was right. I picked up the phone and dialed 911. Starting my day with a visit from Barney Fife was not going to be fun. But the day could only get better from here. Right?

CHAPTER 19

Meghan stopped by around ten-thirty that morning. She looked exactly the same as she had the day before, only this time her black hair was pulled back, exposing several piercings on her ears. "Hey, Ms. Holmes. How are you? I thought I'd stop by in person and see how it was going."

"I'm good." I wiped my hands on my apron and stepped out into the shop. "I called your references and they were quite good."

Meghan nodded and tilted her head a little in expectation.

"Can you start this evening?"

"Yes!" Her expression broke out into a wide smile. She literally jumped up and down on her toes and clapped her hands. "You won't regret this, Ms. Holmes. Seriously."

"Like I said yesterday, there's a memorial service tonight at seven and I'm catering. You'll need to be here by five-thirty. And remember to wear a white button-up blouse, black slacks, and good black walking shoes. No boots."

"Got it."

"I'll also need you Saturday from ten A.M. until four P.M.

The shop is closed on Sundays. I'll post next week's schedule before you leave on Saturday."

"Great!" She bounced.

"Wear your hair pulled back and out of your face. You can keep the eyebrow piercing but don't add to your visible piercings, and no tongue piercings as customers need to be able to understand you when you talk. This is a business and we try to be as professional as possible. The goal is to build customers, not chase them away."

"I understand." Her tone was solemn but her expression shone with happiness.

"See you at five-thirty." I watched her walk out; her happiness lifted my mood. It had been hell dealing with Officer Emry on the vandalism this morning. He'd taken pictures of the painted message and then made scrapings of the paint before he left. It had taken me an hour to scrub the message away. I wondered if I could ask the landlord to repaint the back door along with the front bricks.

The whole episode had pissed my brother off and put me an hour behind. But it was good to know I had help starting tonight. Thank goodness for Sam and Meghan.

Sam showed up at 12:30 P.M. right as I turned the OPEN sign over to CLOSED and marked the BE BACK IN AN HOUR sign.

"Hey." His expression was warm, his mouth turned up and his dark gaze interested. "Are you ready for lunch?"

I took off my apron and grabbed my jacket. It was a black-and-white houndstooth, which matched the black slacks and white shirts that made up most if not all of my wardrobe. "I'm ready." I grabbed the big box full of twelve-inch, gluten-free rolls and jerked my head toward the back. "Let's go out this way."

"Here, let me carry that for you." He took the box and I set the alarm system and locked the door behind us. "Wow, what happened here?" He nodded toward the shot-out back light and the faint impression of silver paint left on the door.

I shoved my hands in my pockets. "I was vandalized this morning."

He drew his brows together and narrowed his eyes. "Are you okay?"

"I'm fine."

"You called the police, didn't you?"

I made a face. "My brother Tim was here. He insisted. So, yes, I filed a police report."

"Good." Our feet crunched on the gravel parking lot. We came out onto the sidewalk on Central. "I hope you don't mind walking."

"No, actually, it's good to get out into the fresh air." I glanced up at the sky, the brilliant blue illustrating that it was too cold now for summer haze. We passed a few trees that had turned color. Their leaves were yellow and red. There was a snap to the air but the sun on my cheek was warm and I walked with a good-looking man.

Sometimes when everything was looking down you had to take a moment and enjoy the small things right in front of you or you'd go crazy. It was something my mom had taught me. I felt a twinge of sadness at the memory.

"A penny for your thoughts." Sam's voice soothed my ears.

"I was thinking how lovely this time of year is, what with the trees and the cool air. Much nicer than, say, August, when the air is so hot you can barely breathe."

"I like this time of year."

"Do you like the long shadows or the spooky decorations?"

"I like the spooky decorations and more important, the hayrack rides." He opened the door to the deli and waited for me to walk in.

"Wow, hayrack rides, I'd forgotten about those."

"The best part is cuddling with someone under the blankets at the bonfire after."

The light in his eyes did funny things to my insides.

"Hi, can I help you?" A young man with blond hair and a crooked smile asked from behind the counter.

"Yes, hi, I'm Toni Holmes. I own the new gluten-free

bakery down the street." I handed him my card. "Is your manager in?"

The boy, whose name tag read Jared, glanced at the card. "Sure, I'll get him." He went to the end of the counter and stuck his head in the kitchen. "Mr. Blake, there's a lady here who wants to talk to you."

I felt the heat of a blush at the kid's shouted words. The diners in the deli stared. Sam wiggled his right eyebrow and I relaxed a bit.

A middle-aged man, shorter than me, bald and about as big around as he was tall came out from the kitchen. He wore a large black-and-white striped apron over a dress shirt and slacks. "Can I help you?"

"My name's Toni Holmes." I handed him my card. "I run the new gluten-free bakery down the street. Sam here offered to take me to lunch at your deli, but I have celiac disease and I can't eat bread unless it's gluten-free. Sam had the idea maybe we could work together to bring you more customers."

Mr. Blake eyed Sam and the box and then me. "Go on."

I gave him my best smile and opened the bakery box. "I specialize in gluten-free baked goods, including bread." I glanced at his selection of deli meat and noted he carried Boar's Head brand, which is GF. "You already carry GF lunch meats and cheeses." I pulled out one of my sub loaves—this one was GF oatmeal. "Smells great, right?" I waved it under his nose. "Now, Jared, is it? If you could take this and cut it I'll show you how to make a GF sandwich."

The young man looked at Mr. Blake, who nodded. He took the bread, got out a deli plate, and reached for the bread knife.

"You'll have to cut the bread with a fresh knife. You don't want to cross contaminate the wheat with the GF."

Jared went to the back and came out with a new knife. He cut it and then added the meats, cheese, and condiments I requested. Then he sliced the sandwich in half and added a pickle and a bag of potato chips and set the plate up on the counter.

"And now I can eat at your deli." I smiled and paid full

price for the meal. "There are several people in and around town who have gluten allergies or sensitivities to wheat or barley. These people currently avoid eating in your deli, Mr. Blake, but if you were to offer GF sandwiches and were careful not to use the same utensils, people would be happy to dine here."

"Really? And where would I get the gluten-free stuff? Your bakery?"

"I would be happy to supply you with a variety of bread types from white to potato to oatmeal."

"And the price?"

"Can be negotiated depending on the number of loaves you purchase."

"I don't know." He shook his bald head. "We're known for our fresh breads."

"I'm a few blocks down on Main and can deliver fresh every morning."

"How do I know these will sell?" he asked as he looked through the box Sam held out for him to inspect.

"How about we do a trial run? I can offer you the loaves for half price for the first week. If you don't see an improvement in sales, we'll call it off. But if you do, you'll order your GF bread from me. What do you have to lose?"

Mr. Blake glanced at Sam, at the loaves, my sandwich, and back to me. "I tell you what, we'll give it seven days, like you said. Then we'll talk again."

"Great!" I smiled broadly and took the box and handed it to Jared, who stared at it as if he didn't know what to do with it. "You can have these on the house today. I'll send over fresh tomorrow."

Mr. Blake's mouth made a firm line and he nodded. "Put those on the counter," he told Jared. "Then put up a sign that says we offer gluten-free sandwiches." He reached out and shook my hand. "Good sales pitch, Ms. Holmes."

"Thank you, it'll be nice working with you."

"On a one-week trial," he said.

"Oh, I think you'll find you want to work together more than a week," I said. As long as no one else got killed.

CHAPTER 20

On our way back to the bakery, I noted the CAUTION signs around the gutters and manholes. "Oh, no."

"What?" Sam asked.

"Grandma Ruth." I stepped up my pace until I was nearly running. "I told her not to do this."

"Do what?" Sam kept up with me stride for stride.

"This." I waved at the caution markers. "Grandma Ruth . . ." I called her name and heard some faint reply. "Bill?"

"They're down in the sewer." A man dressed in white coveralls stepped out from behind a city truck.

I knelt down and stuck my head into the open manhole. "Grandma, what are you doing?"

Bill popped into sight. "We're treasure hunting." He grinned. I guess I shouldn't have been surprised. Treasure to him was a dead animal or an interesting bit of roadkill.

I scowled. "How could you let her down there? It's slimy. She might fall and break a hip."

"I will not fall." Grandma popped into view. "I have a walker." She shook the metal walker at me.

"Oh, Grandma, who's going to clean that?"

"Don't worry." Bill snickered. "It's a loaner." Grandma laughed until she coughed. Bill pounded her on the back. At least they wore coveralls. Thank goodness. I wouldn't have to smell sewer in Grandma's clothes for the next three weeks.

"What are they doing down there?" Sam was on his knees next to me.

"They're looking for possible murder weapons," I said as low as possible.

"Who's that?" Grandma asked.

"Grandma Ruth, I would like to introduce my friend Sam Greenbaum. Sam this is my grandma Ruth and her friend Bill Aimes."

"Hello," Sam said. "Nice to meet you."

"Well, well," Grandma said eyeing Sam. "Toni, you did good." Grandma's eyes twinkled as her cap of orange curls jiggled.

"I hope you have an appointment at the salon before you come to tonight's memorial," I said.

"I do." Grandma looked at her watch and slapped Bill's stomach with the back of her hand. "Bill, we need to get going if we want to be ready for dinner by five. Nice to meet you, Sam. Toni, my watch tells me it's time for you to open the bakery. Scoot, kiddo." She made waving motions with her hands.

I shook my head and watched them both disappear from view. I sat back on my heels and sighed. Then I looked at the city worker. "How did they get down there? I can't imagine Grandma taking those metal ladders."

"There's a set of stairs leading from the bank's basement. We got permission to let them in there."

"There's access to the sewers through the bank's basement?"

"Yes, of course," the city worker said. "But only the sewer department has a key."

Sam took my hand and helped me up. "Thanks." I brushed the dirt off my knees.

"Why are you concerned about there being a sewer

access point under the bank?" Sam asked as we walked around the corner to the back of the bakery.

"There seems to be a lot of talk about connections between the bank and George's murder." I stuffed my hands in my pockets.

"Like what?"

"George was suing the bank and tying up Ed Bruner's sale of the foreclosed farm. Also, there's the fact George was hit by a blunt-force object that no one has found. Grandma was looking in the sewer to see if the killer chucked anything like a pipe or hammer or big rock in there. Now we find out there is access to the sewer from the bank . . ."

"Sounds entirely circumstantial," Sam said as I unlocked the door and disarmed the alarm.

"I know." I pulled off my coat, hung it on one of the coat hooks near the kitchen door, and headed to the front to unlock the shop. "It's why I haven't gone to the police with my thoughts. I know what it's like to be accused based on circumstantial evidence."

Sam followed behind me as I turned the sign around and unlocked the glass front door. Then I made a beeline for the coffee carafes. It was time to brew fresh.

"Do you have your computer back yet?" His voice was comforting even if the question raised my hackles.

"No." I bit my bottom lip and poured water into the coffee machine. "I need to call my lawyer about that."

"What does your lawyer think about you catering George's memorial service?" Sam leaned against the counter and watched me make coffee.

"He has no say." I shrugged and hit the Brew button.

"At least they've taken down most of the crime scene tape." Sam looked out the window. The only yellow tape left was wound around the horse trough. Someone had placed a bouquet of flowers by the trough. It looked kind of sad there all by itself.

"Not exactly an outpouring of love, is it?" I stood beside him and studied the sorry little bunch of carnations.

"I think I saw Sherry Williams put them there."

"Oh." I raised my eyebrows in surprise. "Huh, maybe they had a fling or something."

"Why do you say that? I mean, I can't imagine two more different people."

"Sherry's the one who set up the memorial. She told me it would be good for business. It would help establish the ghost walk tours she wants to start downtown."

"Ghost walk tours?" Sam's eyes were an incredible blue. His generous mouth twitched.

I wanted to breathe him in and hold him in my lungs—more proof that I could not trust my judgment. My divorce had taught me nothing if I was going to fall for the first good-looking guy to pay me the slightest attention. I got back to the subject at hand. "Sherry says they're all the rage and that George's murder is the perfect ending point for walking tours of Oiltop's downtown where they point out all the local ghost legends."

Sam crossed his arms. "Really, like what?"

"Like the fact that on dark October nights you can see devil worshipers in the attic of the old Baptist church."

"Oh my God, I forgot about that old story." His grin grew wide and his eyes sparkled. "Even in Towanda we knew about that. It was something we used to tell our girlfriends to get them to snuggle close as we cruised by the church. Trust me, it was worth the car ride here."

"Then there's Merry Pratt's suicide from the second-floor balcony of the old opera house."

"Opera house?"

I looked at him like he should know about the opera house.

"My parents might have grown up here, but I didn't. They moved an hour south of here before I was born, remember? It's not like I grew up on Oiltop legends."

"It's now the Grey Goose bar and grill. You know, down on the other end of Main Street."

"Oh, right."

"And then there's the town square, where they used to hang murderers and horse thieves after they had been tried in the county courthouse. Rumor is sometimes you can see the white ghostly figures wandering the square."

"And now there's your bakery."

I nodded and drew my lips together in a fine line. "Where George Meister was hit in the head and left to drown in the horse trough." A chill went through the bakery and I rubbed my upper arms. "The price of a walking tour ticket includes a cup of coffee or hot cocoa and a cookie from the bakery at the end."

"Let me guess, Sherry's conducting the tours."

"Yes." The brewer beeped letting me know the coffee was done. I filled the carafe and then set up the second kind of coffee and hit Brew. "I negotiated a 10 percent discount on drinks and cookies as long as she averaged thirty tourists a week. Anything less than that and she pays full price."

"Do you think she'll have that many tourists?"

I shrugged. "The college students might dig it. Then there's the Prairie Port Festival and when the county fair is in town. But even with the new lake, it's not like Oiltop is a booming tourist town. That's why I set the limit at thirty a week or she pays full price. It's just too iffy."

Sam grinned. "I love a woman who knows the art of a deal."

I set the full carafe on the coffee bar and put my hands on my hips. "I forgot to ask. What exactly do you do for a living, Mr. Greenbaum?" I suppose it was a little late to ask him, but it was meant as a friendly if nosey question.

He waved toward his boots. "I'm a cowboy by trade. I run a small spread south of here. But I also do remodeling, carpentry, and subcontracting—a little bit of everything."

"Wow, sounds like you're a handy guy to have around."

"I try to be." His eyes twinkled and my heart pounded a bit too fast. It was dangerous how quickly a girl could get used to having a man around.

CHAPTER 21

Twenty minutes before the memorial was supposed to start, the bakery door jingled.

Meghan gave him a "Hi, how can I help you?" In the two hours she'd been working she'd only gotten a couple of things wrong. I think I was going to love having her. I hope she loved it, too, and the murderers and vandals didn't scare her away.

"I'm here to see Toni." The sound of Brad's voice echoed through to the kitchen, where I was prepping platters and brewing extra coffee.

"Just a sec." Meghan walked into the kitchen. "There's a hot guy out there asking for you. He might be a bit old, but he's still hot." Meghan's eyes sparkled.

"That's my lawyer," I informed her. "Tell him to come on back."

"Will do, Boss." Meghan left.

I poured coffee into extra carafes as Brad entered the kitchen. He literally took up all the space. He wore a black overcoat with gold buttons, a *GQ* suit made of a fine dark navy fabric, a pale blue shirt, and a pin-striped maroon tie.

His thick golden hair was brushed back and curled at the neck. His bright gaze took in the clean but busy kitchen.

"Hey."

"Hey," I answered trying to breathe and act normally.

"I heard you were vandalized again last night. Are you all right?"

"Yes, I filed a police report, like you told me to last time. It's always best to have a record of everything, right?"

"Right." He glanced around at the steel-and-marble kitchen. "Nice design."

"Thanks, I knew what I wanted and the landlord agreed to the remodel. Cooler surfaces help to keep dough from sticking."

"Are you going to have a camera installed on the back door?" He leaned casually against the stainless steel counter. I checked to make sure he wasn't getting anything on his coat. Thank goodness I ran a clean kitchen.

"Have you been talking to my brother?"

"No, why?"

"He asked the same thing." I straightened and wiped my hands on a towel. "I'd love to, but I don't have the extra cash for that expense right now."

"Get your landlord to install it."

"It was hard enough to get him to install these counter-tops. He has no incentive to put in a camera, much less repaint the front bricks and the back door. Those things, I'm afraid, are up to me."

"I noticed the fresh paint on the front bricks."

"I didn't want the spray paint showing for the memorial." I put the finishing touches on the platters and placed the last one on the rolling rack that held them.

"Yes, I can see how that would be bad for business." His gaze followed my every move.

I was very self-conscious and caught myself brushing my bangs out of my eyes one time too many. Why did the man have to be hot? And so very much out of my league? Two hot men in one day were really weakening my resolve.

At least Brad had grown up around my family and would

never consider me in his league. Brad knew the weirdos I came with . . . no, not weirdos, creatives, Grandma Ruth would call us. It was the main reason I had moved to Chicago. It was a big city and no one knew my family. There was something freeing in that. Not that it had helped me pick a better man.

"Why are you here, Brad? Did you come for the memorial?"

"I came to tell you the police are releasing your computer equipment. You can pick it up anytime at the station." His smile warmed my fluttering heart.

"Thank you." I meant it. Relief filled me. I could have my life back. "So I'm no longer a person of interest?"

He winced. "They have no evidence to link you, but you're still their number one suspect."

I sighed. "I didn't do it." I swiped the clean counter with a clean dishrag.

"I know you didn't." Brad stepped in close, leaning against the counter. I could feel the heat from his body even though he didn't actually touch me. It had a strange, comforting effect, causing me to blink back the tears I didn't even know I was holding onto.

"If they still think I did this, then why give me my computer back?"

I looked into his eyes. The corners of his mouth lifted. "I pushed. I told them unless they had hard evidence, you would sue them for defamation of character and harm to your business. I imagine I was pretty convincing."

I think my heart rolled over in my chest. God, he made a good Prince Charming—if only I still believed. I hid my emotions by staring down at the dishcloth in my hands and inhaled. There was something wonderful about expensive clothes that smelled of starch, good cologne, and warm male. "Thank you."

"You haven't gotten my bill yet."

That made me laugh. I looked back up and my heart skipped a beat. There was that moment—that awkward moment when you thought a man wanted to kiss you.

I stepped back and tried to be professional. It was hard because I think I might have kissed him. If he weren't my lawyer. If things were different. I glanced at the clock. "Bill or no bill, thanks. More than half my business is online. It's been eating up a lot of time running to Tasha's inn to use her computer."

"Toni."

"Hmm?" I was double-checking the platters and trying to get my nerves back under control.

"When this is over, I'd like to take you out to dinner."

That got my attention. My head whipped around fast. It took a second for my eyes to catch up. "Excuse me?"

He crossed his arms and sent me a sexy half grin. "When this is over, and you no longer need me to be your lawyer, I'd like to take you to dinner."

"Oh." It's all I could get out of my mouth. I opened and closed it several times like a fish out of water. What a sight that must have been.

His grin grew larger. "Yes, I'm single. I know you're single. And I'm interested, Toni. Are you interested?"

In dating the high school hottie who only got better with age? Duh. I kept blinking like a sleepy-eyed doll. While a tiny voice in my head said no, no dating, an even louder buzzing drowned it out.

"I'll take that as a yes," he said with the confidence of a male who knows where he stands.

"Um, Boss?" Meghan popped her head into the kitchen. "Ms. Williams from the chamber of commerce said to tell you everyone's here and you need to get out there so they can begin the memorial."

"Gotta go." I did something ridiculous, like pat Brad on his beefy arm, then grabbed my coat and headed outside.

"Everyone needs a candle." Sherry handed me a small white candle with a paper drip catch. She gave one to Meghan, too.

I saw Tasha and Craig and stood beside them, far from Brad. "I'm glad you're here. I hope you didn't push things on my account."

"I didn't. Besides, I felt I should be here to support you during this weird thing," Tasha whispered.

"Thanks."

"Here, light your candle on mine." She touched her flame to my wick. The candle burst into light, and I noticed Grandma Ruth and Bill on the other side of the crowd.

If you could call it a crowd; there were maybe ten or fifteen people in attendance including me, Meghan, Tasha, Craig, Grandma Ruth, and Bill. Then there was Sherry and her friends from the chamber of commerce.

"There'll be plenty of food," I muttered.

"How many people did Sherry tell you to plan for?" Tasha whispered.

Sherry had started the memorial by introducing Reverend Jones from the Baptist church George had attended.

"I made enough for fifty." I leaned toward Tasha and kept my voice low.

"The chamber will be eating petit fours and cookies for a week." Tasha giggled and the reverend glared at us.

I bit my lower lip to keep from laughing and started checking out exactly who else was in attendance. If Tasha was right, the killer would be here.

There was Rocky Rhode in the back, flashing pictures. The shots were for the newspaper, I supposed. Great, yet another front-page photo of my bakery. Beside him was Candy with her reporter's notebook in hand, and Mike Smith. I guess Mike was here to thank George for the bump in newspaper sales. Then there was Ralph, Craig's brother, standing in the back with his hands in his pockets, looking cold and uncomfortable. He must have either arrived late or refused the candle. Personally I was glad for the candle, as the soft flame warmed my hands.

"Please bow your heads for a moment of silence," the reverend intoned.

I bowed but kept my gaze on the crowd. There was Ed Bruner from the bank standing near Bill and Grandma Ruth. Todd Woles from the men's shop stood near another very well-dressed man. If I were to hazard a guess, I'd label the other man as Todd's boyfriend. Their shoulders touched and their eyes glistened. Were they tears of sadness or relief? Why go to a memorial for a man you had a restraining order against?

Then there was Brad; Amy, his secretary; Chief Blaylock, and Officer Emry. If I counted the chamber members, there were maybe twenty or more in attendance.

"Thank you. Now, if anyone would like to say any words about George, now would be a wonderful time to share." The reverend looked into the crowd and suddenly people's gazes were on the ground, across the street, or on the person next to them. "Anyone? Sherry?"

Sherry smiled her pageant smile and stepped forward. "Of course, Reverend, I would like to say I didn't know George very well, but my mother did go to school with his mother and I couldn't let this tragedy go by without some kind of memorial to mark George's life in our community. George was an outspoken member of our community who had strong opinions and kept to them."

I glanced at Grandma Ruth and raised my right eyebrow. She shrugged and grinned at me.

"Outspokenness should be cherished in a democratic society," Sherry went on. "But outspokenness should go hand in hand with an open mind and forgiveness, which is why we are having this service tonight. Unfortunately, George seemed to have had a few troubles in his life and, right or wrong, he took them out on others. But all is forgiven, and we stand here tonight remembering the goodness of George and his family and all the things they did to help our community. Thank you, George. God bless you, wherever you are."

Silence covered the crowd like a thick blanket. Sherry smiled her pageant smile. "Reverend Jones will say a final prayer, and then Toni Holmes will speak."

My head whipped around and my mouth fell open. Sherry smiled at me as if I knew exactly what I was supposed to say.

"Bow your heads and pray for God's blessings," Reverend

Jones started. Sherry bowed her head and Tasha elbowed me until I did the same. The reverend droned on about the shortness of life and how man is dust and to dust we shall return. When he was done, he said a prayer.

The sound of my heartbeat in my ears drowned out the prayer. What exactly was Sherry up to? What was I supposed to say? Tasha elbowed me again and handed me a small note card. I took the card. There, in Sherry's neat high school printing, was a small statement. I glanced from the card to Sherry.

"And now, Ms. Holmes," the reverend said. Tasha took my candle and pushed me toward the front. Reverend Jones handed me the microphone.

"Hello." The mic squawked with feedback. I swallowed hard and read from the card. "Thank you all for coming and honoring a member of our community." I took a deep breath and pressed on. "His tragic death will never be forgotten. Please come inside the bakery for fellowship and shared memories. Coffee and treats are provided courtesy of the Oiltop Chamber of Commerce." I waved my hand toward Sherry and Alisa. "Thank you."

And it was over. I handed the microphone to Sherry, and saw that Meghan had slipped inside the bakery to help pass out cups of coffee and hot cocoa and point people toward the platters.

"I think that went very well," Sherry said. "Don't you?"

I flattened my mouth. "Sure, if you say so."

"Shall we go inside and get warm?"

I stepped into the warmth of my bakery, plastered on my happy sales face, and tried to ignore the weirdness that was the memorial for a guy who had been killed while vandalizing my shop. I grabbed a platter and passed it around. "Petit four? They're chocolate and raspberry. And, yes, they are entirely gluten-free. Perfect for anyone with celiac, children with allergies, and the elderly whose systems are sensitive."

"Toni, smile for the camera," Rocky said. I paused next to Todd and his friend and gave my best party smile. The camera clicked and the bulb popped. "Thanks, this will look good on the front page."

Rocky moved on as people ate, shared stories, and drank my coffee. And deep inside, I couldn't help wondering if there was a killer in our midst.

CHAPTER 22

"You should tell Chief Blaylock your theory," Tasha said as she gobbled up another petit four.

"I don't have any evidence." I kept my gaze on Ed. He looked like a normal guy in his late forties: a bit round, a bit wrinkled, and still combing over a few long hairs in the misguided hope no one would notice he was balding.

"There's more to your theory than what the cops have on you," Tasha pointed out.

"What theory is this?" Chief Blaylock came up, snagged a couple of the little cakes, and balanced them carefully on his full plate.

"Nothing, really." I shook my head.

"She suspects Ed Bruner of killing George Meister," Tasha said. I widened my eyes at her, flattened my mouth, and slightly shook my head. She refused to stop. "You see, Ed foreclosed on George's property last month and set up an auction for next Saturday."

"Yes, I know." The chief popped a petit four into his mouth. "These are really good."

"Thanks," I said. "I cater weddings, birthdays, anniversaries . . ."

"And funerals, obviously." Craig stepped in and took a couple of cakes from the plate.

"I was telling Chief Blaylock about Toni's theory of who killed George."

"It's really not a theory," I protested.

"Chief, did you know that when Ed had a couple of interested buyers come tour George's place, George sued the bank? I think it was for more time. George said all he needed was time and he could be caught up on payments, but Ed had buyers who weren't willing to wait."

"Seriously." The chief raised an eyebrow. "You think Ed killed George?"

"Yes," Tasha said in a stage whisper. "You see, George was killed by a blow to the head with a mysterious blunt instrument."

The chief narrowed his eyes. "How do you know that?"

"It's a small town," Tasha said "Everyone knows. And Toni figured out what the blunt instrument was."

"No, I did not. More cake?" I rolled my eyes at Tasha to get her to stop. For goodness' sake, the last thing I needed was for the police to think I had killed George because I had a theory about the bank deposit bags.

"You know what killed George?" Craig asked.

"No, I don't." I looked around to see if I could excuse myself before I got into more hot water.

"Oh, she's being modest." Tasha patted my arm. "She thinks it was a full bank deposit bag. Those things are heavy if you had a day with a lot of change, or are a banker and fill it with rolls of quarters."

The chief stared at me and narrowed his eyes. I felt the heat of a blush rush up my neck. I had to say something. "I merely mentioned how heavy a bank deposit bag was when it was full. Grandma Ruth said that is how they tried to kill the Greek in the classic novel *The Postman Always Rings Twice.*"

"It's ingenious, really," Tasha gushed. "I mean, wham! with the bank bag, then wipe it off and make your deposit. The bag gets emptied and the actual 'weapon' is gone."

The chief swallowed his cake and took a sip of coffee. I could hear his mind working. Or, as my dad would say, he could smell the wood burning.

"So, you see," Tasha continued, "Ed had motive and means. Plus, did you know there is access to the sewer system from the bank's basement? What better place to get rid of evidence, like bloody clothes and junk."

Craig's head bobbed from Tasha to me and back as the story unfolded. I swallowed hard and waited for the chief to slap the cuffs on me.

"Huh," Chief Blaylock said. "Perhaps I should go talk to Ed."

"Even better, you should check all the bank deposit bags for evidence." Tasha's eyes were wide. "I bet you'll find a bag with George's blood on it."

"Ew," I said out loud. "One of the new bags I get tomorrow might have blood on it?" I hadn't quite thought the whole theory out. "I mean, I doubt Ed steam-cleans the bags before he distributes them."

"Excuse me, won't you?" The chief put his plate on the empty platter I still held and moved off toward Ed.

"I can't believe you did that," I scolded Tasha.

"What do you mean? I saved you from being charged."

"Or got me convicted," I stage-whispered, my gaze not leaving Chief Blaylock's wide back. "If Ed has an alibi, then the chief will think I'm really guilty since I know what the murder weapon is."

"Oh." Tasha scrunched up her forehead then wrinkled her nose. "I hadn't thought of that."

"Sounds to me like Ed has more to worry about than you do." Craig patted me on the back. He paused. "If it was a bank deposit bag, do you think they can link it to anyone in particular?"

"I don't know." I tilted my head. "As far as I know, the bags aren't numbered or checked out. I mean, it's sort of an honor system, isn't it? You get six bags and return six bags."

"Too bad." Craig sipped his coffee. "It would be cool if they could link the bag to the killer."

"We don't even know if George was killed by a bank bag. Grandma Ruth said it could be any weapon at hand, which means anything from a rock to a cane to a baseball bat." I tried to bring some sanity back to the discussion.

"The good news is they didn't find anything in your shop." Tasha sipped her coffee and glanced around. "They have no evidence to link you, either."

"Thank goodness."

"You know," Tasha said, "Todd Woles would have access to a bank bag. Wouldn't he?"

"All the businesses on Main get bank deposit bags," Craig said.

"Did you see Todd was here with his . . . friend? Why would they come to the memorial but not even bother to come in for refreshments?" Tasha sipped her drink.

"I have no idea." I noticed some people leaving. "Have a good night, folks, and remember to stop by the bakery for the best coffee and pastries in town," I called after them. I mean, the whole point of the reception was to drum up new customers. Right?

"Oh, good news." I put my hand on Tasha's arm. "Brad says I can pick up my computer stuff from the police station in the morning. Thanks for letting me borrow yours this past week. You're a lifesaver."

"Are you no longer a suspect?" Craig asked.

"No." I gave a short shake of my head. "It simply means Brad's a good lawyer. He threatened them with legal action if I didn't get my stuff back. After all, it is my livelihood." I noticed Tasha flagging me down. "Gotta go, see you at dinner."

The reception had only lasted a little over an hour. Meghan and I boxed up the remainders and sent them home with Sherry and Alisa. I locked the front and turned to find Meghan grinning at me. "That was interesting," I said.

"My first catering gig." She pulled out the last of the trays from the display case. "You actually sold three pies, two cakes, and a couple dozen cookies."

"That's a perk of hosting at the bakery." I hit the switch and turned off the music. Meghan had cleaned the front as people left. The only thing left to do was prep work for the morning. I checked the clock; I had less than a half an hour before I was supposed to be at Tasha's dinner party.

Meghan towel-dried the last of the dishes. "What do you do with the day-old pies and cookies?"

"I take them to the food pantry." I took off my white apron and hung it on the coat rack. "If the bakery really gets going, I might be able to sell discounted day-olds. But right now people are suspicious of gluten-free food, so I have to be sure everything is as fresh as possible."

"Cool." Meghan took off her apron and hung it up. "Do you need anything else?"

"No, I'm good. I'll see you tomorrow morning."

"See ya." Meghan put on her coat and walked out the back door.

"Hey," I said as a thought occurred to me.

"Yeah?"

"Do you have an escort? It's dark out there."

Meghan's eyes flashed and she laughed. "It's because of the dead guy, right?"

"That and someone shot out the back light and spray painted the back door this morning."

"Jesus." Meghan's eyes grew wide.

"Don't worry, it'll pass. But I think you shouldn't go out there alone at least for a while."

"My bike is parked out back." Meghan pointed toward the door.

"Hang on, I'll go with you." I grabbed my coat and purse and walked out. I set the alarm and locked the door, then I walked to where she'd locked her bicycle to the single street-lamp, which lighted the back parking area.

I shivered and glanced around as she unlocked her bike.

"Listen, why don't you toss it in the back of the van and I'll give you a ride home. Okay?"

"Sure." Meghan walked her bike to the van. "This place is kind of giving me the creeps all of a sudden."

"Tomorrow, park your bike out front," I suggested. "There are more people out front to see you when you take off." I opened the back of the van and she lifted her bike inside.

"Isn't the front where the guy was killed?"

I slammed the door shut. "Yes, but more people are around on Main Street this time of night. You know, date night, movies, cruising, and such."

"You think kids still cruise?" She laughed at me when I shrugged.

"What, am I showing my age?"

"A little."

We both climbed into the van and slammed our doors. I hit the lock button and started the van up. Suddenly, someone pounded on my driver's window, scaring me half to death. I think I screamed or maybe it was Meghan; more likely both of us.

A shadowed male's face filled the window. "Open up!"

"Who are you, and why should I?" The van was running. All I had to do was put it in gear and back out. Unless he had a gun, in that case I'd try to run him over first. "Do you have your seat belt on?" I whispered to Meghan.

"I do."

"I need to talk to you," the muffled male voice went on.

"I can't see your face."

He took a step back into more of the light. "It's me. Ed Bruner."

Crap.

"What do you want?"

"I need to talk to you," Ed said. "Open your window."

Since it didn't look like he had a gun or a blunt instrument, I opened my window a crack and hoped I wasn't being like one of those too-stupid-to-live horror-movie girls. You know the ones who hear a noise and go down into the basement to check it out. And everyone yells to get out of there, the killer is down there . . . right before the killer gets her.

"What do you want, Ed? I'm late for a dinner party at Tasha Wilkes's house."

Meghan leaned forward. "And I've got to get home."

"I want to know what the hell you said to Chief Blaylock. He said he'd like to examine all our bank deposit bags and hoped I wouldn't make him get a warrant."

"I didn't say anything," which was the truth. It was Tasha who had done all the talking.

"Now no one's getting their bank bags distributed tomorrow because first thing in the morning the chief is taking them all in."

Welcome to my world, I thought but tried to keep my mouth shut. "Get a good lawyer and you'll get them back in three to four days." Yes, I know, I have a smart mouth.

Ed's face grew red and his eyes narrowed. "Goddamn it! How are people supposed to make their deposits with no bags?"

"I don't know, maybe walk in and give the cash to the teller?"

"I swear to God, if I find out you prompted this—"

"Is everything all right here?" Sam came around the van, his tool belt slung low on his hip. It startled me when he appeared suddenly, but then I was relieved there was another witness should things go horribly bad.

"Not really." I waved at Sam. "Ed was scaring us while expressing his concerns about being a person of interest in the murder case."

"Dude, you all right?" Sam leaned against the van and had his hands in his pocket. He looked calm but in control, which helped lower my heart rate.

"Great, just great." Ed waved his hands in an exasperated gesture. "Even better if people minded their own business." Then he stormed off.

I lowered the window all the way and leaned out to catch Sam's attention. "Thanks for that."

"No problem."

"I didn't know you were in town . . ."

"Mrs. Becher over at the quilt shop saw my truck parked out front the other day and called. Thanks to you, I finished an easy remodel on the quilt shop bathroom."

"Nice." Meghan gave him the thumbs-up.

"I was closing up when I heard that guy shouting. Thought I'd see if everything was all right."

"It is now. Thanks." I took a deep breath to calm my nerves. "I'm taking Meghan home. I didn't think it was safe for her to ride her bike this late at night."

"Good choice." Sam gave a short nod of his head. "Be safe, you two." He stepped back and I threw the van in gear and headed toward Central.

"Wow," was the first thing Meghan said. "I thought Mr. Bruner was going to punch you."

I swallowed. "Kind of hard to do with that much glass between us."

"Good thing he didn't have a gun."

I had had the same thought and tried not to think about it too much.

CHAPTER 23

I arrived bright and early at the Oiltop Police Station on Saturday morning. I couldn't wait to have my computer back. The place looked oddly abandoned.

"Can I help you?" The big cop at the desk narrowed his eyes at me as I stepped inside. Maybe it was the bakery box I held that caught his attention. Cops do like their donuts, right?

"Yes, hi, I'm Toni Holmes. My lawyer, Brad Ridgeway, said I could pick up my computer and things this morning."

The cop looked at me for a long, silent moment. What? Was he going to arrest me for coming in to get my stuff? Maybe the thought was paranoid, but it didn't mean it might not be true. I lifted the bakery box. "I brought pastries."

The big cop stood. "What kind?"

I opened the box. "There's cheese Danish and pecan tarts and cinnamon rolls and apple fritters."

He eyed me suspiciously. "Aren't you the lady with the kooky bakery?"

"Try one." I nudged the box toward him.

"The cinnamon rolls do look tasty."

I took out a napkin, grabbed the cinnamon roll, and handed it to him. He took a bite and his eyes widened. "That's good."

"Of course it is." I placed the open bakery box on the counter. "I need my computer. You see, I have people who order online and the computer is a serious link to my business."

"Hold on," he said with his mouth full. He picked up a sheet and walked through the door to the back. I waited not so patiently, tapping my fingers on the counter. It really was dead in the station.

When he came through the door with a nice big box, my heart soared. "Thanks!"

He handed me the box. "No problem. Take a second and check to see if all your stuff is in there."

I put the box on the counter and rummaged through it while he helped himself to a cheese Danish. "Looks like it's all here." I watched him chow down. "Here, take my card. I open at seven during the week and ten on Saturdays. I bake fresh pastries available every day but Sunday."

"Great." He wiped the back of his hand across his full mouth and took the card.

I picked up my box and had to ask, "Are you the only one here?"

"Yep," he mumbled through the Danish. "Everyone else is at the murder site."

The hairs on the back of my neck rose. "The murder site?" I hadn't seen anyone outside my shop when I left.

"Someone called in a new body about an hour ago." His eyes narrowed and he tilted his head. "Do you know anything about that?"

"No. I had no idea. Who is it? Do they know? Where . . . where did they find the second body?"

"The body was found in the bank drive-thru."

"The bank?" My thoughts went to Ed. Had he killed again? Was he turning into a serial killer? Oh, crap, the dead body could have been me and Meghan. "Do ya'll have any leads as to who did it?"

"No, do you?"

I shrugged. "If a body was found near the bank, and I were the chief, I think I'd be talking to Ed Bruner."

"Can't." The big guy stuffed the last of the Danish into his mouth.

"Why not?"

"Because Ed is the dead body."

CHAPTER 24

Ed was dead. Well, that blew a big hole in my theory that he'd killed George. So I was back to only one suspect and that was Todd. Back at the bakery, I decided not to mention Ed's death to Meghan as I showed her how to mix cupcakes. I thought I'd let her find out for herself.

It was completely creepy that we'd had an altercation with Ed the night before. Sam, Meghan, and I might have even been the last people to see him alive . . . except for the killer, of course.

Leaving Meghan to make a fresh batch of chocolate cupcakes, I went to my office to boot up my computer. It had taken me fifteen minutes to plug the thing back in and reset the desktop the way I liked it. I have to admit, it did sort of freak me out to think someone had riffled through my computer, moving files, peeking through personal e-mails. I shivered. It was a kind of violation even if the person doing it worked for law enforcement. Even though I didn't have anything on the computer worth hiding, it felt weird. After all, I was too busy for sexy e-mails, answering personal ads online, or visiting questionable sites. Who knew my lack of a social life would pay off?

I suspected the boring data was the real reason I had gotten my computer back so quickly. No offense to Brad or his lawyering skills; chances were, I had put the Oiltop PD cyber hackers to sleep.

"Hey, Boss." Meghan stuck her head into my tiny office. "Someone slipped this under the back door." She waved a long white business envelope.

"Why would they do that?" I took the envelope. My name was carefully printed on the front in black ink.

"It's too thin for a bomb." Meghan's eyes twinkled. "I'd watch for white powder, though."

"Stop it." The letter looked completely normal. Why slide it under the door?

"Please, I can't help but think bomb." She shrugged. "I was raised with the Murrah federal building bombing and 9/11. It's a nasty world out there."

"Go check on the cupcakes." I waved her away. "That way, you won't be exposed if there's something deadly inside."

"Yes, Boss." She saluted and closed my office door.

I took out my letter opener and carefully sliced through the top, opening the envelope wide. Inside was a folded note on white typing paper. I pulled it out and opened it.

Typed in black was *Ed Bruner's death is on your hands. Stop poking in other people's business. Or you'll be next.*

A shiver went down my spine. I dropped the note as if it were suddenly on fire, grabbed my phone, and called Chief Blaylock's office.

"Chief's office, this is Mindy, how can I help you?"

"Hey Mindy, this is Toni Holmes down at the Baker's Treat. I received a threatening letter. Someone slipped it under my door a few minutes ago."

"Wow," Mindy said. "That doesn't happen a whole lot in Oiltop."

"What am I supposed to do?"

"I'll call the chief and see what he says. Hang on." She

put me on hold. Kool & the Gang played on the hold music.
When had the police station last updated its hold music,
1980?

I paced my tiny closet of an office, refusing to sit at my
desk or touch the letter again. The words on the paper
haunted me. How was I responsible for Ed's death? Did the
killer know I had suspected Ed? Why not let Ed take the
rap? Unless Ed had known who the killer was . . .

How could Ed have known?

"Ms. Holmes? Thanks for holding. Chief Blaylock said
for you to not touch the letter. He or Officer Emry will be
down later today to take a report."

"Do you have any idea when they're coming?" I asked,
staring at the letter like it might jump up and bite me at any
moment.

"He said sometime this afternoon."

"Great."

"Don't worry, Ms. Holmes, the chief's good at his job."
Mindy hung up, leaving me alone with the eerie threat letter.
If the chief were good at his job, how come there were now
two dead men in town. And why was I still getting threats?

I left the office and closed the door.

"What was in the letter?" Meghan asked.

"A threat." I had to be honest. Meghan deserved to know
what she'd gotten herself into by taking the job. "Did you
see anyone come to the door?"

"No, I was mixing cupcakes like you showed me. Then
when I went for more sugar, I noticed the note sliding across
the floor." She pointed to the black-and-white tile nearest
the door. The back door itself was solid steel with no window, but there was a peephole.

"Did you think to look out?"

"I checked the peep but didn't see anyone. So I picked
up the letter and brought it to you. Did it have white powder
in it?" She wiggled her eyebrows and her piercing
twinkled.

"No." I smiled at her attempt to calm me. "Just a typed
threat explaining that Ed Bruner's murder was my fault."

"Wait, what? The banker guy died?" Meghan wiped her hands on a towel. "The one who threatened us last night? I thought he was the killer."

"Either he was and someone killed him out of vigilante justice or he wasn't but he figured out who the killer was and died for it." I hugged my waist. "Either way, he's dead and he left behind two little kids."

"Creepy." Meghan chewed on her bottom lip. "One more death and the dude becomes a serial killer. Who knew we might have a serial killer here in Oiltop?"

"He's not going to be a serial killer," I assured her. "I called the chief's office. They're sending someone down to look at the letter and record the threat."

"It's weird, but the banker dying kind of makes me feel safer." Meghan leaned against the double stainless steel sink.

"Why, because of the police?"

"No, because if the dude is a serial killer, he'd clearly rather kill men than women. I think we're safe."

I patted her on the shoulder. "You keep believing that. Oh, and I'll be taking you home from now on."

"Whatever makes you feel better," Meghan said. In typical teenage fashion, she shook off the creepy conversation and asked, "What kind of filling are we putting inside the cupcakes?"

I shook my head. "Italian cream."

Officer Emry came in through the front door, scaring the two little old ladies who were enjoying scones and tea, one of whom was the antique shop manager, Celia Warren. Sigh. She gave me a wide-eyed look, and I mouthed that I'd tell her about it later.

It was around 3 P.M. and the letter had been in the closed office for over three hours. Officer Emry shifted his heavy belt up on his hips and swaggered toward the back of the bakery.

"Chief Blaylock says you called in a second threat?" He brushed his thin hair out of his eyes.

"Someone slipped a letter under my back door," I told

him as I walked to my office. "Meghan saw it come under the door and brought it to me." I opened my office and waved for him to enter. "I was in here doing paperwork when I opened the letter."

"That was foolish. Nowadays, everyone knows not to open any letter that's the least bit suspicious."

I frowned. "Yes, Meghan told me. But I didn't want to bother you all if it were something simple."

He picked up a pen and poked at the envelope on my desk. "Do you recognize the handwriting?"

"No."

He moved the envelope and read the letter. "Huh, sounds like someone thinks you're involved in Ed Bruner's murder as well as George Meister's."

I rolled my eyes and hugged my waist. "For goodness' sake, if I were the killer would I keep sending myself threats and calling you in to investigate?"

"Killers do like to insert themselves into the investigation." He gave me the evil eye.

I wanted to slug him. Good thing I had some self-restraint. All I needed was for him to drag me out of here on assault charges.

He pulled latex gloves out of his jacket pocket. "I'm going to have to take this in as evidence." He put on the gloves and picked up the envelope and letter, carefully placing them inside a plastic zip bag. He opened a pouch on his heavy tool belt and slid the evidence bag inside. Then he opened his vest and took out a notebook. "I'm going to have to take a statement from you and your assistant."

"That's fine." I explained again how Meghan had come in and given me the letter, what I did as I opened it, and what I did immediately after.

Officer Emry nodded and sniffed. He finished his notes and looked at me, resting his glove-covered hands on his tool belt. His right hand was near his gun as if he expected me to make a run for it anytime.

"The real question is, what did you do that might have gotten the deceased killed?"

I narrowed my eyes. "The deceased?"

"You know," Officer Emry got impatient, "the banker, Ed Bruner."

"She didn't do anything." Meghan stepped in to defend me. "It was Mr. Bruner who nearly killed us last night."

"I wouldn't say he nearly killed us," I corrected and looked from her to the officer. "He scared us and threatened us, but he didn't try to kill us."

"Wait, you saw Ed last night?"

"Yes, we did." Meghan crossed her arms and looked fierce. "The guy came out of nowhere, pounded on the van, scaring us half to death and demanding we roll down the window."

"Really?" Officer Emry wrote something in his notebook. "What was his attitude?"

"He was pissed off," Meghan volunteered.

"Why was he mad?"

"He thought I had talked to the chief about the possibility of the bank's deposit bag being the murder weapon," I finished before Meghan could embellish. "He said the chief had taken all his deposit bags in for evidence, and he wanted to know what I thought his customers were supposed to do while the police examined the bank bags."

"What did you say?" Officer Emry never looked up from his notebook.

"I told him they could go inside and make deposits like everyone else."

"That's when he threatened to punch her," Meghan nodded. "Luckily, Sam came along."

"Sam?"

"Sam Greenbaum," I stated. "He happened to be finishing a bathroom remodel next door."

"Happened to?" Emry looked up and raised a skinny eyebrow.

"Oh, for goodness' sake, ask Mrs. Becher next door. He told me that she'd hired him to finish the store bath."

"Right, I will. So this Sam Greenbaum was there when Ed Bruner threatened you. Did he get physical with Ed?"

"What? No!" I shook my head and put my palm out. "No, Sam asked Ed to stay away, and Ed left. It was that simple."

"Did you see either man get into an altercation?"

"No," I answered quickly.

"We took off after Mr. Bruner left," Meghan added. "Ms. Holmes drove me home."

"Probably not a bad idea with killers on the loose," Officer Emry muttered.

"Killers?" I tilted my head at his slip. "As in more than one?"

Officer Emry flipped closed his tiny notebook and slipped it into his vest pocket. He sniffed, and studied us both. "There's no evidence to connect the two murders." He adjusted his belt and narrowed his eyes. "Seems like the only thing those two have in common is you, Ms. Holmes."

"Oh, come on!"

"I ain't saying you're a person of interest in Ed Bruner's murder. At least, not yet, but I'd keep on my toes if I were you."

"I'll take that under advisement," I mumbled and swung my arm toward the front door. "Thanks for coming out. Please let me know if you or Chief Blaylock have any idea who keeps threatening me."

"Will do." Officer Emry gave me a two-fingered salute. "In the meantime, don't go out the back alone. Not even in daytime."

"Right." For once, I completely agreed with him. I walked him to the door, then headed back to my office and dialed the security company. "Is this Advent Security? Yes, I called earlier about an appointment for placing a camera at the back door of my business. Is there any way I can get that done today?"

CHAPTER 25

I arrived home to find Grandma Ruth sitting on the swing which hung from the ceiling of my wide Victorian porch. Not surprisingly, a cloud of cigarette smoke enveloped her. She wore a skirt today made from a wild butterfly pattern. The skirt was hitched up across her wide-spread knees to expose the tops of her knee-high hose and her worn Nike tennis shoes. She wore a dark navy pea coat and a dark blue stocking cap on top of her orange curls. The tall, sand-filled pot she used for butts sat conveniently in front of her.

I parked the van and trudged up the side steps, buzzed a kiss on her rough cheek, and sat down next to her. My eyes watered from the smoke. "Hey, Grandma, how are you?"

The fall darkness showed a myriad of stars in the night sky. The two parties had been evening affairs and I was lucky enough to lay out the food and be done by nine.

"The real question is, how are you, kiddo?" Grandma Ruth asked and blew out a wreath of smoke.

"I suppose you heard Ed Bruner was found dead this morning."

"Yep. For the first time in a week, you're not on the front page of the newspaper."

"I'd say yay, but not at the expense of another man's life."

"I agree." Grandma took a long drag. "I heard his head had been smashed in by some sort of heavy instrument, like a pipe. He was left crumpled in a pile in the drive-thru." Grandma squinted her blue eyes at me. "Right by the night-deposit bin."

I winced. "Another crime of passion?"

"No, this one was premeditated," Grandma stated. "It wasn't the same weapon, that's for sure. I understand it left a completely different mark. Plus, there was some sort of metal flakes. The cops sent them to the lab in Wichita for analysis."

My stomach lurched. Premeditated . . . which meant whoever killed Ed had planned the act and could be out there right now planning my demise. I hoped Meghan was onto something and the murderer was only targeting men.

"I understand you got a threatening letter today." Grandma broke into my self-pitying thoughts.

I made a face to express my frustration. "Yes. It said I was responsible for Ed's death. And that I needed to leave well enough alone."

"Interesting." Grandma stared out at the nearly bald elm tree. Its dark branches threw scary shadows on the street. Perfect for Halloween.

I pushed my bangs out of my face. "What do you think it means?"

"I heard you told the chief about your bank deposit bag theory . . ."

"Tasha told him," I muttered and crossed my arms. "I admitted there wasn't any evidence to support it."

"Still, Chief Blaylock went to Ed and asked to examine the bank deposit bags." Grandma was like a hound on a scent.

"Even if they found evidence on the bags, there's no way they could trace it to a killer. Could they? It's not like the bags have serial numbers."

"Ed must have figured out who did it." Grandma puffed on her cigarette. "Or he must have been close enough to make the killer feel threatened."

I shook my head and jammed my hands in my jacket pocket. "I still don't know how that's my fault. I'd never even spoken to Ed until he pounded on the van window last night."

Grandma snapped her head in my direction. "Did he threaten you?"

"Scared me, sure. Threatened me? Maybe a little, but Sam Greenbaum showed up and chased him away." I leaned my head back against the swing and blew out a long breath. "Now Officer Emry thinks I'm involved in both murders, and I just got my computer back."

"Officer Emry is a bumbling fool. Chief Blaylock knows that." Grandma patted me on the knee. "Don't worry. We'll figure this out. Now don't 'cha want to hear about my sewer adventures?"

"Sure." I lowered my eyebrows. "Did you actually find anything while you were down there?"

"Bill found some bones he thought were interesting. He took them back to his shop."

"Bones?"

"Nothing to worry about; some kind of animal, he said. I teased it was an alligator."

I chuckled. Grandma did have a great sense of humor.

"What I found, however, was more than a little interesting."

"Really?"

"I didn't find a murder weapon."

"Oh." Disappointment made my shoulders droop.

"But I think I found an old speakeasy."

"What?"

"There was a door a few feet from the bank entrance. It wasn't on the official sewer system map. Bill and I managed to pry it open. Inside was a ten-by-ten room lit by two old chandeliers, nothing fancy. There were a couple of tables and a few chairs in there."

"A speakeasy, that's crazy cool." Grandma had been a flapper in her youth. She could tell some stories.

"I know, I'm researching now and trying to figure out who ran it. Who attended the parties, etc. It'll make for a great human-interest story. For my blog, of course. . . ."

"Of course." Admiration warmed my heart. "Thank goodness you didn't find a murder weapon. The way Officer Emry thinks, he might accuse us both of being involved."

"Like I said," Grandma puffed on her smoke, "the man's a bumbling fool. I have no idea how he passed the test to get on the police force."

We sat silently for a while, staring out onto the quiet street. Unlike the busy cruising streets of Central and Main, no one but homeowners rambled down the brick-covered roads in the old neighborhoods.

"There weren't a whole lot of people at the memorial," I said, breaking the comfortable silence. "How's your suspect list coming along?"

"Ed was there," Grandma said. "I thought maybe you were right. He made a really good suspect. But now that's out."

"I agree; I don't think his death was suicide."

"Hard to bludgeon yourself in the head. Ed was talented but not that talented." Grandma chuckled low until she coughed. I laughed with her.

"That doesn't leave many suspects," I mused. "Well, there's still Todd but I have no idea why he would kill George now after nearly two years. There's no way Sherry or Alisa were up and dressed and walking down Main Street at 5:30 A.M."

"Right. It takes those two at least two hours of prep before they are decent enough to leave their homes."

I laughed at the thought that Sherry would be mad enough to storm down Main Street in a housecoat and curlers with night cream on her face to whack George upside the head for spray painting the buildings. I sobered. "Who else besides Todd wanted George dead? Wait, is there a neighborhood watch for the downtown area?"

Grandma Ruth frowned and stroked her chin. "Not that I'm aware of. I know there're a few apartments over stores but those are mostly rented to folks who travel around picking up temp jobs. Migrants wouldn't care who was coming or going or stalking around. They have no stake in keeping the downtown nice."

"Huh. Do you think the killer lives above one of the stores?"

"And what, came into town to kill randomly then move on?"

"Kind of creepy to think about, isn't it? But yes. Do you think that's possible?"

Grandma shrugged and lit another cigarette. "Possible, but not very probable. It would mean the murders are random, and those are the hardest to solve."

My shoulders fell in defeat. If this were a random serial killer, the murder would never be solved and I'd spend the rest of my life living under a cloud of suspicion. Even the possibility of never solving these murders made me want to cry.

"Don't worry." Grandma patted my knee again. "Those threats you've been getting mean that someone in town knows something. I'm sure we'll get to the bottom of this soon." She snuffed her cigarette out in the sand. "Let's go in." Grandma stood, rocking the swing wildly. "You can make me dinner while we figure out what to do next."

CHAPTER 26

Twice a month, Tasha and I met for Sunday afternoon coffee. Kip spent the day with his grandma and we were free to have girl time.

My den was cozy with a crackling fire in the fireplace. The coffee table was laden with a tray holding two carafes—one with coffee and one with chai tea. There would have been wine and margaritas if I weren't certain I'd fall asleep after the first drink. Instead there were plates of cookies and cakes and assorted coffee flavors, creams, and sugars.

I had my bare feet up on the edge of the coffee table, exposing my toenails, which I was painting Zombie Black to celebrate the season.

Tasha had foils in her hair for new white streaks in her long blonde locks. I had tried to talk her into pink but she was concerned they would come out too red. Not that there was anything wrong with red hair. "How's the investigation going?"

I cringed. "It's stalled ever since Ed was killed."

"I know he was your number one suspect." Tasha sipped her tea. "So, let's think about this . . . who would benefit from George's death?"

"The only one I've known who's benefited is Mike Smith. Ever since the flour bombing, people in the surrounding counties have been buying newspapers. Grandma Ruth tells me they're thinking of adding extra reporters. She might even get her column back."

Tasha's eyes widened. "That's it! Of course, why didn't I see it before? With every incident, Rocky gets new photos in the paper, Candy gets more readers, and Mike sells more papers."

I frowned. "Are you saying that one of them is killing people?"

She shrugged. "Why not? Did George pick on Rocky at school?"

"Gosh, I don't know. It seems like everyone picked on Rocky during school. It's his parents' fault. They gave him that name."

"Well, Candy could have done it. She wants nothing more than to get one of her articles picked up by the *New York Times*."

I shook my head. "That isn't going to happen."

"Unless the murders continue and she gives this serial killer a name."

An inelegant snort came out of my mouth. "You're reaching."

"Am I? Did you know that Todd Woles once waited four years to seek revenge on a guy?"

I leaned in toward her. "Really?"

"Yes. I asked Phyllis, who talked to Sue, and she said that it's a known fact that in high school Jon Ramsey and a bunch of his thugs grabbed Todd, stripped him, and tied him to the flagpole by the stadium. Coach Hillard found him hours later. The boys were suspended and Todd's parents hired him a bodyguard."

"Oh my God, that's terrible." I swallowed in horror. Poor Todd.

"He waited four years, like I said, but he got his revenge."

"He did?"

"Yes, Todd was driving down Kellogg in Wichita when

he saw Jon waiting at a bus stop. Todd drove his car up on the curb and ran Jon down."

"He hit him?"

"No just chased him for like a mile." Tasha leaned back. "Not that I blame him. Jon was so embarrassed to be seen running screaming from a Smart car that he refused to press charges."

"Wow."

"So, see, it might have been two years since Todd filed that restraining order, but he might have been watching and waiting for his opportunity to exact his revenge." She wagged a newly polished nail at me. Her polish color was Vixen Red.

I studied my toenails as I contemplated Todd's ability to wait to take revenge. "Grandma does think George's murder was one of opportunity."

"See, I just gave you four solid suspects." She sat there in the velvet wing chair with foils in her hair, a mug of tea in her hand, and a superior attitude on her face. "Now, tell me about your love life."

I paused, the glass bottle in one hand and the tiny brush full of polish in the other. "I don't have a love life. Remember? I'm too busy being a murder suspect. But I'm really glad you and Craig are working out. You deserve some happiness in your life."

"So do you." Tasha lasered in on me. "Are you interested in Sam? I get the impression he's interested in you. Have you checked out his muscles? And his backside?" She fell back against her chair, all drama. If it were me, I'd have spilled tea all down the front of me, but Tasha could be dramatic with not even a drop of liquid leaving its container.

"You have a boyfriend," I said, trying not to laugh. "Why are you checking out Sam?"

She batted her eyes at me. "Why, I'm checking him out for you, of course. It's my BFF duty to make sure you have a prime specimen interested in you."

I laughed at her. "What about *my* BFF duty, hmm? Weren't you the one to keep your new boyfriend a secret from me for nearly a month?"

She wrinkled her nose and sipped her coffee. "That was different."

"How?"

"I needed to trust my judgment. You know how bad things have been for me with men. I needed to know I could choose a good one on my own." She rested her elbow on the arm of the chair and flung her hand. "I needed to learn to trust my own instincts."

I raised one eyebrow. "How's that working out for you?"

Her eyes grew big and a secret smile flirted across her face. "Wonderfully. You saw him at the dinner party the other night. Isn't he great with people?"

I nodded and raised my eyebrows in agreement.

"Best of all, he's great with Kip. He knows just how to handle him. Don't get me wrong, I'm sad his little nephew is autistic. I wouldn't wish that on anyone. But I'm happy to find a wonderful guy who doesn't freak out when Kip doesn't act the way he thinks he should."

I leaned back against the brocade of the settee. "Besides how Craig treats Kip, how's he treating you?"

"He's been such a gentleman. It's nice to be treated right for once." Tasha's eyes sparkled.

"Good, I'm glad. You deserve the best, and I appreciate you asking him to keep an eye on me. It's nice to know my friends have my back."

Her face went blank and there was a long awkward pause. "I'm sorry?" Her eyebrows formed a *V* shape and her mouth went a little flat.

"Oh, you know." I waved away her confusion as part of her stress-filled life. "When you asked him to follow me in the car that one time to make sure I got to the bakery safely."

"Oh, right." Relief filled her expression. "I did that because I love you. Plus, Craig is a big guy. He'll scare away the bad guys. It's part of his appeal."

"Right? A girl has to appreciate big guys who scare away bad guys." I made a final stroke on my pinkie toe and shoved the nail polish brush back into the container and twisted it tight. "If Sam hadn't been there the other night, there'd be no telling what Ed would have done." I leaned back and closed my eyes, trying not to think about what might have happened. "I mean, Ed was hopping mad about Chief Blaylock wanting to take all the deposit bags for testing." I opened my eyes and sat up straight, leaning toward her. "If you had been there, you would have thought Ed was hiding something. He scared poor Meghan near to death."

Tasha rested her head against the velvet. "The whole incident sounds scary."

"It was. You should have seen Ed. He was crazy upset. I'm glad I didn't lower the window all the way like he asked. I swear the man would have reached into the car and shaken me."

"If a man does that to a woman, then if you ask me, he deserves to die." Tasha nodded and put her coffee cup down on the table and got up. "Time for me to rinse."

CHAPTER 27

Sherry Williams came into the store early Monday morning. "I put a hold on the ghost walk tour brochure." She was breathless. Her stilettos tapped hurriedly across the black-and-white tiles of the shop.

"Why?"

"To add the bank drive-thru where Ed died, of course." She reached the counter, dressed in an aqua sheath dress with matching coat. A scarf was artfully tied around her neck, its complementary colors creating a Miss America feel. "I'll take a large Sumatra," she ordered. I handed her a wide coffee cup and saucer.

"Anything to eat with that?"

"Dear me, no, we still have goodies at the chamber from the memorial on Friday." She clicked her way over to the coffee bar and poured coffee into her cup, added a splash of nonfat milk, stirred, and took a long sip. "Oh, my, that's good."

"Thank you. Listen, maybe you should hold off on the ghost tours for a few weeks," I suggested.

"Why ever would we want to do that? Halloween is the perfect time to start them."

I leaned against the glass counter. "I don't disagree." I rested my chin in my palm and tried to come up with an argument Sherry would appreciate. "But until the killer is caught, we can't be sure the brochure will list all the proper places."

Sherry frowned and clipped her way back to the counter. "I don't understand." Her perfect hair was sprayed within an inch of its life. It probably would have withstood a tornado. The color sparkled in the morning light coming from the front windows.

"What if the killer isn't done killing?" I suggested. "You can't keep reprinting brochures."

"Oh my goodness." She clutched her throat with her free hand. Her expression was horrified. "You don't think he or she will kill again?"

"There have been two killings now in a week. If it turns out it's a serial killer, then people could keep dropping until he or she's caught."

"Oh, my." She narrowed her eyes and sipped from the giant coffee cup. "Oh, my. How can we give an incomplete tour? Plus you know you get a better discount when you have a larger print run." Sherry shook her head. "Why, I could be stuck with hundreds of incorrect brochures."

I nodded, bit my lips, and raised my eyebrows a bit. "Think of all the trees you would have killed and the money you would have spent, and for what? To only show half the tour?"

"Darn it, you're right." Sherry placed the large coffee cup and saucer on the counter. "I've got to rethink this. I'll be in touch." She wiggled her fingers in the air. "Toodles!" She clipped her way out of the shop.

"Who was that?" Meghan walked in, tying an apron around her waist.

"Sherry Williams from the chamber of commerce. She's setting up ghost tours for Oiltop."

"Cool."

"Not cool if people keep dying," I pointed out. "Hopefully the chief will figure out who did it before another spot ends up on the tour."

"You're no longer investigating?"

"I got Ed killed with my investigation. I almost got *us* killed." I frowned. "I don't want to be responsible for any more."

"Too bad." Meghan checked the coffee carafe and grabbed an empty one to refill. "I thought you were doing a great job."

"Ha! I thought Ed Bruner was the killer. How wrong was that?"

Meghan shrugged. "It was kind of cool to work for a caped crusader. I mean, you could be Bat Woman and I could be Bat Girl." She held two fingers up in a sideways *V*, one under her eyes and one over. "I always wanted to be part of a dynamic duo."

I laughed. "You are silly. Now, when you're done with the coffee, I've got an idea for a seasonal muffin."

"Great, I'll be in back in a jiff."

I walked into the kitchen, put on a fresh apron, and washed my hands. My thoughts churned. Who benefited from killing George? I certainly didn't. Ed did but now he was gone. Todd didn't really benefit, except maybe to extract revenge. Not that revenge wasn't a good enough motive, but it felt wrong. Todd was pretty adamant about not being out of bed that early in the morning. There was Tasha's idea of Mike Smith creating news to sell papers, but then it could be him or Candy or Rocky. I ruled out Candy and Rocky because they really had no reason to frame or threaten me. A thought struck me and I froze. Sherry and the chamber benefited. In fact, she'd started this whole ghost tour thing shortly after George had died, and was all hard-core happy about Ed dying.

Still, I couldn't imagine Miss Kansas, Sherry Williams, hitting grown men over the head and killing them. No, her mode of murder would be more refined, like poison, or convincing your ex-girlfriend to stab you in the back or even blowing up a rival with a bomb in the crown . . . no wait, that was only done in a movie.

Okay, I thought as I dried my hands. Let's keep Sherry as a person of interest. Who else? I came up with bupkes, nothing, nada.

"What are we making?" Meghan came into the kitchen, tied on a fresh apron, and washed her hands.

"Chocolate chip pumpkin muffins," I said. "With coconut flakes."

"Yum. I'll get the dry ingredients." Meghan pulled three bins off the shelf and mixed the proper proportion of flours and starches. "You were here the morning Mr. Meister died, right?"

"Yes." I pureed pumpkin. Fresh was best because you couldn't be certain the canned pumpkin hadn't been processed in a plant with wheat or nuts.

"Were you scared?" She brought the weighed ingredients over and poured them into a big stainless mixer.

"No. I mean, I had no idea anyone was out there." I added eggs and water and honey to the pumpkin.

"But you said you heard something, right?"

"Yes, I heard what sounded like a bird hit the window."

"And you looked out, right?" She placed the measured chocolate chunks and coconut flakes on the counter. "You really didn't see anything? I mean, the guy was murdered a few feet from the door."

I mixed the dry and wet ingredients while she leaned against the counter and watched me intently. "No, it was dark. I didn't see anything." I paused. "Why the fifth degree?"

She shrugged and pulled out muffin pans and began to place paper liners in them. "I'm worried about you."

"You are?"

"Sure. If you saw anything you could be in real danger, like Mr. Bruner." She glanced my way. The sound of paper sliding against paper filled the air as she lined the tins. "I'm not the only one who's worried."

"You're not?"

"No." She finished her task and put her hands on her hips. "Uncle Sam is worried, too. He asked me to ask if you remembered seeing anything."

"Well, you can tell him I didn't. Seriously. If I did, I would have told the police." I folded in the final ingredients.

"Well, what if you remember something suddenly . . . like in the middle of the night or something?"

"Then I'll call the cops." I scooped up quarter-cup measures of the dough and filled the tins. "Trust me. I'm not going after a killer by myself. Now, let's get to work."

By the end of the afternoon, we had experimented with pumpkin muffins and cinnamon apple muffins along with pumpkin cheesecake tarts and mini apple turnovers. The weather outside was bright with a blue sky and a warmth that laughed at the colored leaves. We cracked the bakery front door open and let the smells draw customers in.

Meghan was busy in the front and I was busy on my computer researching any links between Ed and George. I wasn't getting very far. Public records showed they had gone to school together, but that was about it. Then again, they had gone to school with half the people I knew, including Brad Ridgeway and Mike Smith. So that proved nothing. I could get their addresses and even their credit scores if I paid money. Which I didn't have. None of this was getting me anywhere.

After the last threat, this was all feeling very personal— as if all this mayhem were my fault. Now, I knew a rational person wouldn't feel that way, but at that moment, I wasn't being rational. Men were dying. Even though I'd told Meghan I was done investigating, I wasn't. It was pretty clear I was caught up in Ed's death somehow. I couldn't let it happen again. I was more determined than ever to figure out who was threatening me and who had killed these men. Was it the same person?

Maybe if I made a list of everyone I had come in contact with since the day of the grand opening. I decided to give it a whirl and was surprised at what I came up with. Oiltop was a small town, but my list was pretty long.

If the killer were at the memorial, it was a much smaller list. I started a list of memorial attendees with two columns. At the very top of the possible suspect column was Sherry. And the ghost walk business gave her a motive. Then there was Alisa. I put her in the innocent bystander column; she didn't really seem the murdering type. She was more peace-maker than head breaker. I continued down the list, adding Tasha's suspects to the left column. Even then, more people fell into the bystander column than the suspect one. For kicks, I put Officer Emry's name under Sherry's. A girl had to have some fun.

The phone rang and I jumped. I'd been lost in thought and forgotten where I was.

"Baker's Treat, this is Toni, how can I help you?"

"Hi, kiddo."

I sat back and relaxed. "Hi, Grandma, how are you?"

"I'm good. Listen, I was researching public records when I ran across something interesting."

I perked up. "What?"

"Did you know Ed Bruner's bank recently sold Tasha's mortgage on the Welcome Inn?"

"What?" My stomach knotted up.

"Yep, he sold it to a holding group. To make money off the mortgage, the group is changing the due dates to every two weeks or raising the interest rates, Tasha's choice."

"Wait, that's not fair. Can they do that?" I sat up, all thoughts of the murder gone. "Tasha didn't say anything about that."

"I bet she didn't want you to worry. Anyway, she can try to refinance through another bank or credit union before the end of the ninety days."

"Incredible," I muttered, at once worried for my friend and ticked off she hadn't said anything to me about some-thing important in her life—again.

"Thought you should know."

"Thanks, Grandma. Any news on the murder investiga-tion?"

"I'm cross-checking everyone who attended the memo-rial. Don't worry, kiddo, my sources are at work."

I ran a hand over my hair. "I can't help but worry, Grandma. I need to know if Ed died because of me."

"Ed died because someone hit him upside the head with something heavy. You had nothing to do with it. Don't let those notes and threats get to you. You have a business to grow and a friend to help. Got it?"

I sighed. "Got it."

"Good. Besides, Bill and I are helping. We'll get it all worked out."

"I certainly hope so, Grandma. I certainly hope so."

CHAPTER 28

I left Meghan alone at the store and took a big box of muffins and cookies to the Welcome Inn. "Hey, Susy, is Tasha around?"

Susy was a college student interning at the inn. The inn itself was another big old Victorian brick mansion built by the railroad barons, and then had been added onto by the oil barons. It had ten bedrooms and four floors. The ten-by-ten-foot foyer was paneled in solid oak and smelled of lemon wood polish. It gleamed to perfection in the light of the crystal chandelier. A Persian rug softened my footsteps.

Tasha had put an unobtrusive reception desk across from the sweeping oak staircase. She was meticulous about design, and the desk appeared to be made of the same materials as the paneling. In essence, it blended right in, except for Susy sitting behind it in her neat gray-and-white suit. Her brown hair was pulled back in a soft but commanding style.

"Tasha's in her office," Susy said. "Do you want me to let her know you're here?"

"No, don't bother. I'll put the food in the parlor and go

see her." I walked through the square double-door frame with pocket doors. The parlor was huge with a green-and-white tiled fireplace, arts and crafts furniture, and three ceiling-to-floor windows, which let in the afternoon light. There was a small buffet set up beside the fireplace and in full view of the clusters of chairs and tables, meant to allow roomers to gather in small groups or simply come down and feel as if they were in their own living room.

I arranged the cookies and muffins on the sideboard and made a beeline for Tasha's office. The house was arranged in a big square with small rooms and porches jetting off of it. I went through the formal dining area to the kitchen and turned right to the back den, which Tasha used for her office.

"Hey." I walked in without knocking and settled into a green, microfiber, wingback chair close to her desk. The den was also paneled halfway up the wall but Tasha had painted the top portion a light, soothing sage and kept the curtains thin enough to filter light. "I brought a couple dozen cookies and some seasonal muffins I'm trying out."

"Wonderful, thanks." Tasha glanced up from her computer, sent me a distracted smile, and then went back to her work.

"Anyway." Might as well get to the real issue. "I thought we were best friends."

Tasha didn't even look away from her work. "We are."

I curved my mouth briefly in a downward angle. "When did it become an I-tell-you-everything-while-you-keep-secrets-from-me kind of friendship?" I drummed my fingers on the wooden ends of the chair arms.

"What?" She really looked up this time.

I leaned forward. "Grandma Ruth told me Ed Bruner's bank sold your mortgage and now you either have to refinance or you'll get stuck with payments every two weeks or a raise in interest."

"Oh, damn." She sat back, her blue eyes wide. Her mouth slightly opened and trembled. Was that guilt in her eyes? "I suppose I should have told you."

"Yes." I nodded and raised my eyebrows. "You should have

told me. It's not like we haven't spent time together. What's going on with you, anyway? First you keep Craig from me and now you keep this. What else don't I know about you? Are we even really friends?" I was mad. Only yesterday afternoon she'd nosed her way through my entire life. Payback is a bitch.

Tasha blew out a sharp breath and sat back. "With all the things going on in your life, I didn't want to give you more to worry about." She bit her bottom lip and shook her head once. "I've been scrambling to refinance. In fact, that's what I was working on when you came in." She turned her monitor toward me. "See?" There were several online forms for financial institutions.

"I'm not fragile, Tasha, and I might be able to help."

"I know." She turned her monitor back and folded her hands on top of her desk.

"Friendship has to work two ways or it's not a friendship."

"I know," she muttered and studied the top of her desk. "It's just Craig said—"

"Wait, what? You told Craig but you didn't tell me?"

"I see Craig every day. He cares about me and Kip."

I sat back astonished at her words. "And I don't?"

"That's not what I meant."

I crossed my arms. "What did you mean?"

"I meant, Craig sees us more often. He doesn't work as hard as you."

Right. Tears welled up in my eyes. "I thought we were closer than sisters. Hell, you're closer to me than my own sisters. I can't believe you've held out on me."

"I'm sorry." Tasha leaned forward and stretched out her hand. "That was wrong of me."

I wasn't ready to touch her yet, but I wanted to let her know I was not self-absorbed. "How bad is the mortgage thing?"

She frowned. "Bad. I'd been working with Ed about refinancing through him, but he turned me down. Something about the new mortgage lending laws."

"Ed turned you down after selling you out? That rat bastard."

"I'm not one to speak ill of the dead, but I kind of have to agree with you there. He waited a full month before telling me. Meaning I now only have sixty days to figure out what to do next."

"Did you speak to a lawyer?"

"My lawyer said my contract specified Ed's bank could sell the mortgage and when that happened I might have new rules. And I would have ninety days to refinance or accept."

"Can you accept?"

She raised an eyebrow and her mouth made a firm line. "You own a business. Could you accept? My entire budget was run off the mortgage as it was." She put her elbows on the desk and rested her forehead in her palms. "Poor Craig, he said he'd talk to Ed. He tried to reason with him based on their long friendship, but Ed wouldn't budge. He said with the new laws, it was all out of his hands."

"Wait . . . Craig went to Ed? How long ago was this?"

"About four days before Ed died." Tasha shook her head. "If Ed was doing this to other people, I can see why someone would be angry enough to kill him." She looked me in the eye. "Do you think that's what happened? Do you think Ed killed George and someone else killed Ed?"

"Sheesh, I hope not. I'd hate to see people in town taking the law into their own hands. This isn't the 1850s."

Tasha lifted one corner of her mouth. "We are a cow town of sorts. Did you know there's a movement to pass a law so people can openly wear guns on their hips?"

"Crazy people." I shook my head. "What are you doing about the mortgage? Are you applying for refinancing anywhere?"

"I've been filling out the paperwork for one of those online places that's supposed to give you three offers in a matter of days."

I tilted my head. "Really?"

"Yes, as long as your credit is good." She sat back and sighed. "Mine's not great because of the divorces and some crap Kip's dad did to discredit me."

"Wasn't that a long time ago?"

"You have to wait seven years, and even then it takes a while to get the mark off your credit rating, unless you pay someone to fix it. If I could afford to pay someone, I wouldn't have bad credit."

"What happens if you can't refinance?"

"Truthfully?"

My mouth tightened and my gut clenched. "Give it to me straight."

"I'll have to take the increased interest rate. There's no way I can pay every two weeks."

"What will the increase in interest do?"

"It blows my little budget out of the water." She shrugged. "If I can't refinance, I'm going to have to put the inn up for sale."

"But you and Kip live here."

"I know. . . ." She closed her eyes and pinched the bridge of her nose. "We'll be homeless . . . again. You know how hard it is on Kip."

This time I touched her hand. "Don't worry. I won't let you be homeless. That's what friends are for."

She sent me a wan smile. "Craig said Kip and I could move in with him, but I'm not ready for that yet. I'm really not ready to let go of my inn."

"Then let's do whatever it takes to make it work for you."

"Got a winning lotto ticket somewhere?" she asked.

"No, but I can take a couple hours a day off work and ensure you can work on your applications. Meghan's working out nicely. I can run Kip around and supervise here whenever you need me."

"You would do that?"

I rolled my eyes. "All you had to do was tell me and I'd have helped sooner."

"I'm sorry." She winced. "I promise not to keep secrets from you ever again. Scout's honor." She crossed her heart and twined her fingers, raising them in the air.

"I'd believe you, but I happen to know you were never a scout." I stood up. "Seriously. We're friends. Stop keeping things from me. When things are bad for me, you're there. Let me return the favor."

"I will." She rose and gave me a hug.

"Now, do you need anything today?" I looked deeply into her eyes. She looked tired but relieved.

"No, I'm good for now. But I promise to call should something come up."

"Good." I nodded. "I've been your friend longer than Craig. Don't push me away."

"I know." She ran a hand through her perfect hair, which, annoyingly, bounced right back into place. "He prefers we think of each other as a couple now. We should come first, friends after."

I gave her a funny look. "Okay, I know that sounds kind of romantic, but at the same time it also sounds like an abuser. You know, first they get you to fall in love, then they isolate you from your family."

"Craig wouldn't do that." Tasha crossed her arms. "He's really romantic, that's all."

I hugged her again. "Call me if you need anything. I don't care what time it is, day or night. Promise?"

"I promise." She hugged me back and I felt as if the world was suddenly right-side-up again.

CHAPTER 29

The problem with really cool, self-sufficient friends is they forgot to rely on you. Thank goodness my family didn't have that problem. My mom had always been the matriarch of her large brood and, since she'd died and left me her house, I had sort of fallen into the role.

"I made you some rolls and pasta," I said when Tim staggered into the kitchen dirty, grimy, and exhausted from his night shift tossing boxes. It was four A.M., the end of day for him and the start of mine.

"Thanks." He set his lunch box down on the counter, grabbed a big glass of water, and drank like a man out of the desert. "Hey." He jerked his chin toward the answering machine, which now had a flashing thirty on it. "Are you ever going to call Rosa, Joan, and Eleanor? They've started leaving messages on my cell phone."

"Eleanor is in on it now?"

"She gets the *Oiltop Times* online," Tim said, his daisy tattoo peeking out from his shirt sleeve. "They care about you, you know."

"Sure." I hit Play on the message machine.

"Toni, this is Joan. What the hell have you gotten yourself into? My friend Sally tells me that you are a murder suspect. Do you know how embarrassing that is for me?" I hit Stop and raised my right eyebrow.

"Okay." Tim wiped a hand over his tired face. "Joan and Rosa are a bit self-centered. I thought you were at least talking to Eleanor."

"She and Rob took the kids to Disney for seven days," I explained. "They've been saving for that trip for two years."

"But they are your sisters. You shouldn't keep things from them."

"I know." The truth hurt. Wasn't I mad at Tasha for doing this very thing? "I promise to call them all once things settle down."

"Call Eleanor today." Tim filled a giant bowl with pasta. "She'll handle Joan and Rosa."

"You're right."

"I know."

I looked at Tim with fresh eyes. How had he changed so dramatically without my noticing? "Um, listen, I was wondering what you know about Sherry Williams?" I leaned against the counter and sipped espresso.

"The pageant queen?" Tim raised an eyebrow. "Not much. We might have been in the same class in high school, but she ran with the snooty girls." He sat down at the table and dug in. "Why?"

I shrugged. "I have the feeling that she might be connected to the murders."

"Really?" He chewed on the thought for a moment and swallowed. "I can't say as it doesn't seem impossible. That woman is ruthless and everyone knows it. She sets her sights on something and gets it, even if it means knocking off a competitor to do it."

I was surprised by Tim's assessment. "Why do you say that?"

"Oh, God, everyone knows the story . . ." He waved his fork and then dug out more pasta.

"What story?"

"Of how she made Miss Butler County," he said with his mouth full.

"I've never heard it."

He swallowed. "I can't believe that. Were you living in a bubble back in high school?"

"You all were two years ahead of me. Excuse me if I was mired in my own teenage angst." I sipped my coffee.

"Patsy Goodman was the returning runner-up the year Sherry won. According to the people who know these things, Patsy was a shoo-in to win. In fact, Sherry overheard the judges tell Patsy after her interview that she needn't worry. The crown was hers."

"How do you know that?"

"Sherry told Emma Hoote. Emma told everyone else."

"If that's true, it certainly doesn't seem fair. Isn't the interview portion of a pageant the first step? How could the judges have decided already?"

Tim gave me a look that said I was a naive simpleton. "Pageants aren't about who's best. They're about who you know in the business."

I let that sit for a moment and opted not to comment on the fact my brother knew more about the pageant world than I did. That was a topic for another conversation. "If that's true, then how did Sherry win?"

"Rumor is Sherry slipped hot pepper oil into Patsy's makeup the night of the pageant. Patsy's eyes watered and her face swelled up bad enough she had to go to the emergency room."

"You can't win if you aren't in the show." I pursed my lips.

"Exactly. The judges didn't have any idea who to vote for because all the other girls were filler for Patsy's win."

"And Sherry was the next best thing."

Tim forked up more pasta and nodded. "Exactly," he said through his full mouth.

"That's pretty ruthless." But putting hot pepper oil in makeup was more subtle than hitting someone over the head with a blunt object.

"You should hear the stories about how she made Miss Kansas."

I glanced at the clock. Darn it, I had to get to work. "I wish I could, but I don't have the time. Let me ask you this . . . Do you think Sherry's capable of murdering someone?"

Tim sat back thoughtfully and took a swig from his glass. He rubbed his chin. "I suppose she could, if someone got in the way of what she wanted." Tim's mouth went flat. "Are you still poking your nose into George Meister's murder?"

I bit my upper lip and kept my attention focused on picking up my keys and purse.

"Darn it, Toni, didn't you learn anything when you got Ed Bruner killed?"

My mouth fell open. Outrage bloomed in my gut along with a healthy dose of guilt. "I did not get Ed killed. I can't believe you said that."

He shrugged. "I'm just saying what everyone in town is thinking."

"Everyone is wrong." I hoped. Grabbing my purse, I stomped toward the door.

"Do you need an escort?" Tim hollered after me.

"No!" The heat of my anger got me out the door and into the van and down the street before it cooled. Then sadness took over.

How would I ever fit in if everyone hated me? I grabbed a tissue from the box wedged between the seats and dabbed at the tears in my eyes. If I were being honest with myself, fitting in wasn't exactly what I was trying to do in Oiltop. Not really. After all, I had started a gluten-free bakery in the heart of wheat country. I guess in my own way I was still rebelling against the small-mindedness of a small town. But it didn't mean I was responsible for the actions of a killer.

Todd Woles came into the bakery after the morning rush. He wore a smartly tailored Armani suit in dark gray with a pale silver stripe and a pale gray dress shirt to match. His shoes were made of Italian leather and clearly cost more than all my shoes put together. His tie was a pop of color in burnt orange. The man looked as if he belonged in downtown Chicago, not Oiltop, Kansas.

"I've come for the promised free coffee and cookie." He waved my business card in the air.

"I'm glad you stopped in." I put a giant coffee cup and saucer up on the counter in front of him. "The coffee bar is over there. What can I get you to eat? It doesn't have to be a cookie."

"Those pumpkin muffins look great." He took the cup to the coffee bar and fixed himself a drink.

I put a chocolate chip pumpkin muffin on a white porcelain plate and took it over to a small table near the windows. "Here you go. Can I join you?"

Todd waved at the accompanying chair. "Be my guest, it's not like I get a lot of offers in Oiltop."

I grabbed my coffee cup and sat down with him. "It's a small town, isn't it?"

"You mean small-minded?"

I sipped my coffee. "We didn't go to school together, did we?"

"You were four years ahead of me," Todd said. "I thought about leaving. Hell, I tried to leave, but family and fate kept me here." He shrugged.

I laughed. "I know what you mean. I spent the last ten years in Chicago. Then I found myself divorced, my mom died, and here I am. Back in good-ole-boy country."

"It's not all bad." Todd took a bite of his muffin. "At least the food and coffee are good."

"Thanks. How long have you owned the men's store?"

"About six years now. I started off as the general manager. It's a decent living. I enjoy watching the kids come in to pick out prom wear and the young men come to rent a tux for their wedding. Some of the country club set even buy tuxes. It's a good business." He sipped his coffee. "You know men, they don't want to go all the way to Wichita to buy clothes. We offer everything from business wear to tuxes, shoes to wallets."

"I remember going with Jimmy Gaster to pick out a tux to match my prom dress. It was kind of weird since I wasn't really dating Jimmy and didn't know him well enough to dress him."

"Let me guess, old man Shoemaker was no help."

"No help at all. He shoved a tux rental catalog at us and said to wave him down when we knew what we wanted."

"Business is up 98 percent since I took over," Todd preened.

"You must be really good at your job."

"As good as you." He lifted his coffee cup in a toast. "Here's to being misfits making it in a small town."

"Hear, hear." We clinked cups.

I sipped and took the plunge. "Can I ask you a question?"

"Sure." He tilted his head.

"Why did you come to the memorial? I mean, you hated George, right? Didn't I hear you had a restraining order out on him?"

Todd sat back and pursed his lips. "You know about that?"

"It's a small town."

Todd blew out a breath. "Truth be told, it was my friend Phillip who said we should go. He said it would be good closure on a painful episode. He was right."

"I see."

"I'm glad."

Then I had to ask. "Did you really chase Jon Ramsey down Kellogg with your Smart car?"

Todd laughed. The sound was infectious and I found myself smiling. He had tears in his eyes and wiped at them with a napkin. "Yes, I did. You should have heard him scream." He took a deep breath and let it out slowly. "Best day of my life."

"I bet it was. Can I ask you another question?"

"What?"

"Would you do it again if you could?"

He paused and swirled the coffee in his cup, then looked

me straight in the eye. "No." He shook his head and wrinkled his nose. "That incident taught me something."

"What's that?"

"Revenge isn't all it's cracked up to be."

I thought about Todd later that night as I locked the back
door of the bakery. He'd been honest about what he'd done
and seemed truly sincere about his thoughts on revenge.
Time to cross another suspect off my list. "Hey, Toni, you've
got a visitor." Grandma Ruth had come out to the bakery to
ensure I wasn't locking up alone. I followed her gaze and
saw Sam coming around the corner. "At least I'm pretty sure
that nice-looking young man is here to see you and not me."

"Grandma, why don't you go get in the van."

"Why, are you ashamed of me?" Her blue eyes sparkled
and her wide mouth pouted.

"No, of course not."

"Hi Toni, hello, Mrs. Nathers," Sam said and reached
down and bussed a kiss on Grandma's leathery cheek. "How
are you both tonight?"

"I'm better now," Grandma said. "Toni, this boy is a
keeper." She patted his cheek with her wide hand.

Sam winked at me and straightened. "I tried the front
door but you had already locked up, and I thought maybe
I'd catch you around back." He shoved his hands in the back
pockets of his jeans. He wore a Stetson, and his beard was
a rough five o'clock shadow on his strong jaw. He had on a
shearling vest over a work shirt and jeans. His giant silver
belt buckle gleamed in the parking lot streetlight and pro-
claimed him a rodeo champ. "I tried calling a couple of
times, but you didn't call me back. I wanted to make sure
everything was all right."

I flushed at the thought. "I'm sorry, I've been a bit
preoccupied."

"We've been working on our suspect list," Grandma said.

"How's that going?" Sam asked.

"Not as well as we had hoped," she answered.

"If it helps, Mrs. Becher called me and told me that Officer Emry had stopped and questioned her about my remodel work at the quilt shop."

I winced. "Yes, Meghan and I told him you saved us from Ed Bruner's threats the night he died."

"Toni," Grandma scolded. "Did you sic that silly officer on this nice boy? Shame on you."

"Grandma!"

"No, Mrs. Nathers, I'm glad," Sam said. "As soon as Mrs. Becher called me, I went down to the police station and gave a statement. I wanted them to know what I had heard Ed say. If he was threatening you, he might have been threatening the killer."

"Did they believe you?" I played with my car keys. We stood a few feet apart under the repaired lamplight. I got the feeling he'd have stood even closer if Grandma hadn't been there.

"I think so. Chief Blaylock said they found no evidence you or I were involved in Ed's death."

"Thank goodness."

He took off his hat and ran his fingers through his hair. "Listen, I wanted to know if you have time to catch a drink?"

It was only 9:30 P.M. and he had a look on his face that was at once begging puppy dog and alpha male promising more if I wanted it. The spit in my mouth dried up.

"She does," Grandma said.

"Grandma!" I admonished.

"Well, you do." She was stern. "What do you have in mind, son?"

"I was thinking the Chinese Supper Club would have a nice quiet table." He looked from Grandma to me. "Have you eaten?"

"Dinner is a little more complicated than a drink," I pointed out.

"True, but if you were to show up at the Chinese Supper Club, I might be at the bar. If I were to see you at the bar, I'd buy you a drink." He tilted his head, all handsome and twinkly like a charmer with candy. "It's been over a week since we talked."

"She'll go," Grandma decided for me. "Just as soon as she drops me by my place."

I jiggled the keys around in my hand. "I suppose I could go to the Chinese Supper Club."

"Fabulous. Let me walk you both to your van."

The suggestion was silly since I was parked a few feet away. Still, it was nice to walk in the quiet with a handsome man. Grandma's scooter wheels crunched on the gravel. "Wait." Sam touched my arm to stop me.

"What?"

He took a few steps toward the van. "You have a flat."

"A what?" I hurried over to the van. Sure enough, someone had slashed two of my tires. "Damn it!" Tires were expensive and necessary when you made deliveries.

"What is the world coming to?" Grandma asked as she stared at the flat.

Sam did a quick check around the van and made sure all the doors were still locked. "Do you have spares?"

I made a face. "I have a single donut tire, which clearly isn't going to fix this." I waved at the two tires.

"Maybe it's kids pulling Halloween pranks." Grandma crossed her arms in front of her. "I've known some boys to pull some pretty mean things this time of year."

"Let's hope," I said. It was better than the alternative. I pulled out my phone and called 911. By now I had them on speed dial.

"This is dispatch, what is your emergency?"

"Hi, this is Toni Holmes." Again. "Someone has slashed two tires on my delivery van. It's parked behind the bakery."

"Hey Toni, sorry to hear that. Do you want me to send out an officer?"

I glanced at Sam, who squatted down beside the tires and stuck his fingers in the wide gash in the rubber. "Yes, please." I ran a hand through my hair.

"Sure thing." There was a slight pause. "A unit is on the way. Are you alone?"

"No, no, Grandma Ruth and Sam Greenbaum are here with me."

"Good, stay put and an officer will be there in a few minutes."

"Thanks." I hung up. "So much for catching that drink."

Sam's eyes glittered in the streetlight and his jaw was set. "I'm glad you were with Toni, Mrs. Nathers. She should not be in this back parking lot alone. Not with these kinds of things happening." He pushed his hat back and looked me straight in the eye. "I'm glad I was here. What if you'd come out while someone was doing this?"

My stomach clenched. I hadn't thought about it that way. Still, I couldn't give in to the threats or let my life be run by them. Right? Straightening my shoulders, I said, "Now wait. I'm a grown woman with a business. I need to be able to come and go without having to bother other people to come out and watch me."

He rose and stood not a quarter inch from me. I was suddenly aware of the heat that rolled off his chest. The scent of his cologne mixed with man and horse. "I doubt anyone thinks of your safety as a bother." He put his hand under my chin and raised my head up gently until I looked him square in the eye. "This is serious. What if something had happened to you?"

"Then I would kick that person's ass," Grandma said with such ferocity that we all broke out in laughter.

"You know, Mrs. Nathers, I believe you would." He pulled out his cell phone and dialed a number.

"What are you doing?" I asked.

Sam raised his index finger as if to say hold on a moment. "Hey, hi, sorry to call this late but I've got a van with two slashed tires. Can you? Great. We're in the parking lot in the back of south Main Street off of Central." He hung up his phone and I could hear sirens in the distance. "I called in a favor from a friend of mine. He runs a tire shop."

"I don't think you can repair those slashes."

"I agree." Sam rubbed my upper arms. "But Grant has a tow truck. He'll come by and pick up your van. It'll be ready first thing in the morning."

"Oh, thanks." I hadn't thought about what to do after the police report. The squad car pulled up into the parking area and turned off its lights. At least this time it wasn't Officer Emry. Hopefully this was a sign my luck had taken a turn for the better.

The new officer was the same size as Sam, he had blond hair and blue eyes and wore a jacket over his uniform. "Did you call in a report of tires slashed?"

"I did. I'm Toni Holmes."

"Office Bright." He shook my hand and then pulled out a notebook. "And who is with you?"

"I'm Sam Greenbaum," Sam said. "And this is Toni's grandmother, Ruth Nathers."

"Thank you." Officer Bright made a note in his notebook. "What happened?"

"After I locked up the bakery, Sam saw my tires were slashed." I showed him the two flat tires on the driver's side of the van.

"Did you see anyone or hear anything?"

"No." I hugged myself.

"It must have happened before I got here. I walked around the back on foot," Sam offered. "I didn't see anything."

The officer's eyebrows pushed together. "Why did you walk around back? Are you parked back here?"

"No, I'm parked out front. When I saw the bakery door was locked, I walked around back to see if I could catch Toni. It was then we noticed the tires."

"I see."

"Have there been other reports of tires slashed?" I was hopeful this was a different sort of prank. I didn't want to think about the escalating violence of the threats against me.

"Not yet," Officer Bright said. "I see you have a security camera." He pointed with his pencil at the camera mounted near my back door.

"Yes, but I don't think it covers the entire parking lot."

He pursed his lips. "Do you mind if we take a look at the tape?"

"Sure." I pulled out my keys, opened the bakery, and turned off the security alarm. Everyone but Grandma piled into my office.

"Since I can't fit, I'll have myself a little snack." Grandma took her scooter off to the refrigerator, where I kept the Bavarian cream donuts.

I rolled my eyes. "Grandma, you've already had two. Watch your sugar."

"Don't be a nag," she called back. "I'm fine."

I wasn't about to fight her in front of Sam and Officer Bright so I let her be. A quick rewind of the security tape showed only a shadow passing by and the sound of air hissing.

"I'm going to need to take the tape," Officer Bright said.

I made a copy on a scan disc and gave it to him. "Is there anything else you need?"

The policeman thought a moment. "No, I'll start a report and let you know the number. If this is the beginning of a Halloween spree then we need to tie as many of these pranks together as we can. And if it's tied to something else . . . either way you'll have an incident number."

Silence descended as we all contemplated the other thing this might be tied to.

"I've got a tow truck coming to take her van to Knight's Tires," Sam said.

"All right, I'll be in touch." The officer gave me yet another police report number and went on his way. The tow truck driver showed up, and I was sad to see my van hauled off.

"Penny for your thoughts," Sam said as we watched the tow truck turn onto Central.

I rubbed my arms. "I'm wishing I had had the security camera sweep across the parking lot and not simply cover the doorway."

"There was no way you could have known," Grandma said and patted my arm.

"You've had a heck of a couple of weeks," Sam said. "Come on. I'll take you both home."

"Thanks."

We walked in companionable silence around the buildings to where his vehicle was parked in front of the shop.

"The pickup is mine." He pointed to a dark blue heavy-duty pickup with a king cab and a handyman logo on the side. He unlocked the door with a click of his key and opened it for me. I touched the logo.

"Nice. Memorable, actually. Is this what caught Mrs. Becher's eye?"

"Yes."

"It's magnetic?" Grandma asked. "Smart."

"Thanks, I'll tell Paul—Paul Pinkerton. He designed it for me. He teaches graphic arts and such at the college."

Sam helped Grandma into the cab and then muscled her scooter into the back of his truck. I climbed up into the cab and Sam shut the door and walked around the front of the vehicle. The interior was dark leather and smelled of polish and saddle soap. I buckled up and noted the care he took with his vehicle and thought about the care he'd shown with Grandma.

"My friend Tasha is seeing an adjunct professor from the college," I mentioned as Sam climbed in, buckled up, and started the pickup.

"I know a lot of the profs out there," Sam said. "My younger brother teaches physics."

"We have something in common," Grandma said and elbowed me. "My family started the college."

"Yes, ma'am," Sam said. "I know."

"Maybe you know Tasha's friend then, Craig Kennedy? His brother, Ralph, owns the pharmacy across the street."

"I know Ralph. I've seen him out on the golf course."

"You Play golf? At the country club?" Grandma scowled. The American Legion had the only other golf course in Oiltop and it had been shut down the last couple of years.

"I've been known to swing a club or two. Why? Does that surprise you?"

"The country club set is not exactly Grandma's favorite." I tried to head Grandma off at the pass.

"Bunch of hoity-toities," Grandma Ruth groused.

"Live and let live, Grandma, remember?"

Grandma Ruth huffed. "I'd say something about how mean girls never grow up, but I believe the cliché is, If you can't say something nice, don't say anything at all." Grandma crossed her arms over her chest and struck a sullen pose.

Sam waited thirty seconds before he broke the silence. "There's one thing then you should probably know about my family, just in case it makes a difference." He glanced at me as he turned down my street.

"Trust me, when it comes to families mine has little room to talk. Isn't that right, Grandma?"

She snorted her reply and continued to look out the window.

"Really," I continued. "There isn't a whole lot you could say that would ruin my day."

"That's good," he said. "Because my grandmother is on the board at the country club."

CHAPTER 30

Well, now I didn't know what to say. He'd told me he was a cowboy and a handyman. How was I to know his family belonged to the country club? Nothing like putting your foot in your mouth.

Sam took Grandma Ruth home first. He graciously helped her out of the truck and then unloaded her scooter while she sat on a bench in front of her building and smoked.

"Tell him we won't hold his family against him," Grandma said in a stage whisper when I kissed her cheek good-bye.

"Bye, Grandma." I got back into the truck.

"Bye, kiddo." Grandma waved at me. "Thank you again, young man."

"My pleasure, Mrs. Nathers," Sam drawled.

We rode two blocks in silence before he turned onto my street.

"My house is the big Victorian on the corner."

"I know." Sam pulled into my driveway and parked.

"How do you know where I live?"

He turned toward me, draping his arm over the steering wheel. His eyes crinkled in a nice way. "I have my ways."

"Let me guess, you looked me up in the phone book and were doing drive-bys." I was kidding, of course. It's what we used to do in junior high or high school when we had a crush on a guy. Tasha and I would look up his address and check out his house . . . several times a day. Not that we were stalkers or anything.

"You caught me." He raised both hands palm up in surrender and sent me a crooked grin.

"You're not serious." I tilted my head and gave him the once-over.

"Aren't you going to say something about my grandmother and the country club?"

I winced. "About that . . . sorry Grandma and I were snarky." I waved at my house. "My family clearly is not in your league."

"It doesn't bother me if it doesn't bother you." His expression was serious.

"I'm not the one who has a grandma to worry about." I shrugged one shoulder. "Grandma Ruth's certainly not out to impress anyone."

He reached over and tucked a stray hair behind my ear. His touch made my skin tingle. "I'm a grown man, Toni. I don't give a rat's ass what my grandma thinks."

"But you were pretty concerned about getting her just the right platters for her poker party," I pointed out.

"I am happy to help when she needs a favor, but I don't make choices on my personal life to please her. I'm not a trust fund baby. I've got my own stuff going on; I'm not waiting for the old gal to die so I can earn my inheritance."

"Whew." I playacted wiping my brow. "Good to know."

The inside of the cab was a little too close and a little too warm. I scooted to the far edge of the bench seat. "I've got to go. Thanks for all your help tonight."

"I'll walk you to your door."

"You don't have to—" He was out the door and opening mine before I could unbuckle the seat belt.

"Here." He took my hand and I tried to step gracefully out of the high pickup. Luckily I didn't trip or do anything foolish. I did, however, pull my hand back when both feet were safely on the ground.

"Thanks."

"My pleasure." He walked with me up to the sweeping front porch.

I unlocked the front door and things got a little awkward. "I'd offer you a drink but I really need to get to bed. My workday starts at 4 A.M." I winced at how bad it sounded.

He stuck his hands in his pockets. "Are you saying this has nothing to do with my hoity-toity grandma?"

I narrowed my eyes. "Did you say hoity-toity?"

His eyes grew wide. "I did." We both laughed.

"No." I tilted my head a bit. "As I've said, I'm really not in a good place to date anyone."

"Not even Brad Ridgeway?"

"What?"

He had the decency to hang his head. "I heard he's been spending a lot of time with you. I needed to know I wasn't . . . you know."

"What?"

"Horning in on someone."

That made me laugh. "He's my lawyer." I held the door in my hands. "I'll tell you what I told him. I've got to put all my efforts into my business right now. Especially while there's a killer out there trying to take it away from me."

"Are you sure the threats are from the killer?"

I opened my mouth to say I was pretty sure but paused. "No, I'm not sure." I pushed my eyebrows together and wrinkled my nose. "Do you think they are separate incidents?"

He shrugged. "Could be."

"Huh. That puts a whole new light on things."

"Listen, do you want me to check the house before I go? I mean, you've been threatened and your tires slashed. It might be a good thing to have someone in the house with you before you are alone for the night."

I was going to tell him no thanks. Then I thought, isn't that what the stupid girl in all the horror flicks says right before she closes the door and the killer gets her?

"Okay." I gave in and waved him into the house. I think I surprised us both.

"Nice foyer," he commented as I closed the door behind us and flipped on the hall switch. The foyer was smaller than the one at Tasha's inn but no less impressive. It held a space for a Victorian bench and coatrack. There was an antique table in the center, with a dusty centerpiece where people threw their keys and stuff when they walked inside.

There was a curving staircase to the right. The door to the elevator was beyond the stairs and a door to the parlor. The foyer was light and bright. My mother had painted it a pale blue with cream trim and there was a dark blue Oriental rug in the middle of the wood floor. The formal parlor was blue and white and held furniture fancy enough that no one ever used it.

I took off my coat and hung it on the coat tree and put my purse on the table. "Let me give you the nickel tour."

"Sure."

"This is the parlor." I waved my arm like Vanna White as I passed into the den. "This is the den."

"No closets to hide in?" he asked as I rushed through the rooms.

"Those are in the hall." I walked him back into the hall, which linked the foyer to the back of the house. "Closet one and closet two." I opened both doors. One held coats neatly hung. The other was full of boxes and an old but still working vacuum cleaner.

"What's this?" He pointed at the third door.

"That's the elevator."

"Huh, and you thought we were uppity."

We both laughed. "This is the dining room." I switched on the light and he took careful note of its empty state. "And here is a powder room, and finally the kitchen."

"Very nice," he muttered as he checked the pantry door and under the table for lurking strangers. "What's on the other floors?"

"Bedrooms and bathrooms." I shrugged. "Plus there's an office. Can I get you something to drink? I have to warn you my beverages are limited."

"Coffee would be nice. Warm me up for the drive home."

"Coffee I have."

"It's a pretty big house for one person." He leaned against the counter while I made coffee.

"My mom left it to me." I whipped up a couple of lattes. "And my family stays here whenever they want, so I'm rarely alone."

"How big's your family?"

"Huge." I handed him a coffee. "My brother Tim is staying here right now."

"Thanks." He sipped his drink and I waved him to the table in the kitchen nook. "I'm glad you're not alone."

"Tasha thinks I should turn the place into a B&B."

"You are in the historic part of town." He grinned at me.

"You mean the wrong side of the tracks," I teased him.

"Used to be all these old Victorians were the height of fashion. Now everyone wants a new McMansion built out in someone's pasture." He shook his head.

"The newer homes are probably a lot less drafty," I pointed out.

"But the detail and character aren't the same." He sat back, and his thumb stroked the coffee cup. I pretended not to notice how big and sturdy his hands were. "If you ever decide to remodel, give me a call. I love to work on these old places. I've got friends in the area with access to authentic fixtures and such."

"Sounds expensive."

He shrugged. "I could cut you a deal."

I liked the sound of that. The thought of having him around the house every day, wearing work clothes, a tool belt, working with his hands . . . had its own appeal. Then I remembered Meghan's questions and my suspicions grew.

"Thanks again for sending Meghan my way. She's working out great."

"You're most welcome." His eyes went all warm. "It's good to know you're not working all alone."

I narrowed my eyes.

"What?" he asked.

"Did you send her to me to spy on me?"

He leaned back in his seat. "No, why would you think that?"

"Maybe because she was asking very pointed questions today about the murder and what I may or may not have seen?"

"Oh, that . . ." He scrunched his face and colored slightly.

"What?"

"In my defense, I was worried about you."

"And you thought I'd tell Meghan something I wouldn't tell anyone else?"

He put his cup down and raised his hands. "No. Nothing like that. She likes you. I like you. We wanted to make sure you're okay. I'm sorry if I upset you in any way. Forgive me?" He was so sincere. I felt my heart crack.

"This once," I caved. "Don't let it happen again."

"I won't." He rose. "I promise, and you need to get up early. Thanks for the house tour."

I followed him to the front foyer. "Thank you for your concern."

He opened the front door and turned, catching me off guard. Swooping in, he kissed me full on the mouth. There was enough heat and sizzle to tantalize before he pulled away. "Good night, Toni."

The solid oak door was in my hands and I leaned on it as I watched him walk back to his truck. I realized then there was trouble and then there was *trouble*.

CHAPTER 31

"I broke up with Craig," Tasha announced when she pushed open the front door of the bakery.

Meghan was making more coffee after the morning rush. She gave me a look and disappeared into the kitchen to box up the online orders for shipment.

"Sit," I ordered, poured a cup of strong coffee, and brought Tasha a huge cinnamon roll. "What happened?"

She peeled off her jacket, slung it on the back of her chair, and sat down. She then grabbed the sugar container and dumped sugar into her cup and stirred as if her life depended on it.

"Tasha? I thought things were going so well . . ."

"I got to thinking about what you said the other day." Tasha pounded her spoon on the edge of her cup and set it on the saucer.

"What did I say?" A feeling of dread hit the bottom of my stomach. I did have a tendency to speak without thinking especially around my friends.

"You said Craig sounded like an abuser. You know, separating me from my family and friends."

"I did?" I glanced at the floor and frowned. "When? What were we talking about?"

"I was telling you how I didn't tell you things because Craig wanted us to be a couple who relied on each other—not friends. And you said it sounded like he was obsessive and could possibly turn into a stalker."

I winced. It did sound like something I'd say. "But you said he was a perfect gentleman and great with Kip."

"He is great with Kip. Like I said, he has this nephew with autism. He even does a relay to raise money for autism awareness." She picked at her cinnamon roll.

"Then why the breakup?"

"I told him we talked about my mortgage problem and he said my mortgage was none of your business. He got kind of agitated."

"What do you mean agitated?"

"He started pacing and making a fist and flexing his hand and making a fist." She went back to stirring her drink. "I told him to calm down. You're my best friend. I've known you forever. You wouldn't do anything but help me."

"Then he said you were a busybody who needed to mind her own business."

"Wow." I was taken aback. I literally leaned back in my chair as if I had been slapped. "I thought Craig and I were on our way to being friends. I mean, he's been helpful and nice."

"He has." She nodded and sipped her coffee. "But I told him he was out of line. He needed to understand you had been in my life long before he came along and you would be in my life long after."

I winced. "Ouch."

"I know." She made a half frown then wrinkled her nose. "That was a bit over the top."

"What did he say?"

"He got all upset and hurt. 'What do you mean?' he said. 'I thought we were working toward a forever relationship.'"

"Yikes."

"We got our wires crossed. I told him we'd been dating

less than two months and I was still working on the getting-to-know-him part." She stirred her coffee again out of habit. "I mean, who starts thinking forever at two months?"

"I don't."

"Me, neither, too many bad relationships taught me that. So, I told him I needed some time to think things through."

"What did he say?"

"He said it wasn't good for Kip to have men coming and going in his life. That I'm a fool not to realize a good thing when I had it." She paused, her spoon midway between the saucer and the cup. "Is he right?"

"He was angry." I patted her hand. "Whatever happens, Kip will get over it. He's a smart boy. Be honest with him and tell him you and Craig had a fight."

"Why do men make up these stories in their heads?" she asked me. "You know, you say you'll go on one date and suddenly you belong to them."

"Not all guys do that," I pointed out. "Or so I've heard. I can't say as I've had much experience with the ones who don't."

That got a laugh out of her. She rested her elbow on the table. Her long blonde hair brushed her shoulder and she cupped her chin in her palm. "I've got so many worries, what with the mortgage fiasco and Kip. I don't have time to figure out if Craig is a good guy or a bad guy."

"If he's a good guy, he'll figure out you're worth the wait." I lifted my coffee cup to my lips and sipped.

"And if he's not?"

"Then good riddance to bad rubbish."

CHAPTER 32

Grandma Ruth was once again sitting on my front porch when I got home. "Hi." I climbed the stairs and sat down next to her. She squinted at me through her smoke.

"Did Sam stay long last night?" Today she wore a plaid hunter's cap with earflaps and the brim snapped up. It covered her orange hair completely. She wore a man's corduroy coat, a heavy denim skirt that pulled up to her widespread knees, wool knee-highs, and dark Keds.

"How do you know he didn't simply drop me off?"

"Because I believe you are a smart girl." She waggled her eyebrows at me. "A man like that should be invited in for coffee."

"Grandma!"

"Besides, Bill and I happened to come by and saw his fancy truck still parked in your driveway."

I shook my head. "He didn't stay that long."

"I didn't say he did." She squinted one eye and studied me. "Not exactly your usual type."

I leaned back in a huff and crossed my arms. The puffiness of my winter coat made my huff awkward to say the least.

But the season had turned cold, and warmth was more important to me than looks. "Who do you think 'my type' is?"

"I always thought you had a thing for the bad boys."

"Maybe when I was thirteen." I blew out a breath. Neither one of us talked about my ex. I preferred it that way. "Besides, it's nothing. I told him I'm not interested in dating until I have my business on its feet, and that includes having the murder solved." I rolled my head her way. "Got any good leads, Grandma Ruth?"

"As a matter of fact, I do. The speakeasy was first used as part of the Underground Railroad. Did you know that?" She eyed me. "I figure most people in town at the time weren't sympathizers." She looked back at the big elm shaking in the cold wind. "Who knew?"

"I was talking about the murders, Grandma." I rolled my eyes and stood. The swing didn't even rock from my motion, as Grandma had her feet firmly planted.

"Do you know why your mother left you this house?" she asked me as she blew a smoke ring over her head.

"Because I was the only one of her children without a family? Without a life?" I crossed my arms and the jacket puffed out.

"Because she wanted you to have roots, Toni. She wanted you not to get lost up there in Chicago all by yourself. She wanted you here near your family, near me."

"Near you? You have fifty-two grandkids, Grandma. You don't need me."

"I love all my grandkids, Marie, but your mama knew something I'm just now realizing."

"What's that?"

"You are probably the only one smart enough and creative enough to keep up with this old lady." Grandma studied me with a half-smile. "Someone has to be around to keep an eye on me. Who better than you?"

I turned my head, raised my chin, and kept my mouth in a flat line while I thought about what Grandma Ruth said. Truth? I still think it's because Mom knew the other kids would be more practical and sell the old place, splitting the proceeds. I had always had a soft spot in my heart for all things family, from old houses to old ladies. "Are you coming in?" I asked.

"Do you have dessert?"

"I always have dessert." I shook my head. "You know that."

"Good." She put her cigarette out in the sand. "You need to get some pumpkins and maybe one of those skeletons for the front door. Halloween is coming, you know."

Along with Grandma's birthday. She had been born on November 2, the day after All Saints' Day, which was known as All Souls' Day. "Not quite a saint, simply an old soul," she'd say every year. "Makes things more interesting, don't you think?"

"Are you coming over to hand out candy?" I asked as I flipped on the lights, tossed my gear on the foyer table, and took off my puffy coat.

"I come over every year." Grandma Ruth closed the door behind her. "It's tradition."

Ever since she had moved into her apartment in the senior living complex, Grandma dressed up and sat on my mom's porch and scared the living daylights out of trick-or-treaters. The neighborhood kids came to see what kind of monster she'd be. It was something different every year. Grandma Ruth could make the best costumes, every part of them done with her own hands and imagination. No one in my family had ever worn a store-bought costume. Not when we had a talented costumer on hand.

"What are you wearing this year?" I asked, heading straight to the kitchen. When I flipped on the light, I froze.

"I thought about dressing up as George Meister. You know, with a bashed-in skull . . ." Grandma Ruth stopped beside me. "What happened?"

The kitchen had been completely trashed. All my special flours were pulled from the pantry and flung about the countertops and floor. Chairs were overturned. Dishes were broken. The ugly words *Mind your own business, bitch!* had been spray painted across my cabinets in black paint.

"They've never touched the house before," I whispered. My heart sank into the pit of my stomach.

Grandma had her cell phone out of her pocket and dialed 911. "This is Ruth Nathers. Someone has broken into my granddaughter's home and trashed the place. Send a squad car right away."

My first instinct was to rush in and take some kind of inventory, to see what was left of my expensive gluten-free flours. I made a move forward but Grandma's large hand clamped onto my shoulder and stopped me.

"Of course, we won't touch anything," she said into the phone. Her loud voice rumbled through my stunned brain. "No, we haven't checked the entire house. Yes, we're heading outside to wait for you there."

The pressure of Grandma Ruth's hand had me turning around, and we walked what felt like a mile down the hallway back to the front door. I couldn't tell if any of the other rooms had been touched because the hall light didn't shine very far into them. But the idea that someone—with that kind of hatred in their heart—had been in my house made me want to throw up.

Outside, I paced while rubbing my upper arms. I swear it was twenty degrees colder than a few minutes earlier. Maybe it was because I had left my coat inside. Grandma made her way slowly back to the swing, where she settled in and lit a new cigarette. Police sirens sounded in the distance.

Grandma took a long drag of her smoke and blew it out slowly. Her cane rested on her knee. "It does make me wonder whose business you've been into that they would do this."

"I don't know." At that moment, I really didn't. I was stuck on the fact that until now whoever was behind the threats had left my home alone. But now, now they had gone and trashed my mother's house. I realized I wasn't scared. I was mad as hell.

"Don't worry. We'll figure out who did this."

"Oh, I'm not the one who should be worried." I pivoted on my heel.

Grandma Ruth laughed her hoarse, craggy laugh, which always ended in a coughing fit. She eyed me through her smoke. "Got you mad, didn't they?"

"You know, I was upset when they attacked the bakery. But this." I waved my hand. "This is attacking Mom and everyone in our family and that I won't stand for."

"What are you going to do about it?"

"If I tell you, then you'll be an accomplice."

Grandma chuckled then sobered. "How come your brother isn't here?"

"Tim took an extra shift tonight." I yanked my cell phone out of my pocket and dialed Tim's number. "Whoever did this must either know Tim or was watching the house."

"Or both," Grandma Ruth said.

Tim's phone went to voice mail. I left him a message about the break-in and asked him to call me when he got the message, which I knew might not be until four A.M.

The next number I dialed was Brad's office. It was closed of course, but I got his night service and told them to have him call me as soon as he could. A squad car whipped around the corner and I raised my hands to flag them down.

It was Officer Emry. Wonderful. He climbed out of the car and spoke into the radio on his shoulder. Then hitched his belt up and headed toward us. "You ladies have a problem?"

"Yes, someone broke into my home and trashed my kitchen." My hands were on my hips and my feet spread wide as if daring him to say something stupid. I must have looked like a stone-cold gunslinger because he turned twelve shades of red and stuttered, "Are . . . are they still inside?"

"We didn't check." Grandma squinted at Officer Emry. "We did the smart thing, called you and left."

Emry looked up at the four stories of house. His mouth twitched hard to the side. "I'm going to need backup." He turned away from us and talked into his radio.

I looked at Grandma. She shrugged and mouthed, "The man's an idiot." I swallowed my chuckle as he faced us again. "You both stay put. I'm going to do a perimeter check. There's another squad car on the way."

I leaned against the porch rail and watched him dig his gun out of his holster, wrap two hands around it, then figure out he'd need a flashlight to see in the dark. He pointed his gun to the ground and dug out a flashlight, put the flashlight on top of his gun and held them out in front of him. The light wavered a lot.

"Stupid man is going to shoot someone," Grandma muttered from the porch swing where she'd lit another cigarette. "Maybe we'll get lucky and he'll peg Mrs. Dorsky's Great Dane. He lifts his leg on my scooter every time I leave it parked outside."

"First my bakery." I paced to the edge of the porch. "Then my car." I paced back. "Now my home. Something's got to give."

"What happened last night might not be related to the other occurrences."

"What do you mean?" I turned to fully face her as Officer Emry disappeared around the corner of the house. Another siren went off in the distance.

"There were ten reports of slashed tires last night. Chief Blaylock held a press conference. He was pretty sure it was a bunch of drunk high school kids playing Halloween pranks." She shrugged one shoulder. "It happens nearly every year."

I didn't know whether to be relieved or not. "Could be a copycat," I pointed out. "Might have seen the kids at work and thought he'd get away with slashing mine."

"If that's the case, your guy has a lot of time on his hands. He'd have to have been watching the kids and he'd have to have been watching your every move."

The idea of someone watching me, my home, and my business creeped me out . . . a lot.

Chief Blaylock pulled up to the house. Behind him was a county CSU van. "Evening, ladies," the chief said as he approached the house. "Where's Officer Emry?"

"He went around the side to check the perimeter." Grandma Ruth waved her large, flat hands in a sweeping motion as if she were shooing chickens.

The chief stepped off the walk to go after Emry. "Be careful, Chief," Grandma Ruth bellowed. "He has his gun drawn. I'd hate to see you get shot."

The chief looked at Grandma a moment then gave her a short nod of his Stetson-covered head. "Thanks." He strode around the house and hollered, "Emry, put that damn gun away. I'm here to help figure this out."

CHAPTER 33

My cell phone rang as the chief checked the house and the CSU guys hung around on the front porch answering Grandma Ruth's questions.

"Hello?"

"Toni, are you all right?" It was Brad. I stepped off to a more quiet part of the porch. Grandma had started arguing science with one of the techs.

I put a finger in one ear and listened carefully. "Hi Brad, yes, I'm fine. You said to call if anything else happened. Last night, someone slashed two tires on my van, and this evening I came home and found my kitchen vandalized and a threatening note painted across my cabinets."

He muttered something dark. "Did you call Chief Blaylock?"

"Yes." I glanced over to see the chief open my storm door and usher the techs inside. "He's here right now. There's also a CSU unit. I'm out on the porch with Grandma Ruth."

"I can be there in five minutes."

"No." I held my palm out as if he could see me trying to

stop him. "Really, you don't have to come. You said I should call and I did."

"Things are getting serious, Toni." His low voice rumbled through me, at once comforting and compelling. "Maybe you should think about staying with someone else for a while."

I glanced at my house. A tech was using fingerprint dust on the storm door. I winced. It had taken forever to clean up my bakery, I could only imagine what kind of work it would take to clean up the house.

"Toni?"

"Yes." I blew out a breath and turned away from the house. "You're right. I'll call Tasha."

"You said there was a threatening note. What did it say?"

I looked out at the old elms and jiggled to stay warm. "Something about minding my own business."

"Have you been investigating on your own again?"

I rolled my eyes. He sounded like Tim. "No. I've been too busy cleaning up my bakery, catching up on orders, and getting my van towed, buying new tires—"

"Okay, okay, calm down."

Nothing triggered my ire faster than a man telling me to calm down as if I were being a crazy woman. "Brad, someone is stalking me and ruining my business, my van, and now my house. Being calm doesn't seem possible at this moment." My hands waved around like a crazy woman's, but it wasn't my fault. He should have never used that tone with me.

"I'm coming down there."

"Look, do what you want. But I'm not paying for you to come here. Is that clear?"

"Crystal." Oh boy, he sounded mad now. Good. Fine. That's what he got for treating me like an idiot.

"Good," I said. "Do you need to know anything else?"

"Yes."

"What?"

"Are you seeing Sam Greenbaum? Because I heard he was at your house last night. . . ."

I hung up. Lawyer or not, he needed to get a grip. I shoved my phone in my pocket. It rang a few times but I ignored it.

Grandma Ruth stood in the doorway, leaned on the door frame, and shouted orders to the techs while waving her cane. I went over and put my arm around her shoulder. At one time Grandma used to be five-foot-eight. Now, she was hunched a bit and only came up to my armpit.

"We all shrink," she'd said with a shrug. "You will, too. Enjoy your height while you have it."

"Hey, Grandma," I said calmly. "How are you doing? Do you need to sit?"

"I'm fine," she belted out in her best back-of-the-opera-house projection. "Those people, on the other hand, are idiots."

"I have a doctorate in forensic science," Charlie McGee shouted back from his inspection of the foyer floor.

"Yes, well, I've lived twice as long as you, and I'm a lifetime Mensa member. I happen to know a thing or two about science."

"Grandma." I pulled her away from the door. "Let the man work so I can get my house back."

Grandma huffed and worked her way back to the swing. "Ask them to give you a coat. You're freezing."

I stuck my head into the door and Charlie stood there with my puffy coat in his hand. I guess he could still hear Grandma. I took the coat and pulled it on then went to sit on the porch. Grandma and I stared out at the road. The police lights flickered red and blue across the front of the house. The neighbors all had their lights on but were afraid to come out. Instead, they watched us from behind their curtains.

"Mrs. Dorsky is going to have a field day tomorrow." Grandma Ruth lit a cigarette and pointed at the house across the street. The living room curtain fell.

I patted Grandma's denim-covered knee. "Look at it this way. If you play your cards right, you can have an exclusive for tomorrow's paper. If Rocky shows up, your story can be front page."

"No, things this small go into the blotter, kiddo, not the front page," Grandma grumbled and blew a perfect smoke wreath around her head. "After murder, vandalism is too small to sell papers." She leveled her stare at the Dorskys' windows. When the curtains twitched again and the light went out, Grandma chuckled then coughed. I patted her on the back.

My phone rang. It was my brother. "Hey, Tim," I said low into the phone. "Are you on break?"

"What's so urgent you called me at work?"

"Someone broke into the house and trashed the kitchen."

"Holy shit, are you all right?"

"Yes, I'm fine. Grandma Ruth was with me when we found it. We're outside now while the cops and CSU go through the house. Listen, did you happen to see anyone drive by more than once?"

"No."

"Anyone who looked suspicious or knew you would be working a double shift?"

"No one suspicious," Tim said. "My boss and Harold knew about the double shift." Harold had been Tim's best friend since kindergarten. He wasn't very bright, but he was loyal and Tim kept him around.

"I called Brad. He said we should probably stay somewhere else for a while."

"That's a good idea, Toni," Tim said. "I don't think they'll bother the place during the day while I'm there, but I don't like the idea of you home alone at night."

"I know. That's what everyone says, but it's Mom's house. It's the place where we grew up. I can't see why it wouldn't be safe."

"The mess in the kitchen should have shown you enough," Grandma Ruth said, loud enough for Tim to hear her.

"Is there anything missing?"

"Not that I could tell, right off, but we didn't stay inside long enough."

"Fine." I could hear Tim rub his hand through his hair. "Are you going to go home with Grandma?"

"I'm going to call Tasha," I said, then paused when a car pulled along the curb. "Or not. She just showed up. Listen I have to go. I wanted you to know since you have stuff here and all."

"Take care of you, sis."

"I will." I hung up and stood. Tasha parked across the street and ran to the house.

"Holy crap." Tasha grabbed me and hugged me hard. "Are you all right?" She checked me all over.

"I'm fine. Grandma Ruth, tell her I'm fine."

"She's fine," Grandma said without looking. "Bill's here. I guess that means I'm going home." Grandma stood and the porch swing hit the back of my knees as it swung with her movement. Bill came tearing up the walk. I swear I've never seen a man that old and big move so fast.

"Ruth, are you all right?" He took her by the arm.

"I'm fine. My scooter is in the driveway." She let him help her down the stairs. She turned back to me. "Tell the chief I can come down to the station in the morning and give a statement."

"I will." I blew Grandma a kiss and watched Bill walk her to the car. She looked a little more hunched than usual, a little more tired. "Darn it. This thing is worrying her far too much."

Tasha hadn't let go. She squeezed me around the waist and watched as Bill helped Grandma into the passenger side of his Lincoln and then opened the trunk and stuffed the scooter inside. There was no way he'd get the trunk closed, but Bill knew that. He put up Grandma's orange triangle flag to alert other motorists of the hazard.

"It's worrying me, too," Tasha said. "And Kip."

"Kip knows?"

"Honey." She stroked my hair. "The whole town is talking about you. Kip is no dummy."

"I called Brad."

"Good." She hugged me.

"He told me to stay somewhere else for a while."

"Which is exactly why I'm here. You're going to spend the night with me. I was going to hog-tie you and stuff you in my car if you didn't come on your own."

I laughed. "Right. You and whose army?"

"I'm sure she could have a lot of help." Sam's voice came up from the side porch. "What the hell happened?"

"Someone broke into her house and trashed the place," Tasha informed him.

I looked at her with a huge questioning expression. "Wait! How did you know?"

She patted me. "It's a small town, honey. Word gets around fast. You're shaking. We should get out of here."

"I'm not going anywhere until the CSU guys are done and the chief lets me know what he thinks." I glanced from Sam to Tasha. "It could be a long night. Who's with Kip?"

"My mother came to stay."

"Oh no, your mom? I didn't—"

"It's no bother at all." Tasha was firm. "She's the one who called and told me." I made a questioning face and Tasha said, "Mrs. Dorsky called her."

I looked over but there was no movement inside Mrs. Dorsky's house, not even a flutter of the front curtain.

"Listen, I can stay with Toni until the cops are done," Sam volunteered. He looked real cute in his jeans, jacket, and Stetson.

"As her lawyer, it's best if I stay with her." Brad came up the porch steps. He was four inches taller than Sam and wore his *GQ* coat, dress slacks, and wingtip shoes. Tasha looked from one man to the other, her jaw slack, her mouth open.

"I'm fine, gentlemen." I squeezed Tasha's arm. "Tasha will stay with me. Her mom has things covered with Kip and the inn. Right, Tasha?" I gave her a look that said she'd better agree. She batted her eyes at me. I pinched her.

"Ow! I mean, right."

"See? So thanks but no thanks." I held on to Tasha as a lifeline and pretended to smile at the two men.

"You are a stronger woman than me," Tasha said in a stage whisper. I elbowed her in the side and kept on baring my teeth.

The front door opened and Chief Blaylock walked out. He put his hat on his head and studied us. "Whoever did this is long gone."

His words weren't as comforting as he thought.

"What's the damage?" Brad asked.

"They tore up the kitchen right smart." He turned to me. "And they got into your bedroom. It looks like they took a butcher knife or maybe an axe to your bed."

Wow. My knees wanted to buckle a bit, but I mentally ordered them to straighten up and not show fear. If they buckled and I went down, the entire town would know about it in less than ten minutes flat. Which meant whoever had done this would know and possibly get his jollies.

"Toni?" Sam took my hand.

"I'm fine." The words came out a harsh whisper.

"She's fine." Brad gave Sam a look until he let go of my hand.

"Anything else?" I croaked out.

"It appears whoever did this knew what was important to you in the house. Only the kitchen and your bedroom were harmed."

"How'd he get in?" Sam asked, his hands in fists at his sides.

"Broke in through a basement window on the side of the house between the carriage house and the road. This guy knew the house's blind spots." Chief Blaylock gave me a serious look. "Have you been doing more investigating?"

"She hasn't done anything since the note was pushed under her door at the bakery," Tasha said.

"Did anything come of the note?" I asked, trying to find some kind of pony in this pile of manure.

"The CSU guys found yours and your assistant's prints on the envelope. The note itself had your prints and an unknown partial. The partial doesn't match anything at the Meister crime scene."

"Does that mean it wasn't sent by the killer?" Tasha asked. She rubbed the back of my coat and I realized I was clinging to her arm.

"As best we can tell, it wasn't. They're pulling fingerprints from both the kitchen and the bedroom. We'll do a comparison and see what turns up."

"There was a lot of flour on the floor of the kitchen," I said. "Were there any shoeprints?"

"Looks like a size ten, man's shoe. We've taken photos. They can trace the tread to figure out what kind of shoe. It's a start."

"Any sign of the knife that shredded my bed?" I asked. I had a small hope that it had been recovered. I didn't want to think about waking up and finding someone holding it, standing over my bed.

"I'm sorry, no."

"She's staying with me," Tasha told him. "Are there any precautions we should take?"

"I can have a patrol car go by every hour."

"Do it," Brad ordered.

"What about my brother Tim?" I asked. "He's staying here. He'll be home around 4 A.M. Will it be safe for him to stay?"

The chief chewed on a toothpick for a long moment. "I think Tim will be fine. It looks like you were the target. Plus, I doubt whoever did this would strike twice—not with as much police presence as we have out here right now. But I tell you what, you get even the slightest bit scared, you call 911. Someone can be there within five minutes."

"I have you on speed dial." The truth of that was less comforting than it should have been. "Listen, I have to be at work by 4 A.M.," I said. "I have orders to process and a bakery display case to fill."

"Maybe you should consider closing for a day or two." The chief moved the toothpick from one side of his mouth to the other.

"That's a good idea," Tasha, Brad, and Sam all said at the same time.

I narrowed my eyes. "This is my life and I can't let someone threaten me out of it. Seriously, Tasha, could you shut down the Inn for a couple of days? No? What about you, Brad? Could you simply close shop? Sam? Could you not take calls?"

"We understand you're trying to run a business here, Ms. Holmes," Chief Blaylock answered for my friends. "But there won't be a business if you end up in the hospital or worse."

His brown-eyed gaze was sincere and sent a shiver of fear down my back at the idea of something worse than hurt.

"I could carry a weapon." I knew I was reaching, but I refused to be bullied into giving up.

"Concealed carry isn't law yet," Brad said. "Besides, you don't own a gun. Do you?"

"My daddy's pump rifle's in the house somewhere. Or at least it was . . ."

"The CSU guys will be done soon. I suggest you wait until morning to check for missing articles." Chief Blaylock's mouth was grim. "If you can't take a day off of work, then you need to think about having someone with you at the shop."

"I have an assistant. She'll be there from ten until four."

"Not long enough." The chief shook his head.

"I refuse to have to have a bodyguard everywhere I go. My friends and family have lives of their own."

"Maybe then, for their sake, you should think about closing shop until this blows over or we catch the guy doing this." Stubborn should have been the chief's first name.

"You're pretty sure this is a man?" Sam asked.

"Guessing at this time," the chief said. "Why don't you go inside and pack an overnight case then go off with your friends. I'll have a patrolman sit outside your house tonight 'til your brother comes home."

Oh, I was feeling ornery now. The chief thought *he* was stubborn? He should have never pushed me. "If you'll be here, why can't I stay?"

"You haven't seen the mess. Once you look at your bed, you'll want to stay at the inn for a few days." The chief's features were grave. I swallowed hard and took him at his word. Looks like I had to pack my bag.

"Come on." Tasha put her arm through mine. "We'll go in together."

I skipped the kitchen and went straight up to my room. Brad stayed behind to talk to Chief Blaylock. Sam followed behind us, his expression pensive. The stairs looked normal. Squeaky wood, which was worn in the right places from over a hundred years of footsteps. The hall was quiet except for a uniformed officer standing outside my door. I swallowed. He looked daunting in the cheerily papered hallway with his gun on his hip.

I took a deep breath to prepare myself and turned into my bedroom. Two gentlemen wearing dark CSU jackets snapped pictures. The room was trashed. My dresser drawers were opened, clothes tossed about. My underwear was ripped and lying in colorful pieces of silk and satin on the floor. The bed itself was a horror. The blankets were torn and cut with long slashes and hung in rags to the floor. The pillows were ripped apart; stuffing and feathers were everywhere. The sheets and mattress showed such violence that my vision began to blur. If anyone had been sleeping in my bed when the attacker came, they would have been ripped from limb to limb.

"What kind of wacko does this?" Sam muttered.

"How? I mean, that's a lot of work." Tasha wrung her hands. The entrance to my room was thin and tall as old doors are and she had taken her arm from mine to let me enter.

"It's a lot of anger," Charlie McGee added. "Whoever did this was filled with uncontrollable rage." He waved a pencil at the bed. "Something like this is very personal."

I took a couple of numb steps toward my open closet and something crunched under my feet. It was broken bits of porcelain from the handcrafted dressing table set Grandma Ruth had given me when I had turned sixteen. Tears welled up in my eyes. The closet door hung on its hinges. The clothing inside of it had been hacked and tossed about.

"Hey." Tasha took hold of my arm. "Why don't we let these guys do their job? I've got some clean pajamas I can share for tonight."

I couldn't see through the tears. But she and Sam got me out of there. My insides were cold.

"You know," Tasha said as she rubbed my arm and walked me down the stairs, "let's go to the inn. You look like you could use a good drink. I have just the thing in my bar."

"I'll follow you and make sure you get in safe." Sam jingled his keys as we stepped out into the dark, cold October night.

"Where's your bag?" Brad asked.

Sam shook his head.

"I'm taking her home now." Tasha's voice brooked no interference.

"But shouldn't I stay and answer any questions Chief Blaylock might have?"

"The chief's questions can wait until morning." Tasha sent the men a look.

"I'll take care of things here," Brad said. "You go. Get some rest."

"Are you sure?" I glanced from Brad to the chief.

"They're sure." Tasha dragged me toward the driveway. Somewhere the wind blew through dry leaves and rattled the trees. I thought I smelled snow. Another shiver wracked through me. A car pulled up and Rocky stepped out, camera in hand.

"So much for not making the news," I muttered. Rocky snapped a picture as Tasha and Sam stuffed me into Tasha's car.

"Tomorrow is Friday," Tasha said as she started up the car. "You can borrow my clothes. Saturday, we're going shopping. You needed a new wardrobe anyway."

I stared out the window and watched as Sam stepped up to Rocky and said something that had the photographer taking a step back. Then Tasha turned the corner and we were away from the scene. I saw the old houses pass by as we drove. When I was young, I had thought Oiltop was a boring town where nothing happened. A lot had changed since I was a kid.

CHAPTER 34

We arrived at Tasha's apartment in the carriage house to find Tasha's mom, Mary, dozing on the couch. Tasha woke her gently.

"Mom, we're back."

Tasha's mom sat up. Her blonde hair was cut in a soft shag. Her face had pillow marks from the couch cushions. "Oh, oh, dear, I'm sorry I fell asleep." She wiped her mouth and blinked at me. "Are you okay?" She stood and gave me a quick hug. I absorbed the heat from her arms and tried to not think of my own mom.

"I'm okay. I wasn't home when they broke in and Grandma Ruth was with me when we discovered the damage."

She held me at arm's length. Her soft cream sweater had jack o' lanterns dancing across the front in a line. She wore a pair of slacks, her feet covered in stockings, her shoes at the door so as not to track anything into the house. "Are you going to stay with Tasha for a while?"

"The cops thought it was best," I said and cringed at the quiver in my voice.

Tasha gave her mom a look and changed the subject. "How was Kip?"

"He never woke up." She tugged her sweater into place.

"You can stay the night if you want," Tasha offered.

"No, I can't." Her mom headed toward the kitchen to put on her shoes. "I've got to be at work at six. But I'll be around if you need me." She pointed at me. "That means you, too, dear."

"Thanks." Ever since my mom had died, Tasha's mom had decided she would mother me. Right now it felt nice. But I knew she had to go to work. Unlike my mom, who'd had Dad's teacher's pension to live on, Tasha's mom had only her own savings. She supplemented them by working in the school cafeteria. The early lunch shift started at six so that hot meals would go out to the kids starting at eleven A.M. It wasn't hard, and Tasha's mom said she liked the work. It kept her busy and gave her something to look forward to.

I made tea as Tasha walked her mom out. Tasha came back into the kitchen and locked the door. I poured hot water into thick mugs and added chamomile tea bags. "Your mom is so nice."

"Thanks." Tasha picked up the tea and moved toward the living room. "If you don't mind, I'm going to go check on Kip."

"I'll come with you." I followed her down the small hall. I wasn't ready to be alone just yet.

Tasha stepped into Kip's tiny bedroom. I leaned against the door and hugged my warm mug. The scent of the tea wafted around me. Tasha set hers down on the nightstand and leaned down. She tucked the covers around Kip, and softly ran her hand over his hair.

"Mom?" he asked, not opening his eyes.

"I'm right here, sweetie," she said.

"Okay. Sweet dreams." He muttered loud enough for me to catch it.

"Sweet dreams." She planted a soft kiss on his forehead and my heart squeezed. What would it be like to have kids of my own? I guess first you had to have a man in your life.

And since I still wasn't ready to date, that wasn't in the cards for me.

"He's so sweet," I said as she stepped out of the room.

Tasha smiled and sipped her tea. "They all are when they're sleeping."

I slept with Tasha. Rather, Tasha slept while I laid there in her bed and stared at the ceiling. Once the fear and numbness wore off, I got mad. Whoever had done this was a coward. Why couldn't they say what they had to say to my face? I imagined them coming into my room with their big knife and me waiting for them with my daddy's pump-action rifle. The moment he had raised his knife, I would have simply pulled the trigger and let the twin-barrel rifle do its job.

It was a nice thought, one that helped me get up out of the bed and pull on Tasha's clothes. The white tee shirt was too small and the black pants an inch or two short, but the rest fit fine. When we were teens, people sometimes mistook us for sisters, but I think it was simply because we hung around together. Our shapes were not even close to the same. Tasha was a thin blonde and about five-foot-four. I was five-foot-seven and curvy. Ever since she had had Kip, our butts have been the same size, which lent itself to swapping clothes whenever we needed to, like right now.

I grabbed my coat and purse and headed out of the house, ensuring the door was locked behind me. Tim was waiting in the driveway. The sound of my footsteps on the crunchy gravel echoed through the quiet morning air.

"Thanks for picking me up." I crawled into my brother's warm car.

"Not a problem."

"Have you been to the house yet?"

His face was set like stone in the light from the dashboard. "No, but I heard it was bad."

"Are you sure you want to sleep there?"

"If you're asking me if I'm scared . . ." He glanced at me and then back at the road. "I'm not."

"Okay. Good."

"I heard they got in by breaking a basement window."

"That's what Chief Blaylock said." I stared out the window and up at the stars, which twinkled in the black sky.

"It wasn't anyone who knew us."

I turned toward my brother. "What makes you say that?"

Tim's hands were tight on the wheel. "Everyone who knows us knows where we keep the spare key."

My eyes grew wide. "Of course. They would have gone in through the door." I sat back. "That narrows the field a bit."

"Who's so pissed at you he would trash the house but didn't know about the spare key?"

"Good question." We pulled into the driveway. The cop in the squad car got out to check on us as we climbed out of Tim's car.

"Hey." Tim shoved his hands in his pocket and nodded at Officer Bright.

"What are you two doing here this early in the morning?" he asked.

"I live here. Got off work and now I'm going in and going to bed," Tim said.

"I came back for my van. I'm heading into town to start work at the bakery."

"Hate to do this, but it's procedure. I need to check your IDs."

Tim rolled his eyes and I blew out a long breath as I dug through my purse. The officer took our IDs and looked at them with his flashlight. Then he looked at us carefully. "Thanks."

Tim put his ID back in his wallet and tucked it in his pocket. I took mine and put it back into my purse.

"If you wait five minutes, my replacement will be here," the officer said. "I can see you to the bakery before I go home."

"You don't need to—"

"Yes, he does," Tim cut me off. "Thanks." He shook the officer's hand. "I'm going in." He planted a kiss on my cheek and went to the front door to let himself in.

"Don't worry about cleaning up," I hollered after him. "I'm going to call a service."

Tim laughed. "As if I'd do housework." He disappeared into the house and I immediately started to worry.

"It's safe to go in, right?" I asked the officer.

"No one's come or gone since I got here."

Not that that was much comfort, I thought, but kept it to myself. I climbed into my van and started it up. The officer was right. Within five minutes, another cop car came to replace him. Officer Bright drove behind me to work and checked the building. At least for now, all was well.

I was stocking my display case with fresh pastries when I saw him walk by the front windows. My first thought was, that's weird. I checked the time. It was around 5:30 A.M. The same time George had been murdered. Why was Ralph Kennedy walking down Main Street at this time of the morning? I went to the front door and stuck my head out to see where he was going. The streetlights showed he had a bank deposit bag in his hand. The bag looked full and heavy in the lamplight. I checked behind me and the rest of the street was empty. Cold wind blew between the buildings, causing leaves to rise up in little whorls.

Ralph crossed the street and turned into the bank's driveway and out of sight. I looked at the time again and caught a chill. Was it Ralph who had killed George? Why? He seemed like such a well-mannered man. Not the kind to harbor enough rage to bludgeon not one but two men and rip my bedroom to pieces.

I closed and locked the front door and dialed Chief Blaylock's number. I got his answering service. "Chief Blaylock, this is Toni Holmes. When you get a chance could you come down to the bakery? I need to talk to you. Coffee's on the house. Thanks."

I hit End on my cell phone and leaned against my display case. Ever since I had the letter pushed under the back door, I'd been careful to open the blinds when I got to the bakery in the morning. That way, no one could vandalize the front without my seeing them. This was the first time I'd seen Ralph Kennedy walk by. Craig had told me the night George was killed both he and Ralph worked late, or in this case, early in the pharmacy. Maybe this was a regular thing. Maybe Ralph saw who had killed George. If so, why wasn't he coming forward?

I made a fresh pot of coffee and waited for Ralph to pass by on his way back to the pharmacy. It might be worth my while to invite the man in and find out what he knew about George's death.

Twenty minutes later, I'd done all the work in front I could do, and Ralph still hadn't returned. My cell phone rang. One look at the number and I picked up. "Hey, Tasha."

"Where are you?" She sounded mad. "I woke up and you weren't here. You scared the devil out of me."

"I called Tim and he brought me in to work. I told you I was going to go, remember?"

"I didn't think you'd leave in the middle of the night."

"I start work at 4 A.M. I'm not going to change my routine because some insane man hacked at my bed and tossed flour around my kitchen. Besides, Tim is up at that time of night. You were sleeping soundly so I called him. He made sure I was safe."

"You should have woken me up. I would have taken you, or at the very least, made you coffee."

"I'm fine, really." Finally Ralph Kennedy walked by the shop. "Listen, I've got to go."

"Why? It's ten after six."

"Ralph Kennedy walked by. I'm going to invite him in for coffee." I made my way to the front door and unlocked it.

"Wait, by yourself? Do you think that's wise?"

"It's only Ralph," I said. "I've offered him coffee before. Now is as good a time as any to get to know him a bit." I hung up and pushed the door open and stepped out but Ralph was nowhere to be seen. That man could move fast.

"Hey, you're opening early."

Startled, I jumped and glanced to my left. Sam stepped

out of his truck and onto the sidewalk. "What are you doing here?" The question came out involuntarily.

"Mrs. Becher hired me to install shelves in the quilt shop." He waggled his eyebrows. "I think she likes having me around."

"At six-fifteen in the morning?" I hugged myself, as the wind was cold. A crow *caw*ed as it flew over the town.

Sam looked warm in his shearling jacket. "No, the job starts at seven. But I thought I might be able to persuade you to open early and let me have breakfast with you."

"Are you checking up on me, too? Or do you always have jobs that start at seven A.M.?"

"No, I don't always have seven A.M. jobs; sometimes I go to work even earlier. A contractor's work is never done." He opened the door, took my elbow, and escorted me inside.

The bakery smelled of coffee, cinnamon, and pumpkin. The chocolate chip pumpkin muffins had been a huge hit. I had an order for three dozen to be delivered to the senior center at ten A.M. Sam smelled of aftershave and soap. He took off his Stetson and ran a hand through his hair. My cell phone buzzed in my hand. His gaze twinkled at me. "Are you going to get that?"

I looked down to see if it was Tasha calling me back. "No." I stuffed the phone in my apron pocket.

"Then how about some coffee?"

"Okay." I took down two giant cups with matching saucers and handed him one set. "The coffee carafes are full, take your pick." I waved to the coffee bar.

He took me up on my offer, pouring himself a cup and adding a generous amount of cream and sugar.

"You know, come to think of it, your truck always seemed familiar to me," I said as I watched him. "I guess now I know why."

"Why?" He stirred his coffee.

"I've seen you on the road on my way to work."

"I'm sure you have." He took a seat. "There aren't a lot of people on the road at five A.M."

"Wait—" I narrowed my eyes. "Where were you the morning George was killed?"

He laughed. "So, what, I'm a suspect now? Really?"

I didn't say anything.

"Fine." He tipped his head. "If it makes you feel any better, I was in Garden City looking at a couple head of cattle to buy." He reached into his coat. "I've got the rancher's number on my phone. You can call and verify. I bet he's up this early."

"No, I believe you." The heat of a blush rushed over my cheeks. It was hard not to feel stupid accusing a friend of murder. But really, anyone could be the killer, right? My phone rang in my pocket. I ignored it.

"Okay, I answered your question. Now, tell me, how come you aren't answering your phone?"

"It's Tasha. I hung up on her a few minutes ago and now I'm going to have to apologize."

"Really? Why?"

"I saw Ralph Kennedy walk by around five-thirty." I pushed the carafe top, dispensed Sumatra into my mug, added a generous splash of half-and-half, and again tried not to blush at my assumption that Sam could be a killer. "He had a heavy bank bag in his hand. I watched him all the way until he turned into the bank drive."

Sam took a sip of his coffee, his expression thoughtful. "And this made you hang up on Tasha because . . . ?"

"I thought I saw him walk back by. I wanted to ask him in for coffee." I shrugged as if it were nothing. I wasn't about to admit that I had begun to suspect everyone of being a killer. "When I met him, he'd said he'd wished he'd had time to come over and see for himself how good the pastries were."

Sam sprawled out at the table and studied me for a moment. "So you've decided you want to date Ralph?"

"What?" I didn't know what to say. I scrunched up my eyebrows. "No, don't be silly." My cell phone in my pocket rang for the third time. I set my cup down on the table next to Sam's and picked up my phone. "Hey, Tasha."

"I can't believe you hung up on me."

"Sorry."

"No, you're not, or you would have picked right back up. I've half a mind to come down there. Tell me you did not let Ralph Kennedy into the shop with you this morning."

I shook my head at how much she sounded like a mom. "Um . . . no, not Ralph."

"Don't tell me you let in a perfect stranger."

"I wouldn't say perfect . . ."

"Marie Antoinette Holmes! Do I have to call your family?"

"No, just kidding. By the time I got the door open, Ralph was gone. Sam pulled up. He's here now checking on me and having coffee."

"And a donut," Sam called.

"And a donut," I added and made a face. I went to the display cabinet and pulled out a plate and placed two gluten-free spice cake donuts with maple frosting on the plate. "So you see, I'm perfectly fine."

"You are not fine." Tasha all but snorted afterwards. "You are off your rocker. After seeing your bedroom last night, anyone with any sense would have packed up and gone on a long vacation."

"I couldn't pack. All my clothes were shredded, remember?" I set the plate down in front of Sam and took the chair across from him. His open coat revealed a denim work shirt and jeans. "Would you have closed the inn if this had happened to you?"

"We're not talking about me." She sounded angry. "We're talking about you, and I was humoring you when I said you could borrow my clothes. I didn't think they would fit."

I glanced down at the too-tight white tee shirt and flood short pants. "They fit fine."

Sam's gaze wandered over me and he grinned and raised a thumbs-up. I could feel the heat of embarrassment rush up my neck for the second time. I narrowed my eyes at him. He smiled wider and popped the rest of the donut in his mouth.

"Listen, Tasha, if you're calling to scold me, then I'm going to hang up."

"No, wait!"

"What?" I played with the handle of my coffee cup.

"I wanted to ask you to go shopping with me after work tonight. Kip's spending the night at my mom's. I can meet you at six P.M. and we can make a quick trip into Wichita."

"I don't know."

"Oh, come on. You need a new wardrobe. I'll buy dinner. It'll be fun."

I ran a hand over my face. "All right."

"Yippee!" I could hear her clapping. "I can't wait. I found this new shop I've been dying to take you."

"I'm not letting you dress me," I warned. Sam's eyebrows shot up at those words. I sent him a dirty look and turned away from him.

"I promise. I'll only show you the clothes I like. Deal?"

"Deal," I said. "Give Kip a hug for me." I hit the End button and put my phone in my apron pocket. My coffee had cooled and Sam had finished off his breakfast.

"Back to my original question," Sam said.

"What's that?" I sipped coffee and enjoyed its bitter-smooth taste on my tongue.

"Are you dating Ralph Kennedy?"

He caught me with a mouthful of coffee. It wasn't my fault if I spit it all across the table and into his face. "What?"

Sam grabbed a napkin and wiped his face. "Is that a yes or a no?"

"A . . . no." I took more napkins out of the dispenser and cleaned up the table and reached over to dab at his jacket. "Where would you get that stupid idea, anyway?"

"You said you ran out into the street to wave Ralph down and invite him in for coffee. Sounds like a date to me." Sam shrugged and kept his face perfectly even.

He had to be kidding me. "It was not a date." I threw the napkins away. "I wanted to get to know the guy better."

"Sounds like a date." His gaze was intense. "Because you

wouldn't be stupid enough to keep investigating George's murder by yourself after yesterday."

Pictures of my bed torn to shreds went through my head. Fine, the guy did have a point. "I'm not alone." I sipped my coffee and tried to act nonchalant. "You're here."

He tilted his head as one would when talking to a small child. "I kind of figured you would try something like that. It's why I'm here." He shook his head. "I hoped you wouldn't. I hoped you weren't really as stubborn as you come off."

"Who, me, stubborn?" I was not offended. "It's one of my finer qualities."

"Good to know." He lifted his coffee cup.

"Do you think Ralph Kennedy is capable of murder?"

It was his turn to do a spit take. I handed him a napkin. "Little quiet Ralph? Are you kidding me?"

"No, I'm not kidding. You should have seen the heavy bank bag he had in his hand this morning. And, hey, he's not smaller than I am. I mean, I'm tall and all but I'm not as strong as a guy . . . even a guy my height."

"Why would Ralph want to kill George?"

"That's the $64,000 question, isn't it?"

CHAPTER 35

Tasha and I walked into her carriage house apartment, shopping bags in hands, happy but exhausted. I had spent the last four hours purchasing everything from new underwear to two sets of work clothes. I had read somewhere that ten good pieces were the makings of a great wardrobe. I had eight. That would have to do for now.

"Thanks for going with me." I dropped the bags on the floor next to her kitchen island and climbed up on a bar stool. Tasha pulled wineglasses out of her cupboard and opened a bottle of red.

"It was my pleasure. How does it feel to start your wardrobe from scratch?"

I rested my elbows on the granite top and put my cheeks in my hands. "On one hand, it's kind of freeing. On the other, I'm grieving a little. I had a bunch of clothes from Chicago that I'll never be able to replace here."

"That's it then, we'll have to plan a weekend shopping trip." She poured wine into our glasses. "One of the weekends Kip is with his grandma."

"Here's to a shopping weekend in Chicago." I touched my wineglass to hers and took a nice long swallow. The wine was a burst of grape and berry on my tongue. It warmed me as it went down my throat, and I could feel my muscles relaxing. "Don't get me wrong, I'm thankful you loaned me some clothes, but I'm glad to be back into my own size." I waved my hand at the new pair of jeans and long-sleeved V-neck tee shirt I wore.

"I thought you looked cute in my stuff." Tasha pouted, her wineglass in hand. "It really didn't fit you though, did it?" Her smile was contagious.

"You should have seen Bob Meyer staring at my tight tee shirt in the shop. I had to go and dig out a full chef's coat to cover up."

"That's funny." Tasha giggled. "How old is he, ninety?"

"He's seventy-two. He told me so himself when I mentioned I catered birthday parties. For a moment, I thought he was going to order a cake just so I could jump out of it." I slipped off my shoes and enjoyed the wine. "What a long couple of days."

"I know." Tasha pulled her hair out of its professional low ponytail and shook it out. "What are you going to do about your house?"

"I called my insurance company. Tim said they sent over an adjuster this afternoon. I've also hired a company to go in and clean up." I frowned. "I asked them to toss all the clothing. I don't want to ever wear anything that monster might have touched."

Tasha shuddered. "Ugh. I don't blame you one bit. You know, he could have not ripped up certain clothes so you would wear them after he touched them."

"Eww, creepy."

"What about your bed?"

"I have a new one on order. They're supposed to deliver it on Tuesday."

"Yay! A week of girl time."

I sat up straight. "Oh, I'm not going to stay here the whole time. There are five other bedrooms at the house that are empty. I'll take one of them as soon as Chief Blaylock thinks it's safe."

"Oh." She slumped her shoulders and pushed out her bottom lip. "I'd hoped you'd stay with me and help me figure out the mortgage thing."

"I don't have to stay here to help. Listen, the bakery is closed Sunday. I can spend the whole morning working on the mortgages with you."

The back door was yanked open, startling us both. I might have screamed a tiny bit. A man stood in the doorway, his face shadowed. He was breathing heavily as if he had run three miles. It was only six steps, a landing, and six more steps to the carriage house.

"Hello, ladies." He stepped into the light. It was Craig Kennedy.

Tasha stood. "Craig, what are you doing here? Why didn't you knock? Have you no common courtesy?"

"You're the one who should be thinking about courtesy." Craig's voice was low and a bit terrifying. "Where the hell have you been? What is *she* doing here?"

"I don't have to answer that." Tasha raised her chin. "Have you been drinking?"

"You need to leave." I stood and said it firmly as if talking to a stray growling dog. "Go!"

"Like hell I'll go." Craig took a step toward us. "Where's Kip? Have you pawned the poor boy off on someone else again? A good mother would be home taking care of her son, especially a son like Kip."

I stepped between Craig and Tasha. "I said, Go!" I pointed toward the door.

He narrowed his eyes and dropped his forehead like a bull getting ready to charge. "You can't tell me what to do, bitch. This is not your house."

"It's not your house either, Craig." Tasha grabbed the cell phone off the countertop. "You'd better go. I'm calling the police."

My heartbeat pounded in my ears. My hand trembled. I straightened to my full height. "You heard her, now go!"

"You are a meddling bitch. I should have let Ed kill you."

My eyes grew wide and my mouth went dry. I grabbed a heavy frying pan off the hanging rack and took a step toward him. "Get out!"

"What are you going to do, hit me with that?" Craig snorted. "Not likely." He turned his attention on Tasha. "If you dial that number, you're going to regret it."

"Don't threaten me in my own home," Tasha said, and with shaking hands started pushing numbers. "I was right to break up with you. You're insane."

"Don't!" Craig pushed me hard against the counter, knocking the wind out of my lungs. He grabbed Tasha's hand and wrenched the cell phone out of it. Then he knocked her to the ground with a backhand across her face.

Tears sprung into Tasha's eyes. I recovered my balance and rushed him with the pan still in my hand. I might have growled or cursed. I was pretty scared, but I did manage to catch the side of his head with the pan. Too bad all it did was deflect his head about an inch or two. Now he was really mad.

He pivoted on his heel and cuffed me good. My head rung as I slammed into the wall. The worst part was that I couldn't see anything but gray and stars. He grabbed me by the front of my tee shirt and hauled me up. His fist hit my cheek and I bit my tongue. The warm and metallic taste of blood filled my mouth.

A sane person would have run. Clearly, being smacked around had unhinged me because I turned to fight. I wasn't going to let him beat on me. I had enough brothers to know how to defend myself. I ducked his fist, kneed him in the groin, stomped on his instep, and brought my fist up into his chin. He let go of me and staggered backward. I blinked as my vision returned. I couldn't tell if I'd hit my marks right. Shouldn't he have completely crumpled?

He was bent over but looked up at me with death in his eyes. He rushed me, throwing his shoulder into my stomach. The air whooshed out of my lungs and he threw me into the wall. The world went black.

I don't know how long I was out. It didn't feel long. I

woke up to Craig kicking me. Pain radiated through me like fire.

Tasha jumped on his back. "Stop it! Stop hurting her."

Craig was a man crazed. I could barely see straight. Breathing out through my nose was less painful but barely. I heard him knock her off him. I say heard because the only thing I saw was the floor. I realized my cell phone was in my pocket. We needed help if we were going to get out of this alive.

Slowly, carefully, I reached into my pocket and pulled out my phone. Turns out the murders and the vandalism had been a good thing because now I had the police on speed dial. I blinked through whatever was getting in my eyes and hit the speed dial. Craig was shouting. Tasha was screaming. I tried not to moan too loudly. I saw the phone light up. I left it on and pushed it out of the way. Maybe, just maybe, someone at dispatch would hear and send help. Or, at the very least be annoyed enough to investigate.

"I can't believe you chose her over me." Craig slapped Tasha. She fell back against the wall. "After all I did for you. After I killed Ed Bruner for you."

Holy shit. Craig had killed Ed. I didn't dare look at the phone. All I could do was hope the dispatcher had heard his confession. I wished I had taped the incident. I mean, what if Sarah didn't catch on? What if they sent Officer Emry? I should have hit Record.

"Stop it, Craig Kennedy," I shouted. It sort of came out as a high-pitched squeal. "Stop hitting Tasha Wilkes, now!"

I tried to stand. He had grabbed her by the throat and was choking her. "Stop!" I threw myself at him. It wasn't much, but it was all I had. He tossed Tasha aside like a bag of feed and turned on me.

"This is all your fault, goddamn it. If you hadn't interfered, Tasha and Kip would have become my family. My family to watch over and care for." He slammed his fist into the side of my head. My chin came down on the countertop and I discovered how hard granite could be.

Craig grabbed me by the back of my shirt and hauled me

out of the kitchen and into the living room. I saw the panic in Tasha's eyes. "Run!" I shouted. "Tasha, run!"

"No!" Tasha was never one to listen. I saw her struggle to get up and then I was pulled out of view of her and thrown to the floor. Pain blinded me.

"Now you're gonna get the beating you deserve for being a home wrecker." I heard him whip his belt out.

"Like hell," I muttered. My face throbbed and my tongue was swollen, but I couldn't think about that right now. I rolled toward him and tried to knock him down. He stepped over me. I grabbed his leg and bit down hard. Screw it. If I was going to die, then I was going down knowing I had left a mark on the killer.

He screamed like a girl and tried to kick me off. I clung to him as if my life depended on it and clamped my teeth down even harder. If I had to, I'd take a piece out of him. He grabbed me by the hair and yanked me off. Tears sprung to my eyes, but my hands were free and I reached up and clawed the hand that held me by the hair.

He growled and I felt the swing in his body before I felt the electric lick of the belt across my shoulders. I had to get up or get him down. He still had my hair. I scissored my legs and got them behind him and up high enough to knock the back of his knees. He fell forward. The motion pulled my hair harder. Tears blinded me. I heard a mighty crash and suddenly I was free.

I scrambled away and back. My heart pounded in my ears and I wiped my eyes trying to see, to figure out what happened. Someone grabbed me by the shoulder. I reached up and felt a female hand. It was Tasha.

"Come on."

I saw Craig sprawled out on the floor. I put my arm around Tasha, whose face looked like raw meat, and together we staggered to the kitchen. The back door burst open. There was yelling as men rushed inside, guns drawn.

"Freeze!"

The words, the noise was too much. We crumpled to the

floor. Someone big and warm squatted down beside us. "Are
you all right?"

I started laughing. I couldn't see. My mouth was full of
warm, metallic stuff and there was ringing in my ears. "All
right" didn't quite cut it.

"Call an ambulance," the man, whoever he was shouted.
"It's okay," he said softer and stroked my hair. I winced.
"You're safe now."

I realized I hadn't let go of Tasha's hand. I turned to try
to see her through the stinging wetness and tears. She sat
up straight, her back against the kitchen island. Her face
swollen and her eyes . . . her eyes glittered.

"I hope I killed that son of a bitch."

That statement made me laugh like a lunatic. She looked
at me and started laughing, too.

Another man—this time I saw it was Officer Bright—
squatted down. "How did you know?" Tasha asked. "How
did you get here?"

"Ms. Holmes called dispatch. We have the whole thing
on tape."

Tasha looked at me. "How did you do that? I tried to dial
but Craig . . ." A small sob broke out of her. I squeezed her
hand.

"I hab da police on speed dial," I explained as best I could
with my swollen tongue. "I hid one buddon and hid my
phone, hoping id worked."

"And it did." Officer Bright picked up my phone and
handed it to me. "Brilliant move."

"Did you hear it all then?" Tasha asked. "Did you hear
when he said he killed Ed Bruner for me?"

Officer Bright nodded and patted her shoulder. "We've
got it all on tape."

Then the paramedics were there pushing everyone away,
asking questions, shining lights in my eyes, and generally
making the pain worse. Somehow I didn't seem to mind.

CHAPTER 36

Luckily, neither of us had any broken bones or internal damage, but they kept us both overnight in the hospital for observation. Just in case. At least they let us stay in the same room. It turns out we only had badly bruised ribs, horrendously bruised bodies, and needed stitches for our faces. We would both be on liquid diets for a short while.

"I think we need a spa day." I struggled to sit up in the bed.

"Don't make me laugh. It hurts too much," Tasha responded.

"That's what the pain pills are for," I pointed out.

"They didn't give me enough then."

There was a knock at the door, which was odd because in a hospital room people came and went whether you liked it or not. We both turned to find Chief Blaylock at the door. "You ladies mind if I come in?"

"Why not, we're having a party."

He had his hat in his hand. "I wanted to thank you for calling in and giving us Craig's confession on tape. I'm not sure how admissible it will be in court, but now that we know who did it and why, we can put the other pieces of evidence together."

I tried to smile, but it hurt and my cheek was too swollen to move. "Do you think Craig killed George?"

"Well, now, that's the twist, little lady." He ran his hat through his fingers. "Craig says he didn't kill George and there's no evidence he did."

"Shoot." Tasha tried to pout, but it didn't work since her bottom lip was already pretty fat. "There's still a killer out there?"

"I'm afraid that's how we have to look at it. Although, we do have a fingerprint match on Craig and the prints from your house, Ms. Holmes. We're pretty sure he's the one who ransacked it."

"He was probably the one leaving the threats at my store, too."

"More than likely." The chief nodded. "Don't you worry none. We'll see he's put away for a very long time after what he did to you two. We've got him on murder, attempted murder, battery, assault, breaking and entering, and criminal vandalism."

"Great." A weight lifted from my shoulders. "That means I can finally live my life without everyone watching my every move."

"I still need you two to come down and give clear statements about what happened at the carriage house. Now, don't think you have to come down today. But soon, before the memories fade."

"I thought your officers got our statements last night?" Tasha pointed out. She brushed her hair out of her eyes and winced. She had four stitches on her forehead.

"We have solid preliminary statements," he agreed. "But it's always good to come down and see what details you can remember once the shock's worn off."

"Fine." She leaned her head back against her pillow. "I'll have to wait until Kip is in school."

"That will work for us."

"You can borrow Brad if you need a lawyer," I said. I would have patted her hand but the beds were too far apart.

"Now, nobody needs a lawyer, ladies. Everyone in town can see how brave you were."

"It's too bad Craig lived." Tasha shook her head. "He deserved to die."

"You really didn't want to kill him," I said and flashed my eyes toward the chief. "You hit him in self-defense."

"Duh, of course it was self-defense. He tried to kill me. He was in the process of killing you when I hit him. I'm saying it wouldn't have hurt my feelings if it stuck."

"That's the pain meds talking," I assured the chief. "Tasha's a real sweetheart. She wouldn't hurt a fly."

"Lots of things happen in the heat of a moment like the one you two gals went through." Chief Blaylock grinned. "You two take care and come down to the station, all right?"

"We will." I tried to be perky.

"And Ms. Holmes, I'm pretty sure you no longer have to worry about threats and such. I've got the lab going over those bank deposit bags looking for blood evidence and fingerprints. I'm sure we'll have Craig nailed for George's murder as well."

I tried to smile but I think I only managed to drool. "Thanks."

He nodded and headed out. I grabbed a tissue and blotted at my mouth. "Why did you tell the chief you wanted to kill Craig? Are you nuts? He might have to tell the prosecutor and you could be charged with, I don't know, manslaughter or something."

"I don't like to lie," Tasha said calmly, picked up a juice box, and sipped out of the corner of her mouth. Not that much went in because her mouth was as bad as mine. We were quite a sight.

"Can I ask one question?" I rested my head back on my pillow.

"Sure."

"What did you hit him with? I mean, I slammed that pan into him and it barely made a difference."

Tasha's blue eyes twinkled in her black-and-blue face. "I remembered Kip's baseball bat was still sitting in the living room from his last game. You know, sometimes it pays not to do too much housework."

We both tried to chuckle but it hurt too much.

The next morning we were allowed to shower. I washed blood and guck out of my hair, but the sample bottles of shampoo and conditioner did little to save the frizz. My hair and I had an understanding. I'd let it do what it wanted and it wouldn't go too ballistic. Tasha's mom brought us fresh clothes. Getting dressed was a trick with sore ribs and so many bruises that I looked more black-and-blue than white. Why did redheads have to have such transparent skin? I decided against a bra and put on a button-up shirt and slipped on a skirt.

I knew it was chilly out so I took a cue from Grandma Ruth and added knee socks to the outfit and put my feet in slippers. My reflection in the mirror was not much better after the shower, but I shrugged it off. It wasn't like I was trying to make a fashion statement.

We were released around noon with strict orders to rest, to which I rolled my eyes. It might be the weekend but Tasha and I had lives. Besides, my bed was gone, and I couldn't imagine where I was going to be resting. Tim picked me up and drove me home. He helped me up the stairs when I refused to take the ramp. Someone had put carved pumpkins out on the porch.

"Did you decorate?" I asked Tim.

He shrugged and opened the door.

"Surprise!" My family crowded the foyer. My cousin Lucy was there with three of her girls. Grandma Ruth and Bill sat in the fancy wing chairs in the parlor as Tim settled me down on the pale blue settee, which someone had made up with sheets and blankets so that I could be near everyone.

My sister Joan had come down from Kansas City for the day with her five kids. Jennifer and Emma still had fresh scabs from chicken pox. "I promise the doctor told me they were no longer contagious," she said as she leaned in to give me a kiss.

Rosa came in from Wichita with four of her little ones. "Sheila Thompson wants the entire scoop. Don't leave anything out."

"Leave her alone," my brother Richard said. His wife, Phyllis, had come down with him to see if I needed anything.

"Eleanor called earlier," Rosa informed me. "I told her you weren't home yet. She wants to come down to see you as soon as she can figure out what to do with the kids for a few days."

"She doesn't have to come," I protested.

"Of course she does," Richard said. "She's your sister."

It made my head pound. But the house was full of talking and laughter and ribbing. I think the guys had a poker game going in the den. It was a regular Keene family palooza. The doctors would never have released me from the hospital if they had seen this gathering. Rest wasn't possible when the Keene circus was in town.

Lucy had filled the dining room table with food and stacked plates and dishes like a buffet. The house smelled of spice and ham and pies. All kinds of things I couldn't eat.

"I made you some GF pudding," Lucy said as she brought me a cup of lukewarm tea and a straw. "There's vanilla, strawberry, chocolate, and tapioca. I put in the raisins. I think you can eat them."

"Ew, fisheyes and flies," Joan's son Nicholas commented as he ran through the room.

"You be nice, boy, or I'll make you eat that for breakfast," Lucy called after him.

"Stop making me smile," I protested. "All I can do is drool."

She handed me a soft linen handkerchief and patted me

on my shoulder. I tried not to wince. She was being good to me. "You've got visitors coming. I'll go get a wide-toothed comb and help you with your hair."

"Thanks."

Grandma Ruth hobbled over with her cane. She made a motion and Bill got up and pulled her winged-back chair over to the couch so Grandma could sit down. He placed his hand on her shoulder and she patted it. "See what a good man can do for you, kiddo?"

Bill beamed. I tried not to roll my eyes.

"She's a businesswoman, Grandma Ruth," Rosa piped up. "Leave her alone."

"I had eight kids and twenty-four grandkids at her age," Grandma shouted back. "Nothing better to leave to this world than your children and their children."

"Grandma . . ." I managed to get out.

"Tell me how it went down." Grandma Ruth leaned in close, her rectangular face intent. "How'd he get in? What did he do? How did you know he killed Ed?"

The whole room went still. I looked around as everyone leaned in to hear the story. I sipped the tea through the straw, dabbed my mouth, and set it aside. Then I told the tale of Craig Kennedy while Lucy tried to make some sort of sense out of my unruly hair.

I might have embellished a bit on the telling, but not much. Besides, my family likes a good story and embellishments were expected.

"So you see Grandma Ruth," I said, "dating really is overrated." I leaned back against the pillow and closed my eyes a moment.

"It's too bad you feel that way."

I opened my eyes to see Sam leaning against the door frame. With his Stetson in one hand and a bouquet of flowers in another, he looked like every woman's cowboy dream. My heart might have fluttered a bit.

Grandma Ruth got up. "Don't listen to her," she boomed. "She's on pain meds. She'll come 'round once she heals. Come on, Bill," Grandma said. "I need a smoke."

"Are you writing the story for the paper?" I called after her.

She looked over her shoulder and grinned. "My family, my exclusive."

And with those words, everything in my world felt right again. "Come on in, Sam." I waved him over to the chair. "Everyone, this is Sam Greenbaum, rancher and owner of Handyman. He's a friend. Sam, this is my family . . . part of it, anyway."

I watched as my sisters introduced themselves. Sam shook their hands and took Grandma's chair.

"These are for you." He handed me the flowers.

"Thanks, they're lovely." I buried my nose in the fragrance. I love the smell of flower-shop flowers. "I hear there's a ton of food in the dining room," I said. "And the men are in the den playing poker. Feel free to go on in and take their money."

He sent me a crooked grin and my blood tingled. "I came to see you."

Rosa got up and took the flowers. "I'll put these in water."

"Thanks." I waited a moment for her to leave. "This is not my finest look." I hated the idea of how puffy and ugly I was at the moment. At least my Grandma Ruth outfit was covered with blankets. Still, I figured if a man could look me in the eye the way I looked at that moment and still come back, then he might be worth dating.

"You look fine," he said. "I'd say you're beautiful in my eyes, but that sounds corny."

I could feel a blush rising and wondered what the heck color I was with a blush and bruises. "Yes, that was corny."

"I'd like to say you should have let me watch over you, but I think that would piss you off."

"Darn right it would." I bristled and adjusted my shoulders, which hurt. I wanted to bite my tongue to keep from groaning. But my tongue was still a bit swollen.

"I won't say it, then." He kept staring at me until I looked down at his fingers caressing the edge of his hat.

"Good." I looked back at his handsome face.

He studied his hat a moment. "What does the chief say?"

"He says it's over. They got Craig on tape saying he killed Ed for Tasha. They also found evidence it was Craig who trashed my home and ruined my bed."

"What about George?"

I shrugged and winced. Darn it, when was I going to not hurt?

"Here." Joan handed me a pain pill and a glass of water with a straw.

I downed it and the water as best I could and then wiped the drool from my rubbery chin. I guess since Sam didn't make some lame excuse to leave the room, he must be serious about liking me. I rested my head back on the pillow. "The chief says Craig swears he didn't kill George. The lab is still going through all the bank bags. If one was used to murder George, then they'll have Craig for that as well."

"You have another visitor," Rosa said as she carried in Sam's flowers, perfectly arranged and placed in one of my mother's glass vases. She set it on the table as Meghan came into the room. Today she wore her black hair down. Her sixties-girl makeup framed her lovely eyes and bright red lipstick accented her pierced lip. Deftly groomed brows showed off her eyebrow piercing.

"Hi, Boss." She smiled shyly. She wore a vest over a tee shirt, black jeans, and thick-soled black boots.

"Meghan, hi, thanks for stopping by. Everyone, this is my new assistant, Meghan. She's been with me a week and has been great."

"I wouldn't say great." Meghan stepped into the center of the room. "But I haven't burned anything yet."

"Meghan, this is my family and obviously you already know Sam."

"Hey." Meghan gave a short wave and then took the second chair near the settee. "I heard you got beat up pretty bad." Her eyes widened and she put her hand to her mouth. "I mean . . . you look better than people were sayin'." She shook her head and tried again. "I mean, you look good." She clamped her mouth shut. Her piercings glittered in the afternoon light.

"Thanks. I would smile but my face won't move."

"I'll get some ice for that," Rosa said as she passed through, chasing after her son who had a plate full of food and was running through the house.

Having grown up in such a big family, the noise and bustle didn't bother me. I watched Sam closely. He seemed relaxed and kicked his legs out in front of him. Meghan acted a bit uncomfortable, though.

"So—" we both said at the same time.

"Go ahead." She waved at me.

"You owe me a Coke," I teased her. "Listen, I plan on opening the bakery as usual Monday."

"What?"

"Really?"

"No."

Everyone talked at once. I raised my hand palm up and waited for the protests to stop. "Yes, really. Tim can take me in to work and can be my delivery boy for the next week. After that, the doctor assures me I will be fine and able to drive again."

People opened their mouths to speak and I raised my hand again. "And, if Meghan wants to work some extra hours, she can work my schedule and see that if I get tired the shop is manned." That seemed to shut most of them up. "Meghan, do you have time to work the extra hours this week?"

"Are you kidding?" Her eyes twinkled. "That would be awesome. If I want to learn the business, I always knew I needed to be there as long as you."

"It's only for a week, but it will give you a taste of what it's like to run the place."

"Thanks!" She got up. "I'd better go. I've got some things to take care of. What time will you be there?"

"I'll be at the back of the shop at four A.M."

"Cool." She reached out and squeezed my hand. "I promise to be as big a help as I can."

"I'm counting on it."

Meghan pushed through the crowded parlor, then stopped for a second and turned to me. "I have to ask: Did you really think Uncle Sam was the killer and I was spying for him?"

Everyone looked at me; you could have heard a pin drop.

"Maybe." I shrugged. "For a moment."

Meghan's eyes lit up and her smile widened. "That's so cool. Me, a spy. Ha!" She left the house.

"She really is a nice girl." I rested my gaze on Sam and pretended not to be embarrassed by my earlier suspicions. "Thank you again for sending her my way."

"It was my pleasure. Listen, I've got to go, but I can check in on you later."

"I'm good," I said as he leaned down and brushed a feather-light kiss on the one spot on my face that wasn't swollen. My guess was he'd been sitting there the whole time trying to figure out where to plant one that wouldn't hurt.

"I'll be back. You take care now." He said his good-byes to my family and left.

"Knock, knock." Todd Woles stepped into the doorway. "Sam Greenbaum said I should just come on in. Oh my God, honey, your lovely face!" He rushed over and fluttered over me. "That bastard."

I noticed he had roses in his hand. "Are those for me?"

"Oh, yes, I thought you would need something to cheer you." He handed them to me. "Now that I see you, I know you need something."

"I'm fine, really." I enjoyed the fragrance of his orange and yellow roses. "You should see the other guy."

Todd sat down in the wing chair and tugged his waistcoat into place. Yes, the man had dressed to the nines just to come see me. "I certainly hope you kicked his ass."

"We did." I put the roses on my lap. "You look dapper."

"Do you think so?" He brushed imaginary lint off his slacks.

"You always dress better than anyone else I've ever known."

"Well, I do run a men's clothing store." His eyes twinkled at me. "Phil wanted to come but he had a last-minute gig. He sings, you know."

"Really? Professionally?"

"You should check out his website."

"I will."

He leaned over and took my hand and squeezed it. "I wanted you to know I appreciated your coffee invite. Even if it was because you thought I might have killed George."

I felt the heat of a blush. "Yeah, about that . . ."

"No worries." He patted. "You were simply trying to solve a mystery. I would have done the same."

"If it makes any difference, I never really thought it was you."

He straightened and his eyes smiled. "I know."

"Can I ask?"

"What?"

"Is it hard being different and a successful business owner in Oiltop?" I tilted my head and studied him.

He smiled warmly. "Honey, we'll talk when you feel better." He patted my hand.

"Did you ever get threat letters?"

He frowned. "You've gotten threat letters?"

"Chief Blaylock says he's pretty sure it was George sending them. But I wondered if you had ever gotten them."

He paused, his dark eyes misty. "We'll talk when you feel better. Okay?"

"Okay." I took a deep breath, suddenly very tired. "Thanks for coming by. I hope we can be friends."

"Oh, honey, we're already friends." He picked up the flowers. "I'll make sure these get in water. You rest."

My eyes were tired and my lids heavy. I decided it couldn't hurt to rest them a moment.

When I woke up, the house was quiet. A single lamp was lit in the far corner. Brad sat in a wing-backed chair and was reading something that might have been legal briefs. I must have made a sound because he looked up. "Hello." He tucked his reading glasses away. His handsome face held concern and the right touch of horror at my appearance so I knew he wasn't faking it. "Can I get you something?"

"Water would be great." I tried to sit up but felt like I'd

been hit by a truck. I put my head back down on the pillow. He brought me a glass with a straw in it. I grabbed the napkin and sipped the water then dabbed at my mouth. There was pain there, too, which meant I was healing. "Where is everyone?"

"Tim is upstairs sleeping. I guess it's his day off from work. Richard and your sisters left. Lucy put the food in the fridge and told me which puddings were good for you. Do you want something to eat?"

"How long have you been here?"

"About two hours." He put his hand on my hand to stop my protest. "It's all right, I've been working on some briefs."

"Where did the day go?"

"I imagine it went down the pain pill rabbit hole." He raised an eyebrow. "Are you hungry? Do you want anything?"

"I'm good."

"I brought you flowers." His tone was sheepish and I opened my eyes to see that he pointed to another large, lovely bouquet. "Looks like I'm not the only one. Let me guess, Sam Greenbaum."

"I'm—"

"I know, I know, not dating." He crossed his arms over his chest and tilted his head. "You'll let me know when you're ready, right?"

"After my run-in with Craig last night, I may never be ready," I muttered. "He thought he owned Tasha simply because she'd dated him for two months. You should have seen the anger in his eyes."

"Those were his eyes, Toni," Brad said, his tone soft and sad. "Not mine, and I wager not Sam's either."

"I know."

"Do you?"

"I do." Silence echoed through the room. It was awkward and I thought I'd fill it. "What do we do now, oh, lawyer of mine? Do we sue Craig for battery and mental abuse?"

Brad's electric-blue eyes shone and his mouth curved up on one side. "Let's let the prosecutor take his shot before we think about civil charges. Okay?"

"Darn, does this mean it'll be years before I get my millions?" I asked tongue in cheek.

"Sorry to say it, but yes, it'll be years."

"Too bad." I sighed in a long and dramatic fashion. "It would have been fun being a millionaire. I could go to Cabo and lounge about on the beach with cabana boys."

"I like it better when you're here." He sat back. "And I don't fancy being a cabana boy anytime soon."

"What? If I were a millionaire I could get my face repaired and take us both to the beach."

He leaned over and brushed my cheek. "I wouldn't do a thing to your face."

"Then you, Mr. Attorney, need glasses."

"What I need to do is give you your pain pill and let you get some sleep. Are you working Monday?"

"Yes."

"Then get some rest." He handed me a pain pill and my water glass. "And for goodness' sake, stay away from criminals."

"I'll try my best."

CHAPTER 37

It seemed being beaten half to death was also profitable.

Monday was busy. Lucky for me, there had been a surge in online orders. I did a lot of sitting while Meghan made up most of the batters. Time flies when you have a long list, and before I knew it, it was time to open the shop. I have to admit, I made Meghan check to ensure Rocky Rhode and his camera were nowhere in sight.

He wasn't. It seemed whatever Sam said to him had stuck. I didn't know if I was happy or disappointed to no longer be caught by paparazzi.

After we opened, we had a steady stream of curious customers come in, not as much for the food as to get a peek at my battered face. I had dabbed makeup on the worst of it, but my skin hurt too much to get it all. The men whistled at my black eyes, swollen cheek, and stitches on my temple. The women winced. The little boys gawked and the little girls looked away. I was a sight.

Poor Meghan ran around in the back room like a chicken with its head cut off. She had to refill the display cabinet twice. I gave her a break when the crowd dispersed around ten A.M., and she was happy to sit in the back with her feet up on a step stool and a cup of coffee in her hand.

The front doorbell jingled and I stepped out of the kitchen to see Ralph Kennedy come in. "Hi, how can I help you?" I kept it simple even though my heart rate sped up. This was Craig's brother, after all. Would he be mad at me? I fingered the cell phone in my apron pocket.

"Hi, Ms. Holmes." Ralph came up to the front. "I'd like a coffee and a cinnamon roll, please."

His manner was quiet, gentle like all the other times I'd seen him. His eyes looked incredibly sad, a sea of brown despair. I handed him a cup and saucer. "The coffee carafes are over there. I'll be right out with your roll if you want to grab a seat."

"Sure."

I put a big roll on a plate and watched him carefully as he made his coffee and then sat down in the far corner table with his back to the wall and facing the door. He didn't look like he could hurt a soul, and I wasn't going to label him like his brother. That wasn't fair, was it? I mean, I hated it when people lumped me in with some of my brothers' antics. Seriously, you are not your siblings. I took the roll over to him and put it on the table.

"Can you sit with me?" he asked.

"Well . . ."

"I want to apologize for my brother."

"There's no need." I shrugged. "You weren't there. You didn't do it."

"He's still my brother," Ralph sighed and blew on his coffee and took a sip. "Please sit."

I glanced over at the kitchen door. There was no way Meghan could see me here, but I did have my cell phone in my pocket. I took the chair next to him and pulled it out. I had to sit slowly since it wasn't only my face that had been badly bruised.

"Look at you." He shook his head. "I can't believe Craig would do that. Our mama, God rest her soul, must be turning over in her grave knowing he hit a woman."

"Two women," I pointed out. "He beat Tasha pretty bad, too."

"Craig has always had a flash temper and no sense." Ralph sighed and sipped coffee. "It runs in the family."

A shiver went down my back and I glanced at the kitchen door a moment. "Really?"

"Yes, I'm afraid, try as hard as she could, our mama couldn't beat that out of us. One or the other of us was always doing something stupid. Craig was the one who got caught the most. It got so as I would do something and blame it on him. Ma expected him to be the bad one, and she never questioned me about it." He paused and picked at the roll. "Poor Craig took a lot of heat. It's why he's only an adjunct, you know. He was bright enough and educated enough to be a full-time instructor, but his record with the police gave the committee pause. Not that they should have known about it. I mean, juvenile records are sealed, right?"

"He hadn't done anything since he was a kid?" That didn't sound right to me.

"He hadn't gotten caught since he was a kid," Ralph corrected. "Unfortunately, the hiring committee here had several people who knew of his juvenile record. In fact, I'm surprised you and Tasha didn't know."

I hugged myself. "I've been gone for ten years and my memories of Oiltop are hazy on purpose. As for Tasha, she wasn't the kind of kid to pass around rumors. Plus, her mom was always working. They were too busy trying to pay the rent and eat proper to know what the older kids in town did."

"That makes sense, I guess. I told Craig he should have moved away, but he didn't want to be far from the homestead. He was close to Mama, you see, always looking to make her happy. Do you know what her dying words were to him?"

"No." I shook my head, but stopped quickly when pain rattled through my brain like lightning. The pain pills were wearing off.

"'Be a man and get married, make a family, make me happy,'" Ralph said. "I had my wife and boy, of course, but things went bad when my son was diagnosed with autism. Amelia left me to go live with her mother." Ralph shrugged. "I get to see my son at least once a month. I send support money. I look for new treatments, but still I think she blames me somehow for how he turned out."

"Oh, that's not right," I said, leaning forward. "Asperger's and autism have nothing to do with what a parent does or doesn't do."

"I know that. She knows that, but still, a person can't help but suspect and worry. Amelia didn't want to have any more kids. My chance is over."

"I'm sorry, but I don't understand how this has anything to do with what your brother did." I leaned back and crossed my arms over my chest.

"That's what I'm trying to explain," Ralph said. "You see, Craig killed Ed for his lady love, but he didn't kill George."

"He didn't kill George?" I tilted my head. "How do you know?"

Ralph looked me calmly in the eyes, his expression as smooth as an undisturbed pond. "Because I killed George."

Before I realized what I was doing I was out of the chair and had my thumb on the speed dial button for the police. It was an impulse, really. Ralph didn't act like a threat. Still, I'd been through too much not to react when I heard someone confess to murder. Meghan came running from the back at the sound of my chair falling over.

"Now, you don't have to do that," Ralph said to me.

"What's the matter?" Meghan scurried around the counter. I stepped back and put a table between me and Ralph.

Sarah was on the cell phone. "Nine-one-one, how can I help you?"

"This is Toni Holmes," I said.

"Oh, honey, not again. Are you all right?"

Three cop cars came screaming down Main Street and screeched to a halt in front of my store. Unfortunately, the policemen all ran toward the pharmacy.

"I told you, you didn't have to call them." Ralph stood.

"Stay away from me." I put my hand out. "The cops are right outside."

"Ms. Holmes?" Meghan asked behind me.

"Go to the kitchen," I ordered.

"I'm not leaving you alone." She grabbed a broom and held it like a samurai ready to do battle.

"Toni?" Sarah said from what sounded like a million miles away on my cell. "What is going on?"

"Ralph Kennedy is in my bakery," I said. "He just admitted to killing George Meister."

"Oh, crap," Sarah muttered. "I mean, the guys are at the pharmacy now. I'll send them over to you."

"Thanks."

Ralph took a step toward the windows and drew out a long breath. "Don't worry, ladies, I'm going to give myself up. I've been meaning to do it for some time, but I had to take the time to get my affairs in order. You see, I couldn't leave my boy and his mother without any income." He turned away from the windows. "I knew it was only a matter of time before they came for me. You were right." He gave me a sad smile. "I killed George with the bank bag."

"Why?" I trembled, my arm around Meghan. "Why would you do such a thing?"

"It wasn't planned." His voice was quiet. "I was taking the deposit to the bank and saw George starting to spray paint on your building. I stopped him. That's when he said it."

"Said what?"

"He said your bakery was for genetic defects who were born with sin. He said no one who ate here would ever go to heaven." Tears came to Ralph's tired eyes. "He said my boy would go to hell for being born. I didn't even think. I hit him with the bag. He went face-first into the trough and I left him there."

The front door burst open. Chief Blaylock came in with his gun drawn. "Put your hands up!" he shouted. Officer Emry pushed behind him, gun out, and stepped between the men and us. Two other officers entered. They had Ralph on the ground, his arms behind his back and cuffed. When they dragged him to his feet, Ralph had a look of acceptance on his face. "I'm sorry," he said. "For all the trouble you've had."

"Ralph Kennedy, you are under arrest for the murder of George Meister," the chief said. "Take him down to the station."

I clung to Meghan and she clung to me, the broom still in her hand. We watched them hustle Ralph out and into a squad car.

"Did that really just happen?" Meghan asked.

"Are you ladies all right?" Chief Blaylock asked.

"Yes." I nodded. "He didn't touch us."

"Thank God for that," I heard Sarah's voice come out of my cell phone. I lifted the cell to my ear. "Thanks, Sarah, I think it's over now."

"About darn time," she said before she hung up.

The commotion brought people downtown to take a look. Chief Blaylock called the ambulance even though I told him it wasn't necessary. Then he took my statement while Meghan sold coffee and cupcakes.

The shipping guy came in, picked up the online order boxes, and asked what all the excitement was about.

"Just another day at the bakery." Meghan winked at me. "There's always something cooking at Baker's Treat."

"Sounds like a cool place to work," he said with a twinkle in his eye.

"It is," Meghan replied. "It is."

We closed early after selling out everything in the store. I sat through an interview with Candy. She was pretty upset Grandma Ruth had gotten the first exclusive so we let her have the final report. Grandma Ruth came down to the bakery to see me home. Tim drove us both in the van, me in the passenger seat and Grandma strapped in next to her scooter.

"Who knew mild-mannered Ralph would be capable of murder," I said as we pulled up to the house.

"Oh, kiddo, any person in the world could kill if their baby was threatened. It's a law of nature," Grandma Ruth said and winked. "You'd know that if you were to have any kids."

I shook my head and carefully climbed out of the van. Bill was there to take Grandma Ruth's scooter out of the van. Tasha and Kip were on the front porch waiting for me. Tasha looked pretty beat-up as she swung on the porch swing, but she still wore a lovely blue dress and denim jacket. "We came over to help you eat all the food Lucy left."

I smiled. It hurt less. I don't know if it was the pain pills the ambulance guys had poured down my throat or if I was healing. "We sold out today," I said as I climbed the stairs. "I think the bakery is starting to really get a toehold in the community."

"You really should think about turning this house into an inn," Tasha said as I unlocked the door and let everyone inside. "Whoever buys the Welcome Inn could use some stiff competition."

I studied her face. Her expression was serene and accepting. "You put the inn up for sale?"

"Had to," she said with a shrug. "Everything happens for a reason." She took my arm in hers. "I think now is as good a time to admit this as any, but I never did ask Craig to follow you."

"You didn't?" I drew my eyebrows into a confused frown. "But when I told you he followed me, you acted like you knew."

"The key word there is *act*." Tasha took a deep breath. "At the time I thought if I told you I never asked him to do that, you'd worry or worse . . . you'd judge me."

"I'd worry, yes." I squeezed her arm. "But you have to know I wouldn't judge you."

"I do know. I saw a counselor today and she told me that my worry you were judging me was a natural reaction to Craig's isolation. She told me to tell you the truth from now on."

"She is a smart woman."

"We have to look at the good and not dwell on the bad, right? Besides, I'll have more time for Kip."

"What are you going to do for work?" I asked.

"I talked to Don Becher over at the Ramada. He's been looking for a general manager. If I take it, he's promised me weekday hours and free time to run Kip where he needs to go."

"And where will you live?"

She looked at me and I understood. "Welcome home." I squeezed her until we both hurt. "You can have the fourth floor for as long as you need it." There were two small bedrooms, a bath, and a small bonus room up there.

"It should only be a few months before I'm back on my feet, depending on how the sale of the inn goes." Tasha smiled. "Besides, I think we'll be a lot safer now. I mean, we have solid reputations in taking down bad guys together." She raised her arm and made a weak strong-man muscle. "Anyone would think twice about breaking and entering now."

I laughed until it hurt, which didn't take much. "Plus, Tim is installing a security system. We'll let the security company keep the police on speed dial. Anyone breaks in and the alarms will go off and the cops will be here before you can pick up your bat."

"Sounds good to me," she said and put her arm around Kip and walked to the kitchen. "Come on, love, let's see what Aunt Toni has to snack on."

Grandma Ruth walked with me into the den where we sank into the velvet wing chairs. "Gotta love a good mystery," she said, her eyes twinkling. Bill turned on the gas and lit the fireplace.

"I'd settle for a nice glass of wine and a good book," I said. "Real life causes too much bruising."

Grandma Ruth chuckled. "It's good to know you won't be alone, kiddo." She patted my knee. "With Tasha here, I won't be popping over so much."

"You and Bill are welcome anytime." He might be annoying and a freeloader, but it was pretty clear he loved my grandma and that would have to be good enough for me.

"Got any of those scones you need to get rid of?" Bill sat down on the settee.

"Yes, I do."

"And cookies?" he added.

I laughed. "And cookies. Help yourself, they're on the kitchen counter."

Bill got up without complaint and I could hear Tasha and Kip in the kitchen. For the first time since my mom had died, the house felt like home.

BAKER'S TREAT RECIPES

I know how difficult it is to bake gluten-free food—especially if one of your hobbies, like mine, is baking. The following recipes use some of my favorite gluten-free mixes. I recommend you start with a mix. Once you get used to baking gluten-free, you can experiment more with almond flour or creating your own all-purpose mix from a variety of your favorites.

Enjoy!

Kip's Favorite Gluten-Free Chocolate Chip Pumpkin Muffins

MAKES 6 MUFFINS

1 ¼ cups preferred gluten-free baking mix (such as
    Pamela's or Bisquick)
1 teaspoon cinnamon

¼ cup water
1 egg
¼ cup honey or sugar
1 teaspoon gluten-free vanilla
½ cup gluten-free canned pumpkin
½ cup gluten-free chocolate chips or chocolate chunks
    made from your favorite gluten-free chocolate
½ cup coconut (optional)
¼ cup pecans or walnuts (optional)

Preheat oven to 350 F. Grease or line a muffin tin with paper liners and set aside.

Mix first eight ingredients together. Fold in chocolate chips and optional ingredients. Using a ¼-cup measure, spoon into prepared muffin tins, filling each two-thirds full. Bake in preheated oven for 20 to 25 minutes until tops bounce back when touched.

Note—Once baked, muffins can be frozen and reheated in microwave for 40 to 45 seconds for a fresh, hot muffin every morning.

Toni's Chamber of Commerce Gluten-Free Mini Salmon Quiches

1 tablespoon extra-virgin olive oil
¼ cup diced onion
½ teaspoon salt
⅛ teaspoon pepper
4 ounces smoked salmon
2 large eggs, or ½ cup egg substitute
⅔ cup half-and-half

3 ounce ⅓-less-fat cream cheese, cubed
1 tablespoon dill

Preheat oven to 400 F. Lightly coat a mini-muffin tin with cooking spray and set aside.

Heat oil in a nonstick skillet over medium heat. Sauté onion for 2 to 3 minutes or until soft; add salt, pepper, and salmon. Remove from stovetop and set aside to cool.

Combine the egg/egg substitute and half-and-half in a small bowl and set aside.

Place two small cubes of cream cheese in each cup, followed by 1 tablespoon of salmon mixture. Pour egg mixture on top, until each cup is three-quarters filled (do not over-fill). Top each cup with a sprinkle of dill.

Bake quiches for 15 minutes at 400, then reduce heat to 350 F and bake 5 to 7 minutes more.

Tasha's Gluten-Free Mini Quiches

MAKES 60 MINI QUICHES

SHELLS
6 ounce cream cheese, softened
1 cup (2 sticks) butter, softened
2 cups gluten-free all-purpose flour or Gluten Free Pantry piecrust mix

QUICHE MIXTURE
1 ½ cups grated cheddar cheese
8 slices bacon, cooked crisp-crumbled
3 eggs
1 ½ cups half-and-half
½ teaspoon salt

1 cup finely chopped spinach (optional)
1 cup feta cheese (optional)
½ cup mushrooms (optional)

Mix butter and cream cheese together until smooth. Add flour and mix only until a soft dough forms. Overworking dough can make it tough. (This is less likely, however, with gluten-free flour.) Refrigerate 1 hour.

Preheat oven to 350 F.

Form dough into 60 walnut-sized balls. Press each ball into muffin pan, ensuring sides and bottom are covered.

Mix all quiche ingredients together. Pour 1 tablespoon into each muffin. Bake until tops are browned, 15 to 20 minutes.

Tip: Quiches can be cooked and frozen, and reheated at a later date.

Toni's Famous Gluten-Free Danish

MAKES 1½ DOZEN

1 cup (2 sticks) unsalted butter, softened
4 ⅓ cups all-purpose gluten-free flour, such as Better Batter or Pamela's Baking Mix, divided
2 ¼ teaspoons (1 packet) active dry yeast
1 ¼ cups milk
¼ cup sugar
1 teaspoon salt
1 egg
½ teaspoon lemon extract
½ teaspoon almond extract
Preserves or cream cheese for filling
Egg white, for brushing

In a medium bowl, cream together the butter and ⅓ cup of flour. Roll between 2 pieces of waxed paper into a 6 x12-inch sheet. Refrigerate for at least 20 minutes.

In a large bowl, mix together the dry yeast and 1 ½ cups of flour. In a small saucepan over medium heat, combine the milk, sugar, and salt. Heat to 115 degrees F, or just until warm but not hot to the touch. Mix the warm milk mixture into the flour and yeast along with the egg and lemon and almond extracts. Stir for 3 minutes. Knead in the remaining flour ½ cup at a time until the dough is firm and pliable. (Dough may be sticky due to gluten-free flour.) Set aside to rest until doubled in size. Approximately 2 hours.

Roll dough out to a 14-inch square. (Dough can be rolled between waxed paper to keep from sticking.) Place the sheet of the cold butter onto dough, and fold the dough over it like the cover of a book. Seal edges by pressing with fingers. Roll each piece out to a 20 x 12-inch rectangle, then fold into thirds by folding the long sides in over the center. Refrigerate for 15 minutes. Repeat rolling into a large rectangle, and folding into thirds. Wrap in plastic and refrigerate for at least 30 minutes.

Remove from the refrigerator and repeat rolling and folding process two more times, chilling between each fold. Return to the refrigerator to chill again before shaping. If the butter gets too warm, the dough will become difficult to manage.

Roll dough out to ¼-inch thickness. Cut dough into 4-inch squares and place a tablespoon of filling in the center. Fold two of the corners over the center to form a filled-diamond shape. Or, fold the piece in half, cut into 1-inch strips, stretch, twist, and roll into a spiral. Place a dollop (approximately 1 tablespoon) of preserves or other filling in the center. Alternatively, cut into 2-inch circles and place a dollop of filling in center. Place Danish on ungreased baking sheet, cover with lint-free towel and let rise until doubled approximately 2 hours.

Preheat the oven to 450 F.

Brush Danish with egg white; this will ensure a shiny finish. Bake for 8 to 10 minutes, or until bottoms are golden brown.

Danishes can be served immediately or cooled and dusted with powdered sugar or piped with a glaze made of powdered sugar and water.

Danish dough can be frozen for up to three weeks before it is filled, then filled and baked when needed.

Apple-Cinnamon Raisin Muffins

MAKES 6 MUFFINS

1 ¼ cups gluten-free baking mix (such as Pamela's or Bisquick)
1 teaspoon cinnamon
¼ cup water
1 egg
¼ cup honey or sugar
1 teaspoon gluten-free vanilla
½ cup applesauce
½ cup raisins·

Preheat oven to 350 F. Grease a muffin tin or line with paper liners and set aside.

Mix first seven ingredients together. Fold in raisins. Using a ¼-cup measure, spoon into prepared muffin tins, filling each two-thirds full. Bake in preheated 350 degree F oven for 20 to 25 minutes until tops bounce back when touched.

Note—Once baked, muffins can be frozen and reheated in microwave for 40 to 45 seconds for a fresh, hot muffin every morning.

Gluten-Free Blueberry Coffee Cake

FILLING
   ¼ cup sugar
   ¼ cup brown sugar
   2 teaspoons cinnamon
   1 cup walnuts or pecans (optional)
   1 cup blueberries

CAKE BATTER
   ⅔ cup (10 tablespoons) unsalted butter, softened
   1 cup white sugar
   2 large eggs
   1 teaspoon vanilla
   2 cups all-purpose gluten-free baking mix, such as
      Pamela's (I have a recipe for making your own. You can
      find it at www.nancyjparra.com)
   1 cup sour cream

GLAZE
   1 cup powdered sugar
   ¾ teaspoon vanilla
      2–3 tablespoons water (add more or less to make it
      creamy and pourable)

Preheat oven to 350 F. Grease a 9-inch springform pan and
set aside.

Prepare filling: Mix all ingredients except blueberries and
set aside.
   Prepare batter: Cream butter until fluffy. Add sugar and
mix well. Add eggs one at a time, then vanilla. On low speed,
alternate baking mix with sour cream until incorporated.
   Spoon half of the batter into prepared pan, covering the
bottom. Sprinkle half of the filling over the batter. Sprinkle

blueberries over, then spoon remaining batter over the top of the berries. Sprinkle remaining filling on top. Insert a butter knife straight down into batter, moving up and down in a zigzag motion to marbleize cake. Do not smooth out. Bake for 45 to 50 minutes, or until toothpick inserted in cake comes out clean. While warm, run a knife around the edges. When cool, remove from pan and glaze.

Someone wants to bake a killing.

~~~~~~~~

FROM *NEW YORK TIMES* BESTSELLING AUTHOR

JENN MCKINLAY

RED VELVET REVENGE

A Cupcake Bakery Mystery

It may be summertime, but sales at Fairy Tale Cupcakes are below zero—and owners Melanie Cooper and Angie DeLaura are willing to try anything to heat things up. So when local legend Slim Hazard offers them the chance to sell cupcakes at the annual Juniper Pass Rodeo, they're determined to rope in a pretty payday!

But not everyone at Juniper Pass is as sweet for Fairy Tale Cupcakes as Slim—including star bull-rider Ty Stokes. Mel and Angie try to steer clear of the cowboy's short fuse, but when his dead body is found facedown in the hay, it's a whole different rodeo…

INCLUDES SCRUMPTIOUS RECIPES!

"I gobbled it up."
—Julie Hyzy, bestselling author of the
White House Chef Mysteries

facebook.com/TheCrimeSceneBooks
penguin.com